Dawn of the Superhero Age

Book 1 of the Superhero Age Series

Damien Benoit-Ledoux

DBL Books / Purple Spekter™ LLP | Press

DAWN OF THE
SUPERHERO AGE

BOOK 1 OF THE **SUPERHERO AGE SERIES**

DAMIEN
BENOIT-LEDOUX

DAWN OF THE SUPERHERO AGE

The Superhero Age Series

Part of the Spekter Superhero Universe™

Work of Fiction

This story is a work of fiction. Names, characters, places, and incidents are the product of the author's imagination or are used fictitiously. Any resemblance to actual persons, living or dead, events, or locales is entirely coincidental.

Contents

To my son, Aurelien.

Papa loves you so very, very much.

The Story So Far

T his special recap is for 1) those who have never read **Guardians** (gasp!) and 2) those who did and can't quite remember everything amazing that happened in those books.

The Superhero Age series picks up after the amazing events of the **Guardians** five-novel series. Don't worry, you won't need to read those books to understand what's going on. (But don't let me stop you from reading the origin story. It's awesome!)

In an announcer voice: "Last time, on Guardians..."

September

Sixteen-year-old best friends Quinn McAlester and Blake Hargreaves wander into the woods during a family camping trip on Labor Day weekend in Rangeley, Maine. They explore an underground cavern (later identified as an orgone reactor core, a secret facility designed to harvest and store orgone energy from the atmosphere) and accidentally trigger a reaction chamber event that irradiates them with orgone energy. (Although all they see is a cool light show.) Terrified, they run back to their campsite, but pass out and never make it.

Oops.

Three days later, they awake in a hospital room, but something seems off. A strange man named Victor Kraze questions them, but the boys doubt his intentions and withhold the entire truth. Playing their game,

1

Victor tells the boys they survived a lightning strike from a midmorning thunderstorm. Even more lies surface when Victor finally allows them to see their parents.

Back at home, mild-mannered Quinn discovers he can manipulate water in the shower while Blake figures out how to manifest heat and fire. Realizing something has happened to them, they confide in their comic-loving science teacher Ron St. Germain and ask him for help. Ron excitedly agrees and coaches them along as new abilities surface.

Victor appears in Portsmouth to check on the boys and begins a recruitment campaign. He promises to secure the boys' safety in exchange for their membership and loyalty in a secret global organization known as The Order. Immediately sensing Quinn's skepticism, Victor focuses his energy on Blake, who proves much easier to manipulate.

Wait, am I really trying to summarize five books in a few pages? At the pace I'm writing, I'll have a book within a book. So, let's speed this up.

Quinn and Blake have superpowers. Yay!

Oh no, their superpowers are different at first.

But wait!

They can both sense each other's presence, become invisible, are impervious to knives and bullets, have super strength, speed, sight, hearing, and more.

Quinn has a major crush on a boy named Keegan, who doesn't seem to know he exists. Blake doesn't know who he likes and doesn't have time for romance because (he thinks) his abusive domestic life makes him too moody—but their mutual friend Ravone is crushing hard on Blake.

The boys decide they need answers, so they skip school (how naughty!) and return to Rangeley only to confirm their worst nightmares: a secret underground base really exists, and the cavern they discovered over Labor Day weekend gave them superpowers.

October

Back in Portsmouth, a man named Hector Rodriguez accidentally falls off a drawbridge tower, forcing Quinn to reveal his superhuman side to the world. Incidentally, the hero-save totally screws up his first date with Keegan. (Clearly this is the bigger problem for Quinn.) The police become cranky because there's an interfering vigilante in town. Catching wind of the situation, the Department of Homeland Security (DHS) quietly moves in and tries to capture the vigilante who's already earned a superhero moniker: Blue Spekter. Sick of being treated like shit and hunted like a criminal, Blue Spekter directly appeals (and appears) to Police Chief Applegate—but she's not having it.

Evil Victor finally seduces Blake with promises of power and dark justice. Quinn, however, sees right through Victor's nefarious lies and panics over the loss of his best friend to the dark side. Quinn's fears don't stop Blake from quietly exercising dark justice while Quinn—as Blue Spekter—performs heroic acts like preventing a massive air force KC-135 Stratotanker from crashing into Portsmouth. He also stops a crazy-man bomber from blowing up a crowded Market Square.

The rifts between Blake, his alcoholic parents, and his best friend widen as Victor works his manipulative magic. On the upside, Quinn and Keegan (finally) become boyfriends. Despite Victor's successful divide-and-conquer strategy, Quinn convinces Blake to return with him to Rangeley to stop Victor and destroy the facility, but, as Admiral Ackbar once said, it's a trap. The Order is waiting for them, ready to implant a control chip in Quinn's brain. After a tenuous battle that incapacitates most of the facility, Quinn retreats without Blake, who betrays their friendship by siding with Victor.

Evil 1, Good 0.

November

The DHS and Portsmouth police finally figure out Blake is behind the mysterious events (murders) Blue Spekter vehemently denies. With two superhumans on the scene, it takes herculean efforts to keep the press at bay and the truth hidden until they can devise a plan.

Blake gets cocky, and despite his cavalier attitude toward Victor, he trains and fights alongside The Order's highly trained militia. Victor sends him on several eye-opening missions, fueling his anger and confusion about the disorder in the world.

The DHS steps up their game and ensnares Blue Spekter with special weapons called TaseBolts—think Tasers on steroids—but Blue Spekter barely defeats them before passing out. Thankfully and conveniently, science superhero mentor Ron lives across the street and quietly rescues Quinn. A mysterious woman name Ana María García reveals herself that night and her similar, orgone-enabled superpowers, claiming to be the only surviving failed experiment of The Order's first attempts at creating superhumans back in 1965 at the height of the Cold War.

Shortly thereafter, Ron—whose brother works with advanced and indestructible fabrics—presents Quinn with his first iconic (and blue) superhero suit, and it's a hit.

Surprise!

Quinn discovers another secret reactor core hidden inside the supposedly abandoned Portsmouth Naval Prison. Quinn begs Ana María for help, but she refuses, believing knowledge of her existence would only fuel The Order's resolve to restart Project Genesis, the secret joint-CIA effort that created her. Determined to get help any way he can, Quinn finds allies in unsuspecting places and begins building a team that agrees to help him research and take down The Order and Blake, now revealed to the world as the super villain Dark Flame.

December

Enraged by the brutality of the world, Dark Flame embarks upon a campaign of destruction and death in the name of justice. When Victor tries to control him, Dark Flame lashes out and nearly kills him. Shortly thereafter, Dark Flame tracks down and ruthlessly murders the upper echelon of The Order, opening the path to ascension and domination ahead of an angry Victor.

Quinn and Blake share a tense conversation, and Quinn realizes Victor's mad scientists secretly implanted a control chip in Blake's head. Quinn believes the control chip is malfunctioning because it explains Blake's unusual and violent behavior.

Victor sulks. Realizing something is wrong and that he can no longer control Dark Flame and needs help, Victor takes matters into his own hands. He orders his technicians to irradiate him with orgone energy. Despite the number of abysmal failures resulting in death, Victor's infusion process luckily succeeds, and he becomes the next superhuman.

Blue Spekter, who has finally earned the trust and cooperation of the local police and the DHS, leads a successful operation with marines to capture the secret orgone reactor facility inside the abandoned naval prison. This infuriates Dark Flame, who tries to take back the prison on his own, but the marines overwhelm and capture him, thanks to those handy dandy TaseBolts. Unfortunately, Dark Flame escapes and plots his revenge.

After Dark Flame does some unconscionable and destructive things, Blue Spekter and Dark Flame battle over Portsmouth at night, eventually finding themselves fighting on the grounds of the naval prison, where Blue Spekter gains the upper hand. As Dark Flame accepts defeat, he reaches out through the dense mental fog obscuring his conscience and begs his best friend to save him. Blue Spekter risks everything and uses his superpowers to obliterate the malfunctioning control chip in his best friend's brain, inadvertently killing him.

But Blue Spekter has no time to grieve, as superpowered Victor and two superpowered henchmen arrive, ready to kill Blue Spekter and take back the naval prison. With the help of the TaseBolt-wielding marines, Blue Spekter dispatches the two henchmen.

Blake unexpectedly heals and recovers during the intense battle, then fights alongside his best friend against Victor, who is surprisingly strong. But just as Blue Spekter is ready to deliver the killing blow, Victor uses Blake as a human shield, killing him by ripping his heart out.

Victor barely survives Blue Spekter's grief-fueled onslaught and retreats. To this day, no one knows who truly won that battle.

January

Quinn and his friends discover the holidays suck when you grieve a loved one. Quinn and Ana María argue (again) about principles and morality because Ana María still refuses to reveal herself. Realizing Victor already has the power to create super villains, Ana María concedes her position and agrees to help Quinn, adopting the superhero moniker Catamount. This turns out to be a good thing, because Victor attacks the naval prison and the nearby naval shipyard in broad daylight. He lifts a nuclear submarine out of the water, threatening to drop it on top of the marine-held naval prison. Blue Spekter and Catamount defeat him and avoid nuclear disaster, but just barely.

Frustrated with how unprepared he and the DHS are for a full-scale superhuman attack, Blue Spekter trains hard with Catamount. Together, they strike back at Victor and The Order by finding and extracting Dr. Madison, his lead scientist.

Victor, who earns the super villain moniker Nightmare, retaliates by activating the weaponized Rangeley orgone energy array, targeting Portsmouth on New Year's Eve. The net effect of the attack incapacitates the city's population and emergency services until the array deactivates. In the calamity, Quinn discovers Nightmare used the attack as a cover for his true purpose: to kidnap Quinn's family and boyfriend.

Desperate and defeated—exactly where Victor wants him—Quinn sits down with his team and devises a plan to save his loved ones and defeat

Victor once and for all. That's when Agent Hartman says the following words:

"Ladies and gentlemen, make no mistake, the world has irrevocably changed. Today we stand witness to the dawn of the superhero age."

The rest, as they say, are spoilers. But don't let that stop you from discovering the spoilers yourself by enjoying over thirteen-hundred pages of action-packed superhero adventures in the **Guardians** series novels! You can also buy all five books in one in the **Guardians Origin Story Omnibus.**

Now, let's begin **Dawn of the Superhero Age**, shall we?

Chapter 1
Run!

T hunder rolled across the skies as he ran for his life through the dark and thickly wooded forest. His sore bare feet trampled the dense, icy underbrush. It scratched and whipped at his legs, but terror and confusion urged him forward, away from the shouting soldiers pursuing him. Wild, unnatural lightning relentlessly flashed overhead.

Who is chasing me? he wondered.

Moments ago he had awoken, dazed and confused. His eyes had sprung open in the darkness as he gasped into consciousness in the dark of night. Cold winter air had filled his unusually tight lungs, and his warm breath had steamed with every exhale. Wheezing and shivering, he had drawn his arms around his body.

To his surprise, he wasn't clothed except for a pair of yellow-and-blue plaid boxer shorts. The pungent scent of forest decay had filled his nostrils as he glanced around, struggling to focus on the tall, shadowy trees ahead of him. When he heard the shouting and barking, he had leaped to his feet and hadn't stopped running since.

Low and leafless tree branches whipped him in the face, and his lungs ached. He grunted in pain as an unyielding branch scratched his cheek. Cold ice rain fell around him, the forest canopy barely offering protection from the powerful storm. Distracted, he yelped when his bare left foot struck a sharp rock. It pitched him forward, sending him into a tumble across snowy roots and stones. Something sharp jabbed his back, and he cried out in pain.

"Over here!" someone shouted.

He frantically looked around for signs of movement, but the foggy woods made them impossible to spot. A bright flash of lightning blinded him, and a crack of thunder pierced the night sky. Gritting his teeth and ignoring the pain, he pushed himself to his feet and raced deeper into the forest.

"Which way did he go?" someone else hollered.

"This way! Look, snapped twigs and branches," a female voice yelled back. "We can't let him get to the river, or the dogs will lose his scent in this mess."

"Then unleash the dogs."

He cursed as the distant sound of dogs' paws crashing through the underbrush reached him—exceptionally loud sounds he didn't think he should hear yet. Another flash, another crack of loud thunder.

Are they closing in already?

His lungs heaved as he ran without concern for the cuts on the soles of his feet. Branches of all sorts whipped against his face and torso, but he ignored the pain and pushed on. Sweat trickled down his face and stung his eyes. The coppery taste of blood filled his mouth. He blinked in frustration and spat but pushed on. He only trusted the overwhelming feeling that whoever chased him must not find him.

Why are they chasing me?

A gunshot rang out and whipped through the branches overhead. Startled, he ran faster. A rocky cliff overlooking some rushing rapids ten or more feet below surprised him, and he instinctively leaped, hoping to land in deep water. To his surprise, he easily cleared the thirty-foot-wide river and landed in the shrubs on the opposite bank.

Open-mouthed, he turned and stared at the steep riverbank he had leaped from. "How did I—"

"He's over there! Flares!" A moment later, several red flares shot into the clear sky, illuminating the river and its banks. Several snaps of lightning flashed over the river, and thunder shrieked across the sky. The wind howled through the adjacent forest, bending the tall trees, and ice rain pelted his bare skin.

"There he is! Get to the bridge."

A gunshot echoed across the river, exploding the oak tree trunk behind his head.

He yelped and ducked.

"Hold your fire!" someone shouted. "Radio the team on the other side."

Panicked and shivering, he turned and ran away from the river, covering his head as the flares fell around him. He cursed as one landed to his left. The woods thickened again, slowing his pace.

Why am I running from them?

The sounds of urgent chatter, radio squawks, running footsteps, and panting dogs filled his ears. Then the sounds of car engines—no, diesel engines—and stressed suspensions and struts reached his ears.

But how?

Realizing he must be near a road or clearing, he ran faster. Even if his pursuers found him on the open road, he irrationally thought the open road increased his chances of escape. Revving engines and shouting men echoed around him, but in the aural confusion, he couldn't place how near or far they were.

But more importantly, who am I?

Lightning sizzled into the nearby forest, followed by the immediate crashing of thunderclaps. This time, he felt the lightning—a momentary, euphoric sensation that confused him. Something smashed into his chest, making him grunt. It threw off his balance and made him stumble, but he didn't fall. Glancing down, he caught the object in his trembling hands—a squarish and soft yellow beanbag.

"Ow." He winced at the pain. Bright lights startled him to a sudden stop. With his left hand, he tried to shield his eyes against the glare.

"Get down on the ground!" someone shouted.

A second beanbag struck him in the stomach, knocking the wind out of him. He gasped and doubled over, fighting to breathe and stay on his feet. Wild lightning flashed nearby, blinding everyone. The third beanbag pelted his shoulder, sending him reeling until he collapsed on the road. Strong winds swirled around them as thunderclaps rolled and crashed above them. Two men dressed in dark gray tactical gear emerged from the woods, weapons aimed at him.

"Get down on the ground, get down on the ground," they chanted aggressively.

Cowering, he covered his head with his hands and rolled to his knees. Crouched on his elbows, he placed his hands over the back of his head. Another forked lightning bolt illuminated the sky.

"Stay down on the ground!"

He sensed a powerful energy rising within him, but he didn't understand what it was. More lightning, more thunder.

Several more soldiers emerged from the forest and surrounded him, and a second vehicle pulled to a stop. Soldiers jumped from the cab and cargo bed and ran to surround him, their weapons aimed at his head.

"We've got him," someone shouted into their radio. Someone on the other end squawked an unintelligible response as three fearsome German shepherds arrived and stopped short of him, snarling and barking.

"Lie on your stomach," a soldier shouted, but his voice was lost in the commotion that overwhelmed his senses. Another pickup truck and more soldiers arrived.

Just make it stop, he thought. Arcs of lightning danced around them, and the skies roiled with raw power—but the ice rain abated. Yellow motes of raw power formed on his skin and swirled around his head and body.

"What the fuck?" someone shouted. The dogs ceased barking and whined with fear. They backed off, and the soldiers took a step back with them.

A savage crack of lightning erupted from his back and shot skyward, immediately followed by a massive crack of deafening thunder. The dogs yelped, and the soldiers cried out in horror. He felt intense heat radiate from him, followed by a powerful yellow shock wave that exploded from his body. Fallen leaves and twigs erupted from the ground. The soldiers screamed, and the dogs squealed in panic as the energy flung them all ten to twenty feet through the air. They all landed with thuds, unmoving.

A few small trees toppled and lost their leaves, while others swayed when the immense force passed through them. The pickup trucks bounced on their shocks, blew tires, and short-circuited. Their engines ground to a halt, and their lights exploded or switched off. When the shock wave dissipated, only darkness surrounded him.

At last, it was quiet.

He shook with fear and pulled his hands from his head. An owl hooted somewhere nearby, breaking the silence, but no one moved. Looking around, he cautiously pushed himself up to his knees, making sure no one had survived to capture him.

Capture me. Why are they trying to capture me? And what the hell did I just do?

A twig snapped behind him, and he jumped to his feet, startled. A moment later, a damaged tree fell, landing with a loud thud that shook the ground. Confident no one else had reacted to the falling tree, he chose not to wait for enemy reinforcements to arrive.

Enemy. These people are my enemy. But why?

He ran.

A very specific alarm blared from one console's speakers, echoing through the quiet and lightly staffed operations center of the Superhuman Task Force (STF) beneath Hangar 227.

The U.S. Air Force had built the nondescript Hangar 227 at Pease Tradeport in Portsmouth, New Hampshire, in the 1950s, and it had become one of the United States' strategic air command bases. The air force had performed heavy maintenance on bombers and tankers there before selling it to Pan American World Airways, who had used it for about ten years to maintain their fleet.

But what the government had secretly built and maintained beneath the old, abandoned Pan Am hangar rivaled some of the best special effects in modern movies and television shows, specifically those of Marvel's *Agents of S.H.I.E.L.D.* Built into solid bedrock and New Hampshire granite, the STF base could withstand aerial bombardment and nuclear bombing. They had stockpiled it with enough food to support a full complement of personnel for months—including potential babies. Its systems could recycle air and water and generate electricity while maintaining a suitable climate-controlled environment via geothermal energy.

The on-duty graveyard shift soldiers jolted from their relaxed state, all staring at one unmanned workstation. Petty Officer Bruno rolled his chair to the empty workstation, rubbed his tired eyes, and stared at the flashing red warnings on the monitors.

He muttered a curse, then announced, "Satellites just detected a powerful orgone energy bloom!"

"Now? Where?" Lt. Cassidy asked as three soldiers closed in and hovered behind him. The lighting in the operations center automatically brightened after detecting their movement.

"Is Nightmare firing up one of his reactors? Did we find one?" another asked, using the super villain moniker for Victor Kraze, a dangerous individual linked to a secret and sinister globally organized group only known to intelligence agencies as The Order.

"Uh, no. Look, this reading is above ground."

"Shit, then it's probably a superhuman. Where are Blue Spekter and Helion?"

13

Bruno shot Cassidy a perturbed look. "It's 0300 in the morning on a school night. They're in bed, sir."

Unfazed, Cassidy said, "Right. And Catamount?"

"Probably still in Europe, not the Blue Ridge Mountains."

"Where are those mountains?"

"Virginia, where this explosion took place. Specifically... hold on, refining—" He tapped a few keys, and the satellite image enlarged and enhanced. "There. Near Spec, Virginia."

"Where the hell is that?"

Bruno shifted the map around. "Just over two hundred miles southwest of D.C. And given this energy metric and dispersion rate, it was a level one. Maybe a level two. However, according to the weather reports, an unexpectedly severe thunderstorm has rolled through."

Cassidy swore. "Then there's an orgone reactor nearby, and we're probably dealing with a *new* superhuman. Better wake Director Potter."

Chapter 2
The World Is Changing Again

"**W**here is he?" Director Potter asked, marching to the center of operations, an empty coffee mug gripped tightly in his hand. He stopped and studied the live infrared satellite feed of Spec, Virginia, and the surrounding area on the massive wall monitors in the operations center.

Lt. Cassidy pointed to a small blue dot. "There, sir. Crossing the mountain range now."

"Good. Put Blue Spekter on the speakers."

"Yes, sir." Cassidy nodded and tapped some keys at his station. "Channel open, sir."

Potter folded his arms over his chest, coffee mug dangling from his fingers. "Blue Spekter, this is Director Potter. Report, please."

"Morning, Director," Blue Spekter replied, his sleepy voice booming over the loudspeakers. "I'm circling the area. It's really dark and quiet, given it's four in the morning."

"Jesus, turn that down," Potter barked, wincing at the loudness. Lt. Cassidy nodded and lowered the volume. "Where are you going? Tracking shows you're not where you should be."

"The cellular signal sucks, and I can't see anything. Can someone guide me in?"

"Cassidy," Potter grumbled, attempting to sip from his empty cup. He frowned.

"Yes, sir. Blue Spekter, this is Lieutenant Cassidy. Head southeast from your current position."

"All right."

A minute and several directions later, Lt. Cassidy said, "There, you should be on top of the orgone bloom we detected."

"Confirmed, Lieutenant. I can feel it. The orgone concentration is much higher here. Oh, wow."

"What is it?" Potter asked.

"One sec."

Potter sighed impatiently. "Blue, could you turn on the video feed from the headset camera we gave you?"

"Sure." A moment later, a picture-in-picture window appeared on the wall monitors as the satellite connected with the livestream transmitted from Blue Spekter's micro-camera. Unfortunately, since it was four in the morning, the video feed was underexposed.

"Damn thing needs an infrared mode," Potter grumbled.

"It has one," Lt. Cassidy said. "Blue Spekter, please tap the Mode Select button once."

"Okay."

A moment later, the feed switched to infrared.

Potter grunted with frustration. "The image isn't super clear. Blue, you'll have to describe what you see."

"Bodies. At least fifteen, and several trucks. There are some big dogs here too. German shepherds, I think."

"What are they doing?" Potter asked.

"Nothing. I think they're all dead."

"Jesus."

"There's like a... I dunno how to describe it." As Blue Spekter spoke, he pointed so they could easily see what he described. "It's like a radial or circular pattern in the ground. Like a crop circle maybe? It's hard to see in the dark. Its center is over here, and it—wow, the orgone is intense. Also, someone or something flattened all the surrounding trees. If I didn't know better, I'd say a push or explosive blast power caused this—and that could explain the orgone bloom."

Blue Spekter landed and walked over to one of the fallen soldiers. "Aw crap, they're wearing uniforms like the ones worn by Victor's men up at Rangeley. I bet they work for him—which means he can't be far. That means he survived the battle over Rangeley."

"Let's not jump to conclusions, Blue Spekter. Can you sense any super-humans nearby?" Director Potter asked.

"No, I can't. So, either they know how to cloak themselves, or they're gone."

"Understood."

"Gonna start circling, see if I can pick up anything."

"All right," Potter replied, smiling at an ensign who brought him a fresh mug of coffee. "Thank you," he whispered.

"You might wanna get some people down here before the locals wake up," Blue Spekter said. "I don't think you want this on the news today."

Potter gestured at Lt. Cassidy, who nodded and issued commands at his console. "Already scrambling, Blue Spekter. But before you take off, please check the status of the bodies. Are they unconscious or deceased?"

"Hang on, I'll check a couple of them out." Blue Spekter checked several bodies for pulses but sensed no heartbeats with his fingers or super hearing. "I think they're all dead, Director. Wait, I just heard one of them groan. He's pretty far back. Oh, shit, there's a big branch sticking through him. Ugh, so much blood. So gross."

"Keep it together, Blue Spekter. I need you to talk to him. See what you can discover before he dies."

"Uh, gruesome, but okay. If this is one of Victor's henchmen, I have an idea."

A moment later, Blue Spekter's headset camera aimed toward and fo-cused on a pale, dying man. His body lay reclined, legs on the ground

17

and back resting against a tree trunk, his bloodied stomach impaled by a solid oak branch.

"Hey, buddy, can you hear me?"

The man groaned hoarsely. "Are you one of us?"

"Yes," Blue Spekter lied. "Nightmare sent me when no one checked in. Tell me what happened. You've lost a lot of blood and probably won't survive."

"God dammit," Director Potter muttered over Blue Spekter's earcomm.

The man moaned in despair, then licked his bloodied lips. "We were chasing him."

"Who?" The soldier eyed Blue Spekter with suspicion. Realizing he might blow his cover, Blue Spekter improvised. "I don't know the details of your operation."

"The kid. We thought he was dead, but he wasn't. When he disappeared prior to incineration, we realized he had crawled off the table."

Blue Spekter maintained his composure and swallowed his shock. "And not only did he survive, but he used his powers against you?"

The man coughed. "Didn't expect that."

"Then I better find him and bring him back to Nightmare. Give me a clue. What does he look like?"

The man coughed several times and wheezed. "Seventeen. Brown hair, brown eyes. Answers to Carlos. Only wearing boxer shorts." The man's eyes glossed over.

Blue Spekter gently shook the man's head. "Stay with me, now."

The man's eyes snapped to attention.

"How tall is the kid? How tall is Carlos?"

"Five foot eleven maybe, and really skinny."

"Does Carlos have a control chip?"

"Of course. They all do."

"Why is Nightmare experimenting on high school kids?"

The man shot Blue Spekter a strange look. "You don't work for Nightmare, do you?"

Blue Spekter shook his head. "No."

The man cursed.

"Why do you work for him?"

"The money is good."

"It doesn't bother you he wants to take over the world?"

"You would think that, wouldn't you?"

"I'm more than thinking about it. You work for the wrong side, buddy. Look where it got you. Death by an oak tree, maybe that's what they'll write on your tombstone."

"Fuck you."

"Where is he making them? Where is the reactor?"

The man smirked and coughed. "Like I'd tell you."

"Either way, it will be found and destroyed."

"Do your worst."

The man's eyes widened, then he sputtered frothy, bloody saliva. He coughed again, then exhaled his last.

Blue Spekter sighed and bowed his head. "Uh, guys? He just died."

"I understand, Blue Spekter," Director Potter replied. "Thank you for pulling that information out of him. I'm sorry you had to experience this."

The sudden squeal of a barn door hinge in desperate need of lubrication abruptly roused him from sleep. The potent smell of hay and sheep triggered a memory, but he didn't understand why. Had he been here before? A chilly breeze swept over his naked body as an older man humming a tune cleared his throat at the entrance to the barn.

Panic paralyzed him. He didn't know if he could trust this man. As unusually loud footsteps approached, he waited and watched.

The sheep he had slept next to for warmth bleated, then scrambled to its feet and nuzzled the locked gate with its snout.

"I'm a-comin', Mabel," the older man's voice announced.

He pushed himself to a seated position, then scurried back, his left foot slipping on the hay. He glanced around the rugged post-and-beam barn interior. Strange-looking tools and equipment hung on the walls from wooden pegs, and someone had stacked several bales of hay to one side—probably for Mabel.

He swung his gaze around, and his eyes widened with fear when the unshaven, white-haired old man appeared outside the pen. He wore a faded buffalo plaid flannel shirt over a thick sweater, and a tattered red knitted hat on his head.

The older man stared at him, seemingly unfazed by his presence or nakedness. "Where are your clothes, boy?" He spoke slowly, his words rolling with an Appalachian accent.

He glanced down and saw only the tattered elastic waistband of his boxer shorts around his waist. Suddenly feeling embarrassed, he shifted his legs and covered himself, wondering which thicket had torn away the last scrap of clothing he owned. Then he remembered running from soldiers and the strange place he couldn't remember going to.

He stared at the older man, unsure of how to answer. The farmer didn't seem dangerous, so maybe he could trust him. Mabel bleated again. The man looked at the sheep.

"You and Mabel, uh, didn't, uh... you know?"

He looked at Mabel, unsure of the question. Mabel sniffed the air and bleated again. He shook his head and cleared his throat. "I was just... cold."

The farmer chuckled and nodded. "Well, sheep's good for doinkin', but we frown upon that in these parts, contrary to what most people believe about us."

"Uh-huh," he said nervously.

"So, where are your clothes? Did you lose a bet with your friends?"

"No. I don't know."

The older man smacked his lips with amusement. "How did you end up in my barn?"

"I—I was running away from… I don't know."

"Huh. What's your name, son?"

"My name is—" Tears formed when he couldn't remember. "I don't know that either."

"You don't know your name?"

He wiped tears from his eyes and shook his head. "No."

"Mine's Jesse."

"Okay."

"Well, you need a name. How about Ethan?"

"Okay," Ethan replied, shivering.

Jesse waved his hand. "Come with me to the house, Ethan. You can't spend the day bollicky bare-ass in the barn, not in this cold weather. Come inside and take a hot shower. You can borrow some of my son's clothes." He pulled off his flannel shirt and tossed it at him. "Put that around your waist. Don't need you givin' the missus a fright with the size of that thing, one way or the other."

Ten minutes later, Jesse set a pile of folded clothes on the small bathroom sink. Ethan watched him through the transparent plastic shower curtain. He still shivered under the hot water that mixed with dirt and dry blood on the bottom of the antique white porcelain clawfoot tub.

Jesse studied him a moment, then averted his gaze. "You don't have any bruises." Ethan glanced at his body, but said nothing. "Come downstairs when you've finished and dressed. Janie's cookin' up some flapjacks for you. I reckon you might be hungry." He paused, and a strange expression crossed his face. "Uh, you do like flapjacks, dontcha?"

"Yeah," Ethan replied with a nod, but he didn't know what the farmer had asked him.

After Ethan had scrubbed off the dirt and blood, he dried himself in front of the dusty vanity mirror. His face seemed familiar, but he stared at his nude, toned body because it appeared different than expected, or as his memory suggested it should look. He flexed a few times, wondering why he appeared more muscular and less scrawny than he remembered.

As he towel dried his medium-length brown hair, he caught the fresh scent of something familiar, but he didn't know why.

Laundry detergent!

He sniffed the towel again and wondered if he used the same kind. He dressed, noting how his chest and arms filled out the white undershirt Jesse had given him.

He made his way downstairs, the unexpectedly familiar smells of coffee and bacon filling his nostrils. His stomach gurgled with excitement. The floorboards creaked and announced his presence, but he still knocked on the doorframe when he saw Jesse nose-deep in a newspaper. A woman in a simple blue dress and yellow apron—presumably Janie—focused on the stove, her back toward him. She had tied her gray hair up in a neat bun.

Jesse flipped the newspaper down, and Janie turned to study him. "Mornin', Ethan. Hope you feel better," Jesse said. "There's fresh coffee in the hot pot."

"Uh, hi. Thanks."

"A healthy boy like you looks like he could eat a lot of flapjacks, eh?" Janie asked, also speaking with an Appalachian accent. She peered at him over the top of her silver glasses.

"Yes. At least, I think so. I don't know what flapjacks are."

"You don't know what a flapjack is?" she echoed, stunned.

"It's a pancake, Ethan," Jesse added.

Ethan smiled faintly. "Oh, then yes. I love flapjacks."

Jesse encouraged him to get coffee and have a seat. Ethan gratefully poured himself a cup and sat opposite Jesse.

A moment later, Janie set a healthy stack of flapjacks down in front of him, then slid a plate of bacon and scrambled eggs toward him. Janie offered him a kind smile. "There you are, Ethan."

"Eat up. You're gonna need your strength today," Jesse added.

"I am?"

"A bird in the hand is worth two in the bush. Until you remember who you are, it's best for you to stay here. Besides, I could use the help of a strapping boy like you for a couple of days."

Wondering what birds in bushes meant, Ethan shot him a confused look. "Oh?"

Jesse chuckled. "Did the threat of farm chores suddenly jog your memory?"

Ethan smiled faintly again. "No, sir, it did not."

"Hmm. Good. It's good you're not afraid of a little honest work in exchange for food in your belly and a roof over your head. You don't have to sleep with Mabel tonight. You can use the spare bedroom."

"Thank you."

"Later today, we'll go into town and see if the sheriff knows anything about a missing person."

"Okay."

Janie rolled her eyes with amusement. "A young man of many words, I see."

"Sorry. I just, I don't know who I am. I don't know where I am."

"You're in Spec, Virginia. Ever heard of it?"

After a moment, he shook his head. "No, I don't think so."

Jesse laughed. "Doubt it's the amnesia. Most people haven't."

Chapter 3
More Questions Than Answers

Nothing looked familiar. Despite the warm jacket Jesse had lent him, Ethan hugged himself in the cold air while studying the simple, almost nonexistent town of Spec. His breath fogged around him, and he frowned in frustration.

"You comin'?" Jesse asked, a polite smile on his face.

"Yup." Ethan followed Jesse into the sheriff's warm office.

A slender brown-haired deputy sat at the front desk, regarding Jesse with curiosity. Behind him, a small radio played soft country music. To his left, Ethan could see an older, portly sheriff through the reinforced glass windows of his office, speaking with someone on the telephone. The deputy leaned back and cleared his throat. "Afternoon, Jesse. Who's your friend?"

"Afternoon, Deputy Davis. I call him Ethan. Found him in my barn this mornin'."

"Trespasser?"

"Hard to say. Can't remember himself."

"Do you need me to take him off your hands?" Deputy Davis asked, eyeing Ethan with suspicion.

"Nah. Just wondering if you got any missing person's reports from these parts."

"No, not yet. What's your name, son?"

"I don't remember, sir."

"Do you live here?"

"I don't think so."

Deputy Davis pursed his lips. "Where are you from?"

"I don't know."

The deputy frowned. "Well, what do you know?"

"That I like flapjacks."

They stared at one another for a moment until Deputy Davis shot Jesse a strange look. "This kid firing on all cylinders, Jesse?"

Jesse shrugged. "I think so. Just can't remember much. Strong as hell. Ethan helped me stack all the hay in the barn this mornin'."

"Really? So, we're calling him Ethan?"

"I reckon it's as good a name as any until we figure out who he is."

"How much can you bench, Ethan?" Deputy Davis asked.

"Bench?"

"Lift. How much can you lift? Don't tell me you don't lift weights, given the size of your upper body."

Ethan looked down at his arms and well-developed, muscular chest. Even through the plaid flannel shirt, his chest seemed larger than it had this morning when he dressed himself. "Uh, I don't know."

"Do you play football?"

Ethan looked at the deputy with confusion. "Maybe?"

The deputy's gaze lingered. "Damn, you really don't remember anything, do you?"

"I don't, sir."

"Huh. Polite. So, do you live here?"

Ethan chuckled. "I remember you asked me that already, Deputy, but I don't think so. Nothing in town looks familiar to me."

"Huh."

Jesse scratched his head, and Ethan shoved his hands into his pockets.

Deputy Davis sighed. "Well, I'll pull the state and federal missing person's reports this afternoon. Ethan, come back here so I can take your picture for reference, since we don't know your real name. I'm gonna take a set of fingerprints too. Slim chance that'll bring up your identity, though."

"Okay." Ethan walked over to the mugshot wall and waited. Deputy Davis fiddled with the camera settings and took front and side profile pictures. They sidestepped to the digital fingerprint machine, and Deputy Davis rolled all ten of Ethan's fingers over the biometric scanning plate.

The curious sheriff came out of his office and approached. "Howdy, Jesse. Who's this? You booking him, Davis?"

Deputy Davis shook his head. "Naw, he ain't done nothing wrong, Sheriff."

"Mornin', Sheriff Dollard," Jesse said. "Found him in my barn this mornin'. Kid can't remember a thing."

"Ain't never seen you before. How'd you get in old man Jesse's barn, son?" Sheriff Dollard asked.

"Uh, I don't really remember, sir. I woke up when he found me."

The sheriff grunted. "You should know how you got there."

"I, uh—"

"Kid was bollicky bare-ass when I found him in the barn. No clothes, nothing on him. Can't even remember his name."

Sheriff Dollard frowned and repeated, "Can't remember your name?"

Ethan shook his head and gestured to Jesse. "Uh, no. We're calling me Ethan until I can remember who I am."

Jesse quickly explained what he knew to Sheriff Dollard. Deputy Davis made his way back to his desk and worked at his computer.

"Ethan, eh?" the sheriff asked with a grunt. "You don't look like an Ethan. You Hispanic or sumthin'?"

Ethan shrugged. "I guess? Maybe?"

"Well, when I look at your skin compared to ours, it's browner. Maybe you're Italian. Nah, you're Hispanic. I'd put money on it."

"Okay."

"Well, whatever he is, Sheriff, he's a lost boy who needs his family. He can stay with me and Janie until we figure out who he is."

"That's mighty kind of you, Jesse," Sheriff Dollard said. Then he looked squarely at Ethan. "I hope you understand the immensity of this man's generosity."

"I do, sir," Ethan replied.

"He does. Kid's been earning his keep. Stacked my hay this mornin', and he's gonna be splittin' and stackin' my wood for winter burning. He's not afraid to sweat."

"Good. Cuz I don't want any trouble from you up at the farm or in town, ya hear me, boy?"

Ethan nodded. "Yes, sir."

"Good. Afternoon, Jesse." Sheriff Dollard nodded at them before disappearing into his office.

Jesse nodded back. "Sheriff."

Deputy Davis spoke up. "Well, Ethan, I've run your prints through several databases. Good news is, you're not a felon. There's no record of your fingerprints in the state criminal database either. It'll take longer to run them against all the federal databases, but it appears we have the time." Deputy Davis paused as an idea formed in his mind. "Do you drive, Ethan? You look like you're over sixteen."

"Uh... maybe? I don't know."

"Okay. I'll run your picture against facial recognition at the DMV too. If you have a Virginia driver's license, we'll find it."

"Thanks, Deputy. Uh, what's a DMV?"

"The Department of Motor Vehicles. They manage driver's licenses. You need one to drive a vehicle."

"Oh."

"Well, unless you need anything else, Jesse, you boys can head home. I'll call you as soon as I find anything out."

Jesse nodded. "Thanks, Deputy. Much obliged. Have a pleasant afternoon."

"You too. Take care, Ethan. We'll figure this out, don't you worry."

Ethan smiled half-heartedly. "Thanks."

Blue Spekter landed at Hangar 227 with a scowl on his face, almost forgetting to decelerate to avoid cracking the tarmac.

The plainclothes soldiers watched him land with awe. The sight of a blue-glowing superhuman still amazed them.

When the elevator doors opened at the underground operations center level, he marched straight to Director Potter's office. The morning crew had been called in early, and the center bustled with activity. Officers and investigators of various ranks attempted to paint a picture with almost no information.

"What's going on, Quinn?" Director Potter asked as Blue Spekter plopped into one of the two chairs opposite the director.

"Victor's not dead. He's up to something. I know it." He pushed his cowl off his face and head and tousled his sweaty, matted hair.

Potter leaned forward and steepled his fingers together, elbows resting on his gunmetal-gray desk. "Yes, it would seem so."

"Clearly, there's another superhuman on the playing field. We still know nothing about where or how Victor makes them. How do we still know nothing?"

The director pursed his lips, then dropped his hands. "Quinn, they hid a secret orgone energy reactor on the same island as a high security naval base. Victor, through The Order, has access to significant finances. He also wields a weaponized orgone arsenal that has the potential to destabilize and change the world forever."

Quinn sat forward, excited. "Aha! We do know something. So, why the hell can't we find The Order?"

Potter pursed his lips and nodded. "Because they're unlike any enemy anyone has faced, perhaps in the world's history."

"What do you mean?" Quinn asked, leaning back.

"Normally, one nation fights another nation. A group of people battles another group of people for resources or dominance. Each nation has a capital or headquarters that lends itself as an automatic target. The Order isn't a nation with a capital or headquarters—they're decentralized. How do you find someone who could be anywhere and everywhere at the same time?"

Quinn sighed, and his shoulders slumped.

Director Potter cleared his throat and continued. "Believe me, I know it's hard. Orgone is such a strange and nearly undetectable energy. It could be all around us, and we'd never know it. You sense orgone the way I sense a cool breeze, but we don't have sensors that can detect the energy signature before Victor does something incredible—or devastating."

Quinn sat upright, seething with frustration that bordered on anger. "No, you don't understand. I fought those superhuman assholes here and over Rangeley. To save the world, I had to kill them, and I'm only seventeen! Whatever took out those soldiers in Spec did it in one fell swoop. I can't tell if it was malicious or accidental, and it's bugging the shit out of me. And now, the potential for another fucking Dark Flame just became real."

"You're right, Quinn. I don't understand what you've gone through, but I know you've taken the right steps to work through it. It might get easier, it might not. This morning's discovery shocks all of us. We knew it was coming, but we hoped it never would."

Quinn sighed and slouched into the chair.

Potter's shoulders relaxed. "Look, Quinn, I'm not trying to be dismissive. Down here, we all feel the invisible, crushing weight of Victor and The Order. Most have yet to understand the threat The Order poses to the world. Back in the sixties, after their initial efforts at making superhumans failed during the Cold War, they shifted their focus to weather manipulation. But it took them fifty years to figure out how to control the weather. Then the world changed when Blue Spekter arrived."

"So, it's my fault?" Quinn asked, his expression wary.

"Of course not. But from the little intel we've gathered, The Order under Victor's direction has refocused its efforts to create superhumans."

"But why? What is the point of creating evil superhumans?" Quinn asked.

"Then or now?"

Quinn shrugged. "Well, I know The Order supposedly wanted to create superhumans to defeat the Soviet Union during the rising threat of nuclear war, but now I'm honestly not sure if they were allied with American interests. What if they sold their 'product' to the Soviets?"

Director Potter smiled. "Now you're getting it. From what we know, The Order's goal is global domination."

"What does global domination even mean? Seems like that's what every super villain in every comic wants... that or horrific destruction."

"It's about control. They believe freedom and choice are illusions, an opium of the masses, to paraphrase Karl Marx."

"Who?"

Potter chuckled. "Uh, he's not important right now. The Order believes humanity craves direction just as much as they crave power. Imagine an entire globe under the boot of a communist regime."

"No, thanks."

"We need to be careful, because that's where we're headed, with or without superhumans in the mix."

"Do you believe The Order still wants to make money from the sale of superhumans?"

Potter shook his head. "No. The Order wants to emerge as the ruler of a new world order."

Quinn nodded with understanding. "That's what Victor promised Blake: the opportunity to build a brand-new world that would be safe from bombers and terrorists and everyone else who wants to blow someone up in the name of hate or religion."

"And who would be in charge?"

"The person with the biggest guns?" Quinn asked.

"Which right now is the U.S., Russia, and China. But introduce superhumans, a thirst for power, and the absence of moral leadership? Earth's mightiest nations would have no choice but to fall in line or face devastating consequences."

"Damn."

"So, we both agree it is imperative to find Victor and take him out. It is imperative we discover and understand how The Order works, and it is imperative we stop them both."

Quinn nodded. "No argument there."

"Victor is a scheming idealist. Someone in The Order saw his potential and seduced him with a lie similar to the one he used with Blake. But Victor outsmarted his superiors and defeated them with their own tactics. He's at the top or close to it, and he uses the same tactics to win people over. After all, he had already recruited and created the superhumans you defeated over Rangeley."

"But did we get them all?"

"There's a good chance we did. He likely miscalculated and threw all his forces against the three of you."

"Wait, so do you think the orgone bloom was Victor or someone else?"

"We already know he has created more superhumans. That dying guard thought you were on his side."

Quinn scratched his chin. "If there were guards in Spec, wouldn't that suggest a nearby reactor facility?"

"That's a strong possibility, and we're retasking several satellites to sweep over the area and beyond."

Quinn sat up with excitement. "Can I help?"

"Yes. It's Thursday. You can help by going home, showering, and going to school."

"What?"

"I'm serious. The fate of the world won't be decided today. If you wanna fly around Spec again this weekend, I won't stop you."

"But—"

"No buts. We must avoid alarming Victor. We're sending in plainclothes officers with the new orgone detectors Dr. Madison developed. They've never been field tested, so who knows if they'll help us. Our folks will look like tourists and locals, so they won't raise ire or suspicion."

Quinn sighed, crestfallen. "Fine."

"You gotta go to school, kid. You may be Earth's mightiest defender, but you still need your education. Even Iron Man has his diplomas."

Quinn chuckled and rolled his eyes. "You sound like my dads."

"Well, I know your dads would be furious with me if I authorized a day off from school so you could look for a needle in a haystack. When I need you, I'll call. I promise. We got you out of bed before the sun rose, right?"

Quinn stood and saluted half-heartedly. "Yeah, yeah, you're in charge. I'm not. See you later, DP."

Quinn turned and made his way out of Director Potter's office.

Potter smirked and shook his head. "Teenagers."

"I heard that!" Quinn shouted, smiling back at the director.

Chapter 4
Two Truths and a Lie

E than split wood the way Jesse had shown him. He lined up the quarter log on the trunk, aimed, raised the axe over his head, then swung the sharp blade in a graceful arc and split the wood in two. The halves fell to the ground, and he tossed them onto the nearby pile. Every so often, he wiped his sweaty forehead with his forearm.

Jesse ambled toward him on the footpath with two mugs of steaming hot liquid in his hand. "Maybe I should've brought you lemonade instead of hot cocoa," Jesse hollered.

"I'll take the hot cocoa," Ethan shouted back. The white undershirt he wore had become soaked with perspiration. But despite feeling warm from his chores, the sunny winter air still felt cold, and he couldn't shake an unusual chill.

Ethan lined up another quarter log and swung the axe. He stuck the axe in the trunk as Jesse approached and handed him a mug. They both enjoyed sips in silence.

"She melts down the milk chocolate, ya know," Jesse said. "We don't use that powdered crap in our hot cocoa."

Ethan smiled. "This tastes familiar. I must like it."

Jesse smiled. "A man's heart is found through his stomach. If food jogs your memory, then maybe you'll remember more at dinner. Janie is making her famous pot roast."

"I don't know what that is, but I assume it's delicious."

Jesse studied him for a moment. "You don't know what a pot roast is?" He sipped his cocoa.

"No. I didn't know what hot cocoa was until I drank it."

Jesse shifted his weight to his left leg. "What do you remember? You know how to walk and talk, and you're a quick study. I reckon you're a smart kid in school who gets good grades and all that. Did you remember the sky was blue, or did you discover that as well?"

Ethan chuckled. "It's like... well, I didn't recognize my body in the mirror this morning. I don't look the same, but I can't remember what I looked like. Things look normal to me—the color of the trees, the way the wind blows through the leaves. It's like I'm noticing it all for the first time, but it's not strange or new. But specific things you name, like hot cocoa and pot roast.... Or when Deputy Davis asked if I drove a car, I only knew what he meant because I rode in your truck. Experience jogs my memory."

"Damn."

"They said I might be Italian or Hispanic. I know the words, but I don't know what they mean. I don't know why my skin is, as Dollard said, 'browner' than yours. Is that a thing? I honestly don't know."

"You've never met a Black person before?"

"A what?"

Jesse's eyes bulged with shock. He pointed at his face with his free hand. "A person with... black, err, dark brown skin. It's usually much darker than yours."

Ethan itched his nose. "So, a Black person can be white?"

Jesse frowned and scratched his forehead. "Uh, no, that's not what I meant."

"Oh."

They stood in silence for a moment until Jesse spoke up. "So, what you're saying is, if you saw a Black person, it'd seem normal?"

"Probably. Before you taught me, I didn't know what splitting wood was. I understand it's for heating your home in the winter. I just don't understand what I'm doing here or why everything seems, uh, newish to me."

"Huh. Well, uh, Deputy Davis called a few moments ago."

"Oh?"

"Unfortunately, he doesn't know who you are either. Your face doesn't appear in the DMV database, which means you're probably not from Virginia. Or, you just don't have your driver's license yet."

"Okay." Ethan's heart sank with the unpleasant news.

"And your fingerprints didn't show up in the, well, the other government databases, either, which means you're not a criminal. There's a kindness about you, even though you don't know it." Jesse shot him a quizzical look. "Do you know what a criminal is?"

Ethan felt uncomfortable with the word. "The way you use the word, I think it's a bad person."

"Yep. It's someone who has broken the law. Anyway, that's not you. So, look, Ethan, you've been more than helpful today. Take a walk in the woods. There's some trails across the property, over yonder. Have some you time and see if anything comes up. Come back before the sunset, though. Janie's pot roast and mashed taters wait for no man, and you don't want to miss supper."

"Sounds good, Jesse."

"Eh, but don't get lost, okay? Stay on the trails. It's easy to lose your way in the forest."

"Will do."

Ethan crossed the field and found the trailhead. He meandered through the woods, sipping his cocoa. Unlike the other night when the soldiers chased him through the woods, he enjoyed the forest serenity and its rich smells, pine trees and crisp winter air. Unfortunately, nothing triggered his memory, but he recognized the differences between the scavenging chipmunks and squirrels that scurried by.

Several minutes later, a whooshing sound passed above him, through the tall pine trees. He glanced up and saw nothing, so he dismissed it and kept walking.

Ethan suddenly cried out in pain. He dropped the cocoa mug and cradled his head in both hands, doubling over before dropping to his knees on the trail. An overwhelming awareness of someone else filled his mind—and it hurt. Somehow, he knew they approached him through the trees, probably just up the trail. The sensation faded, and he grabbed his empty cocoa mug before straightening up.

A young woman emerged from a thicket of trees down the trail and smiled brightly at him. Wide-eyed, Ethan stared at her, realizing she was the person he had just sensed. She took several excited steps forward and said, "Hi, sweetheart!"

Ethan took a step back and raised the cocoa mug defensively. "Who are you? How did you do that?"

Confused, she paused and raised her hands, suggesting she meant no harm. "Do what?"

He pointed to his head. "I could feel you… in my mind. I still can."

"Because we're special. You can sense the others like you, others like me."

"Who are you?"

The young woman frowned. "You don't remember me?"

Ethan studied her features. Her most prominent feature was the striking frizzy, wavy red hair that fell to her chest. Her wide green eyes watched him with wonder and excitement. Beneath her light brown leather jacket, she wore a thick ivory turtleneck with skinny-fit dark-wash jeans and coffee-brown leather dress boots. He shook his head. "No, should I?"

"I'm someone special to you. I'm your girlfriend, and I've been looking for you."

"My what?" The scent of a light, flowery perfume hit Ethan's nose. It seemed familiar, but who she was remained lost on him.

"Your girlfriend. We're romantically involved."

"Girlfriend," he repeated, confused by the suggestion. "We are?" Unlike everything else he had remembered, nothing in his thoughts suggested she was important to him.

She frowned. "Do you remember me?"

Ethan shook his head. "No. What's your name?"

"My name is Vanessa. Do you know your name?"

Her name still didn't trigger memories about her or their relationship. He shook his head. "I don't. The couple who said I could stay with them call me Ethan."

Vanessa raised her eyebrow. "The couple you're staying with?"

"Yeah. It's complicated," he replied, wondering if he could trust her. Unlike Jesse and Janie, something about her didn't sit right in his gut.

"Oh. I like that name, but your name is Carlos Domínguez."

"Carlos," he repeated, and the name settled within him. "My name is Carlos."

"Do you remember that?"

Ethan—Carlos—smiled. "Yeah."

She took a step forward. "We work for a brilliant man named Victor Kraze."

The name triggered an uneasy feeling within Carlos.

When Vanessa noticed, she took another small step forward. "He's our friend, Carlos, and he made us special. We're part of an elite squad of individuals who—"

"Like the police?"

Vanessa regarded him with surprise and took another step forward. "No, not exactly. But we were conducting a training exercise. Something went wrong, something we still don't understand. You disappeared, and we've been searching for you since. I'm glad I finally found you."

"How long have I been gone?"

"A few days."

"The sensation in my head... is that linked to our specialness?"

"Yes. We can do some pretty amazing things."

37

"What else can we do?"

Vanessa drew a deep breath and studied him for a moment. "I'd rather not discuss that until you remember more. Are you staying at the farm on the other side of the field?"

"Yeah, why?"

She stepped forward again. "I'll report back that I found you. I'm so relieved. You need to stay there until we get new orders."

"I'm not going anywhere with you." He shook his head and took two steps back.

Shock fell across Vanessa's face. "Babe, why not?"

"If I've been missing, why couldn't the deputy find a missing person's report?"

"Because we didn't file one. People like us exist outside the law."

"How old am I?"

Vanessa's eyes widened. "You're seventeen."

"So I can drive," he murmured.

"What? Of course you can."

"Where did you come from?" he asked, becoming more suspicious.

She pointed to the trail behind her. "We've been searching the woods. It's taken time, but I'm glad I found you."

"For how long?"

"About two days."

But I woke up in the barn this morning. He swallowed. "I'm gonna go now. You do whatever you want, but I don't know who you are."

"Babe, I promise it will all make sense. Maybe we should just go back—"

"I said no!" The forcefulness of his voice startled both of them. He felt hot and pulled at his collar. After a moment, he softened and asked, "Am I from Virginia?"

She shook her head. "No. You're from Portsmouth, New Hampshire."

Carlos reflected on that revelation, but no memories stirred. However, it did sound familiar. "Thanks."

"I'm gonna get going and check in with leadership. But before I go, can I give you a hug? Maybe that will jog a memory."

He studied her smiling face for a moment but chose to listen to the uneasiness in his gut. "Uh, no. Not yet."

"Oh," Vanessa replied, appearing crestfallen.

"I just don't know you. Like, at all."

"All right, then. I'll leave you be." She winked. "Don't you be following me now." She turned and made her way down the path.

When Vanessa disappeared past the thicket of trees, Carlos still knew where she was in his mind and could imagine her walking away—until she was gone and it was quiet around him. Confused, he jogged down the trail after her for several minutes, but she had vanished just as mysteriously as she had appeared.

"The hell?" Carlos muttered, drawing a deep breath of fresh air before making his way back to the farmhouse.

Janie watched Ethan curiously as he toyed with the melting butter on his mashed potatoes. "What's wrong, dear? Do you not like smashed taters?"

"Oh, uh, I do, Janie. They're delicious. It's just that, well… I had a strange encounter in the woods."

"I see. Do you want to talk about it?" she asked kindly.

"Uh, sure. Well, I met a girl in the woods."

"You what?" Jesse asked, startled. He nearly dropped his fork on the table.

"Oh my," Janie added.

"I met a girl in the woods," Ethan repeated. "Her name is Vanessa, and she claimed to know me and that we were—uh, are—romantically involved, but I don't remember her, like, at all. I've recalled things after you showed them to me, but I can't remember her at all."

"A random girl in the woods. Doesn't that seem strange to you?" Jesse asked, shoveling a forkful of beef into his mouth.

"I think so. Is that not normal?"

Jesse shook his head. "Just about as normal as finding a bollicky bare-ass boy in my barn."

Ethan chuckled. "So, no."

Jesse shook his head and shoved another forkful of pot roast into his mouth. "Definitely not normal."

"Don't talk with your mouth full, dear," Janie said absentmindedly, her gaze fixed on Ethan.

Jesse grunted.

"What did this Vanessa say?" Janie asked, lowering her fork to her plate while regarding him with concern.

"Basically told me who I was, that she's my girlfriend, and that I was out here on a training exercise that went wrong and I disappeared."

"A training exercise? Are you in the military?"

"I don't think so. She said I'm seventeen. Can you be in the military when you're seventeen?"

Janie shook her head. "No, you can't enlist until you turn eighteen."

"Oh."

"Where is Vanessa now?"

Ethan shrugged. "She went back into the woods."

Jesse shot his wife a concerned look. "You're certain this Vanessa person is real? Are you hallucinating?"

Ethan chuckled. "I don't think so, but I understand how bizarre it sounds. I met her on the trail near a bunch of trees. I didn't see which way she went. When I ran after her, she was gone. But she knew I was staying here with you."

"Hmmm," Jesse murmured with concern. "Did she say anything useful?"

"She told me I'm from Portsmouth, New Hampshire, and that my name is Carlos Domínguez."

"Carlos! That's a lovely name," Janie said, a wide smile dancing on her face. "It's a pleasure to meet you, Carlos."

"Thanks," he replied with a sheepish smile.

"And Domínguez. How exotic!"

"Domínguez," Jesse echoed quietly. "So, you're Hispanic, or Spanish."

"I guess? I recognize it as my name, but it doesn't trigger any memories of my family."

"Well, we can call Deputy Davis tomorrow and give him this new information. Maybe you're registered as missing in New Hampshire."

"Yeah, uh, Vanessa said the reason deputies won't find a missing person's report is because I'm part of a special group that operates outside the law."

Jesse stared at him for a moment. "What?"

Carlos shrugged. "I don't know what it means either. She tried to take me with her, but I refused. That got her all upset, and it seemed to confuse her. She's supposed to check with someone to figure out what to do, something about needing new orders."

"Maybe you should stay out of those woods. Make her come to the house. I'd like to ask this Vanessa a few questions."

"I will, Jesse."

"At any rate, we should speak with Deputy Davis tomorrow morning and tell him who you think you are. No need having him run a wild goose chase, right?"

Carlos stared blankly at Jesse. "Is chasing a goose related to figuring out who I am?"

Janie chuckled, and Jesse's mouth fell agape. "It's an expression, son." He explained the colloquialism, and they shared a laugh. As they finished dinner, Carlos listened to their small talk and appreciated how they tried to include him in the conversation. Unfortunately, he had no reference points for current events or much of anything else they tried to talk with him about.

After cleaning up and doing the dishes by hand with Janie, he sat with them in the living room and watched a show called *I Love Lucy*. A fire crackled in the fireplace, casting a soft glow and spreading warmth across the family room.

Later, after Jesse and Janie had fallen asleep (and snored a bit) in their recliners, Carlos went upstairs to shower, studying the unfamiliar family pictures hung in the staircase along the way.

Carlos relaxed under the hot stream of water, letting its heat seep in and soothe his muscles. He thought about nothing for a few minutes as he ran the bar of soap over his wet body. A powerful urge overcame him, and he willingly surrendered to the much-needed and familiar distraction until his body tensed with toe-curling delight. He grunted quietly with the cascading pleasure and felt an unusual and unfamiliar power surge through his body. And out of the corner of his eye, he swore he saw an arc of yellow electricity snap across his arm. The vanity lights flickered wildly until the moment faded. Staring down at himself in disbelief, he shook his head, somehow realizing that it was impossible.

Understanding the farmhouse was old, he shrugged it off and washed up. Stepping out of the tub, he stared at himself in the mirror, noticing his body appeared more muscular—even from earlier that morning. His chest, back, shoulders, and arms had swelled and seemed larger, and his abs had tightened into a visible eight-pack. His quads, glutes, and calves were bigger too.

He finished drying his hair and pulled on a pair of gray sweatpants, then climbed into bed. He lay on his back, hands clasped behind his head as he stared at the ceiling, but sleep eluded him.

He thought about how his body looked and wondered if there was any truth to what Vanessa had said about him—them—being special. After all, he had caused the explosion that killed his pursuers. And unlike Vanessa, of the handful of people he had met that day, from the deputy to the folks at the corner store, none of them had triggered that strange sensation of awareness that let him locate her.

Was she like him, and if she was, did it explain the mysteriousness of her sudden appearance and disappearance?

And why didn't he remember her romantically? Everything he had experienced—from sheep, stacking hay, splitting wood, and hot cocoa—felt familiar after someone introduced it to him.

But her?

Nothing. Not a hint of recognition or attraction. She was pretty, and he'd be lucky to be with a woman like her, but he didn't know her or the Victor guy she had mentioned. But New Hampshire felt familiar, which meant she had told him something truthful during their exchange in the forest.

He sighed and closed his eyes. Eventually, sleep overtook him for the night.

Chapter 5
What Is Real?

T he next morning, Jesse and Carlos met with Deputy Davis to share the information gleaned from Vanessa. They waited patiently as the deputy tapped at his computer. Jesse leaned against the counter, and Carlos fidgeted nervously with his fingers, hopeful to discover more about his identity.

Deputy Davis smiled. "Found it. Chief Tina Applegate of the Portsmouth Police Department authorized the missing person's report on Monday of this week. However, hmmm, that's odd. Someone—there's no name here—marked the report as completed yesterday. Unfortunately, there's no note, so I don't know why they closed the report."

"Maybe it's because Vanessa found me," Carlos said.

Deputy Davis shifted his stance. "Tell me more about her, Carlos. You said she appeared and disappeared on the trail?"

Carlos nodded. "I'm sure it sounds crazy. It does to me. I was all alone, and then she was there. And when I wouldn't go with her, she left saying she needed to check in with her boss or someone like that. Then she was gone. I tried to follow her, but I couldn't find her."

"Okay. I'll still send someone over to check it out. And you don't remember if she's your girlfriend?"

Carlos shook his head. "I think I have a girlfriend back home. That word triggers something warm in my heart, but it's definitely not her. I have no idea who she is. Does the report say anything else about me?"

Deputy Davis studied the report on the computer screen. "Yes, that a Mrs. Yolanda Domínguez filed the missing person's report."

"I recognize that name."

"Says here she's your guardian and, uh, ab… abuela?"

Recognition clicked within Carlos. "Yes, that's right. She's my abuela, my grandma. We live in Portsmouth, in a brick house."

"Atlantic Heights?"

"Yup, that's in my neighborhood. Oh my gosh, that's where I'm from!" Carlos said with a smile.

"Do you live with your grandma?" Jesse asked.

Carlos nodded enthusiastically. "Yeah, I think so."

"No parents?"

Shaking his head, Carlos said, "I don't think so. I don't remember why, but I don't think they're around."

"I'm sorry," Jesse replied.

"I don't know if that's a bad thing." Carlos shrugged. "Just the way it is."

"There's a phone number here. Would you like to call her?"

Carlos nodded again. "Yes, please."

Deputy Davis wrote the phone number on a piece of scratch paper, then pointed to an empty desk behind him. "You can use that phone there to call your grandma."

Carlos dialed the number from the desk phone. On the third ring, a woman answered. "Hello?"

"Abuela, it's me, Carlos."

"Carlos!" Abuela squealed, causing Carlos to pull the phone away from his ear. She continued in Spanish, and Carlos realized he also spoke Spanish.

"What happened, Carlosito? Where did you go? Why did you leave? Where are you?"

He replied in Spanish that flowed naturally from him. "I'm sorry, Abuela, I have amnesia. I don't know what happened."

Both Jesse and Deputy Davis stared at him in surprise. Carlos covered the mouthpiece, shrugged, and said in English, "Apparently I speak Spanish."

Abuela became impatient. "Where are you? Where is area code 757?"

"I'm in a small town in Virginia." He spoke in English out of consideration for the two men who observed his side of the call.

"Virginia! What... why are you there?"

"Abuela, I don't know what happened. Yesterday morning, I woke up in a barn." To avoid alarming her, he deliberately left out the fact that he had been naked. "A kind man and his wife welcomed me into their home, and we've been working with the police to find out who I am."

"Who you are? What do you mean you don't know who you are?"

"I remember nothing. I have amnesia."

"Well, come home, Carlosito. You've missed a full week of school!"

"I know, Abuela. I just have to figure out how to get home."

"Who brought you there? You tell them I said to bring you home right now!"

Carlos bowed his head in frustration. "Abuela, I don't know how I got here. I didn't know my name until my supposed girlfriend tried to get me to come with her."

"Your girlfriend? What does Everleigh have to do with this?"

"Everleigh is my girlfriend?"

Jesse and the deputy exchanged glances.

"Of course," Abuela said. "What do you mean she tried to come get you? She's at school, worried sick about you."

"She didn't. It was someone named Vanessa."

"Who is Vanessa?"

Carlos rubbed the bridge of his nose. "Ugh, the girl pretending to be my girlfriend, I guess."

"You are cheating on Everleigh?" Abuela shrieked.

"What? No, Abuela, it's not like that at all. I'm not cheating on Everleigh. I didn't remember her until you mentioned her name."

"Why are you talking like a crazy person?" Abuela asked.

"Abuela! I have amnesia, and I remember nothing. I didn't remember you until the police down here in Virginia found the missing person's report you filed."

"How could you forget your abuela, Carlosito? I've cared for you since you were five years old!"

"Because I did, okay? I'm sorry you're not understanding right now, but I need money to get home."

"How will you come home?"

"I don't know, hold on." He pulled the mouthpiece away from his face and looked at the deputy. "How far am I from home, and how would I get there?"

Deputy Davis and Jesse stared at one another for a moment. The deputy took a shot at the answer. "It won't be easy without some form of identification, which you don't have. That rules out planes and trains and leaves the bus systems. You're about four hours south of Washington D.C. From there, you'd have to bus to Boston and likely take another bus to Portsmouth, but you'll have to research that. Never been there myself. You're looking at the better part of a day of travel, I'd say. Maybe two, depending on how the buses run."

Carlos nodded. "Thanks." He brought the phone close to his face again. "Abuela, it's going to take a day or two to get home, but I don't have any money for tickets."

"You know we don't have the money for expensive travel. Where are you now?"

"I'm at the sheriff's office in town."

"Sheriff? Are you in trouble with the law? Did you get arrested?"

"What? No!"

"We don't need a repeat of last year, Carlosito."

47

Carlos frowned, confused by her statement. Having no recollection of what she meant, he ignored it. "Abuela, Deputy Davis has been helping me figure out who I am. That's how we got your number—from the missing person's report you filed."

A moment of silence passed. "I'll have to ask some friends for some help. Figure out how much you need to come home, mijo. I'll wire the money to the sheriff's office for your bus tickets. Put the deputy on the phone, please."

"Okay." Carlos stood and extended the phone in his hand. "She'd like to speak with you, Deputy."

Deputy Davis nodded and traded places with Carlos, who shoved his hands in his pockets and went to stand near Jesse.

"So, that's your grandma?" Jesse asked.

"Yeah. I remember her."

"She sounds upset."

Carlos chuckled. "That obvious?"

"Just a bit. Don't worry, it's gonna work out. We'll get you home, one way or another."

Several minutes later, Deputy Davis hung up the phone. He rubbed his temples and smiled politely at Carlos. "She's, uh, intense."

Carlos smirked.

"Jesse, do y'all have a computer with the Internet?" Deputy Davis asked.

"Nah, I ain't got that fancy modern stuff."

"Carlos, I can't believe I'm going to ask you this question, but do you know how to use a computer?"

Carlos shrugged. "Maybe?"

Deputy Davis rolled his eyes. "Look, I'm gonna do you this one favor since you're being so kind to Jesse and Janie. And honestly, you just need to get home. I'll research your way home and purchase the appropriate bus tickets. Then I'll call your grandma and tell her how much she needs to wire us for the tickets."

"Thank you," Carlos said, wondering if money was going to be a problem.

Jesse tipped his hat. "That's mighty kind of you, Deputy."

The deputy chuckled. "Don't thank me yet, Jesse. Buses to D.C. don't pass through here every day. He might be around for a while."

Unfazed, Jesse grinned. "There's plenty more wood to chop and stack back at the farm."

Jesse steered the truck up the dirt driveway. Both he and Carlos noticed a blue Subaru Outback parked in front of the house.

"Who's that?" Carlos asked.

"Don't know. Never seen that fancy a car before."

Carlos's hands shot up, and he squeezed his temples. "Ouch!"

"What's wrong?" Jesse asked, alarmed, as he parked the truck.

"It's her. She's inside. I can sense her."

"Who?"

"Vanessa. The girl from the woods I told you about."

Jesse cursed.

A moment later, the intense sensation faded. "I think they're sitting and talking."

"How do you know that?"

"Well, I have an awareness of Vanessa. She's sitting at the kitchen table, in the seat next to the window. I can't sense Janie, though. Nor you."

"Strange."

"She's strange. If I can sense her, she can probably sense me. We should go."

Jesse grabbed Carlos's arm gently. "Listen, if you don't trust her, don't be quick to volunteer information."

"What do you mean?"

"It's just a hunch. Don't tell her you spoke with your grandma, and don't tell her your real girlfriend's name. Listen to what she has to say. That'll help you understand how much is truth or lies. Like how much you can trust her, ya know?"

Carlos nodded. "Sounds like a plan, Jesse. Thanks." The two men entered the house together.

When Carlos followed Jesse into the house through the side door into the kitchen, a brightly smiling Vanessa jumped to her feet. "Babe! I've missed you."

Jesse grunted as Vanessa crossed the kitchen and excitedly hugged Carlos. Her warm hug seemed familiar and welcome but felt irritating at the same time for reasons unknown.

"Isn't it wonderful?" Janie asked, staring at her husband. Carlos politely smiled at Janie and detected the slightest hint of concern in her eyes.

"Mmm," Jesse grunted.

Carlos's gaze shifted to Jesse, who returned the same worried look to his wife.

After letting go of Carlos, Vanessa turned to Jesse. "I'm sorry, sir. I'm Vanessa, Carlos's girlfriend."

Jesse nodded curtly and shook her hand. "A pleasure."

Vanessa turned back to Carlos with a cheery smile. "Babe, what have you been up to?" she asked, rubbing Carlos's arms.

"Trying to figure out how I got here."

"Oh, I can tell you that!"

"Yeah?"

"We've been working with the impoverished—" She stopped when she saw Carlos's confused expression. "Oh, you know, doing mission-ary work for our church youth group, and we—"

"Missionary work?" Carlos asked, confused.

Janie shot Jesse and Carlos a doubtful look that Vanessa didn't notice.

"Yeah, we're repairing run-down houses for people in the area who can't afford much. We belong to Faith Baptist Church, and our youth group is called Christ's Light."

Carlos drew a deep breath and nervously shifted his stance. "Who are you, Vanessa?"

"What do you mean?" Vanessa asked, appearing confused.

"Who are you to me?"

"I'm your girlfriend. Why don't we sit down, and we can talk?"

"Would you like us to give you some privacy?" Janie asked.

"No," Carlos replied quickly.

Vanessa's expression flashed with irritation before reforming into a pleasant smile. "Then let's sit."

Carlos, Jesse, and Vanessa sat at the table with Janie, who pushed the coffee pot toward them. "Coffee's still hot if you want some."

"Thanks," Carlos said, pouring himself a mug. Jesse moved a mug across the table, and Carlos poured him a cup too. "So, mission work, huh? Where?"

"In the next town over, Lithia. We're working with the Lithia Faith Baptist Church."

Carlos glanced at Jesse, who nodded. "Then why didn't you tell me this yesterday?"

One of Vanessa's eyes twitched. "Yesterday?"

"Yeah. When you mysteriously met me on the trail on the other side of the field. You told me we're part of some elite squad that was out doing a training exercise. Now we were doing—"

"Missionary work is what we're doing here, Carlos," Vanessa interjected sternly. "We're not in the military."

Carlos drummed his fingers on the table. "All right, so tell me how I wandered off and wound up in Jesse's barn."

"Well, I wasn't with you when that happened." She shot Janie a concerned glance. "The boys snuck out of the cabins and went, I'm sorry to say, ma'am, skinny-dipping in the river."

"Oh my," Janie commented, covering her mouth in shock. Jesse rolled his eyes, and Carlos couldn't gauge Janie's sincerity.

Vanessa placed her hand on her heart. "I know. I'm sorry to admit that in front of you, Mrs. Collins. The church frowns upon that sort of behavior, I assure you."

"Of course," Janie replied. "But why did they skinny-dip in the middle of February? The water is deathly cold."

"I went winter skinny-dipping with other church boys?" Carlos asked, eyes wide with shock.

"We'll talk about that later, babe. Yes, Mrs. Collins. The boys took part in the unofficial polar swim. It's not a summer frolic, though. They rush in, submerge themselves, then rush out. Whole thing probably takes less than ten minutes."

Janie shook her head, a worried look falling over her. "Oh my, jumping into the river at this time of year sounds absolutely dreadful."

"Indeed. Anyway, they thought everyone had come back, and no one realized you were missing until yesterday morning, when you were nowhere to be found."

"So, where is the minister?" Jesse asked.

"An excellent question, Mr. Collins. When I explained to Pastor Kraze that I had found Carlos but he was suffering from the most horrible case of amnesia, he became concerned. But I told him Carlos was staying with kind people, and he trusts me to bring Carlos back to the flock."

"Pastor Kraze?" Carlos asked.

"Yes. Pastor Victor Kraze is our youth pastor. He's in charge of the discipleship and missionary programs at our church too."

Once again, the strange name did not sit easily with Carlos.

"He must be so worried," Janie said, an expression of concern spreading across her face. She wrung her hands together nervously. "Why don't you invite him over?"

Vanessa immediately shook her head. "No, but thank you for your hospitality. Pastor Kraze would like me to bring Carlos back to the flock."

She looked at Carlos and grasped his hands. "Your friends and family are worried about you, Carlos. They were relieved to know I found you, just as much as I'm relieved that you're back. My heart was so twisted with sadness when we thought we'd lost you. I know you'll remember everything soon. You just need to see what's familiar to you."

"My family?" Carlos asked innocently.

"Your mom was not thrilled with Pastor Kraze after he told her you went missing. I was sitting nearby, being consoled by some of our sisters in Christ, when Pastor Kraze made the phone call. I've never heard your mom so angry."

"And my dad?"

Vanessa squeezed his hand. "Your dad is the strong, silent type. I don't know what he said on the phone, if anything. Last night, he answered the phone when I called to share the good news that I had found you."

"You spoke to my dad yourself?"

A wide smile spread across Vanessa's face. "Yes, praise be to God. Your parents are elated. Once we rejoin with the youth group, you and I are going home. We need to see a doctor for your amnesia."

"And nobody knows how I went from skinny-dipping in the river to... missing?"

Vanessa shook her head again. "We were hoping you could tell us."

"I remember nothing."

"Did you get lost in the dark? Did you hit your head on something? Did the other boys play a mean prank on you?"

"I honestly don't know, Vanessa."

"I understand. You must've hit your head or something. You're so lucky to have found Mr. Collins's barn. Otherwise, you could have died of hypothermia." Tears welled in her eyes, and her face wrinkled with sadness before she regained her composure. "But I'm guessing you don't have a concussion."

"What's a concussion?" Carlos asked.

53

Jesse cleared his throat. "It's when you hit your head hard. You see stars and shit in your vision, and you can't be allowed to sleep for a while, to make sure nothing worse happens. But I found him sleepin' in my barn, and he showed no signs of concussion, Miss Vanessa."

"That's wonderful, Mr. Collins. So, I apologize, but I have to ask a troublesome question. Carlos, when will you be ready to come back to the camp?"

Carlos shook his head. "Not today."

"What?" Vanessa asked, her voice trembling.

"I told you yesterday, I don't know who you are."

"But we've been together for almost a year."

Carlos shook his head again. "New words, sights, and facts all trigger my memory in seconds. You don't."

"Does our pastor's name ring a bell? Do you recognize the name Victor Kraze?"

"Vaguely."

"Well, praise be to God, that's a start."

Carlos frowned. "He's someone I don't trust. Or like. I'm not sure which one yet."

"What?" Vanessa asked, shocked. "You love him! He's one of your top ten favorite people."

"Mmm… I don't think so. Look, I need time to think about things. Have my dad call me. Janie can give you the phone number here. Hearing my dad's voice should trigger my memory. If my parents confirm you are who you say you are, and I remember things, then heck yeah, I'll go with you. I'm just not ready to leave the only thing I know right now. Besides, I've got some more wood to stack for Jesse."

Vanessa suddenly looked furious and pursed her lips tightly. "Can I talk to you outside, alone, for a moment?"

"Uh, sure."

They got up and headed toward the front porch. Carlos felt Jesse's and Janie's concerned gazes as he followed Vanessa onto the porch.

When the door shut behind Carlos, Vanessa rounded on him. "Freeze asset one!"

"Huh?" Carlos replied, looking confused.

Vanessa regarded him with surprise. "Aw, crap."

"I'm sorry?"

"Carlos, you need to come with me. No more games. These old people mean nothing to you."

"They sheltered me and gave me food and clothing."

"So, thank them for their kindness, and let's go."

"No."

"Why not?" Vanessa nearly shouted.

"The fact that you're so desperate to bring me somewhere I don't even belong, for starters."

"But—"

"Have my mom or dad call me. Or call the Spec Sheriff's Office. They know how to get in touch with Jesse."

"Why did you go to the sheriff's office?" Vanessa asked, somewhat alarmed.

"I went yesterday with Jesse to find out if anyone had filed a missing person's report. But no one had."

"Well, of course not, silly. I had already found you. You hadn't even been gone a full day yet."

"Uh-huh. Well, goodbye for now, I guess."

Vanessa became cross. "You're making a mistake, Carlos. Come with me right now."

"No. You need to leave me the hell alone until I know who you are, understand?"

"That is not how you speak to your girlfriend."

"If that's even who you really are."

"How can you say that? That's so mean!" Vanessa asked, wiping a tear from her eye.

"I told you, I don't remember you. I have no idea who you are."

"I knew it was a mistake getting involved with you. Everyone warned me you were nothing but a jerk. I should've listened to my friends."

Carlos rolled his eyes. "If we're nothing more than missionaries, why can I sense you in my head? I can't sense anyone else."

"I told you yesterday, you and I are special."

"That's not what you told me in there," Carlos said, jerking a thumb toward the house.

"Of course not. I can't risk Janie and Jesse knowing what we truly are."

"Then what is real?"

"Our connection is real. Come back with me and meet Victor."

"Is that guy a youth pastor? Is there even a church?"

"No. He's something more than that."

"Uh-huh. Have my dad call me, okay? Have a nice day, Vanessa."

He turned and went back inside, never giving her a second glance. He watched from the kitchen window as she drove away and kept watching until her presence faded from his mind.

Behind him, Janie washed the coffee mugs in the kitchen sink. Jesse still sat at the table, staring at nothing in particular, though he appeared frustrated. Carlos turned, and they stared at one another.

"What a crock of horseshit." Janie shook her head. Carlos's eyes popped open with surprised amusement when Janie angrily cursed. "That girl sure knows how to lie, hun. I don't trust her."

"Me either, Janie," Carlos said. "If you guys can put up with me for a few more days, I'll get on that bus and head home. I want nothing to do with her or the supposed minister guy."

Janie crossed the room and embraced him. "Stay as long as you need, dear. I've enjoyed your company, and Jesse much appreciates your help with the wood and other chores around the farm. We're not getting any younger these days."

"Yep, much obliged," Jesse added. "These bones are gettin' old, slow, and sore."

Carlos sighed. "I need to think."

"Why don't you and I head to the Barley Shack this afternoon?"

"Jesse, he's seventeen!"

"Oh pish-posh, Janie. I wasn't suggesting he drink a beer. He can have a Coke."

"Oh," Janie said.

Carlos smiled. "I don't know what that is, but I'm probably gonna like it."

Chapter 6
Uninhibited

After lunch, Carlos accompanied Jesse to the Barley Shack, the town's only pub. The aged and beer-stained wooden paneling on the walls betrayed the sins of patrons who had come before, and the venue smelled of buttery popcorn and beer nuts. They sat at a weathered but highly polished bar under dim, incandescent Edison-style lighting. Classic rock music played on hidden speakers. Some quiet locals who seemed to make a day job out of drinking sat nearby. Others occupied the dimly lit booths along the walls, and two retirees played pool in the billiard area.

The bartender delivered their drinks, and they each took a sip—Jesse, a cheap pale ale, and Carlos, a Coke. Jesse set his beer down and spoke first. "So, there is a Baptist Church in Lithia, but its membership is dying off. It's not one to, uh, commune or work with other churches. They keep to themselves when it comes to prayin' mostly, but when the menfolk come in here, they pretend not to recognize one another."

"Why?"

Jesse chuckled. "Most Baptists don't drink alcohol. It's a strict no-no."

"Oh."

Jesse frowned, then swirled the beer in his glass. "I don't mean to alarm you, so don't look right now. A man in the corner is staring at you. I reckon he's fixin' to do something."

"Uh, okay?"

"Hold on, he's just getting off his phone. He's got a brown T-shirt with a John Deere on it."

"A what?"

"It's a green tractor. Can't miss him. Okay, look now."

Carlos whipped around and spotted the man Jesse had referred to. He turned back and shrugged. "I don't know who that is."

"I wonder if he's one of your not-girlfriend's people. You know, the special squad thing she intentionally avoided mentioning this mornin'."

"Maybe. There's, um, something I didn't tell you."

Jesse furrowed his eyebrows. "Aw, hell, Carlos."

"Vanessa might be right about the squad thing."

"Why's that? You think you're in the army or sumthin'?" Jesse sipped his beer.

"I don't remember everything, but a few things stand out in my mind. The night before you found me, I woke up deep in the woods. I don't know where that was in relation to the barn. There were soldiers chasing me, and I was running from them, but I don't remember from where. I remember crossing a river, and—" Carlos's voice quivered, and he hesitated.

"You can tell me, son."

Carlos cleared his throat and pushed his Coke away, losing the taste for it. "They almost caught me, but I did something I don't think people should be able to do."

"What was it?"

"Somehow, I exploded."

"Huh?" Jesse asked, his face wrinkling with confusion.

"They had me surrounded, at gunpoint. I was down on the ground on my hands and knees, and then... I just... well, some kind of energy exploded from me and knocked everyone back. Nobody moved, so I ran."

"Are you pulling my leg?" Jesse asked, slightly irritated.

"No, sir. I ran, and then I woke up in your barn when you opened the door. That reminds me, I should oil that hinge before I go."

Jesse laughed. "That hinge and I go way back. Don't bother with it. Mabel would be all out of sorts if she didn't hear me comin'."

"All right, I won't. Anyway, I must have found the barn and cuddled with Mabel to keep warm before I passed out."

"You're stronger than a boy should be, for your age," Jesse said. He sipped his beer.

"I am?"

"You pick up the hay bales with one arm, like it's a bag of cotton balls. My boys could never do that, and they were rugged outdoorsmen."

"Oh."

"Not only that, you split every log with one swing of the axe. That's a learned skill."

"Huh."

"And when I found you, you were this scrawny kid, a skin sack hanging on a skeleton. Now look at you. You've filled out and look like one of those Olympic athletes, all muscles and strength."

Carlos nodded. "I noticed that change too."

"One thing's for certain, Vanessa ain't part of no Jesus camp from around here. There's more truth in what she tried to cover up—what she told you in the woods—than that fake missionary bullshit she tried to sell us. She thought we were two stupid hicks. Shame on her."

Carlos chuckled.

"Took balls to ask her to have your parents call you. Part of me is curious if she'll drum up some fancy actor to play your dad."

"Right," Carlos said, reaching for and sipping his Coke.

They chatted until the main door opened, jingling a small brass bell that hung from the door. Four tough-looking, rugged men wearing black boots, tactical pants, and leather jackets entered the pub, drawing the attention of the locals and the bartender. Two of them wore fingerless gloves.

"Can I help you?" the bartender asked, wiping a beer glass.

The newcomers didn't respond. Instead, they glanced at the man in the brown T-shirt, who pointed to where Carlos and Jesse sat. They approached, determination in their footsteps.

"Carlos Domínguez?" one of them asked.

Carlos put down his Coke. "I think so."

"Freeze asset one."

"Excuse me?" Carlos replied, unsure of what that meant.

The man pursed his lips. "You need to—"

"Are you boys from the church?" Jesse asked, cutting the man off.

"What?" the man in the lead asked with derision, side-eying Jesse.

"The church mission trip Vanessa said Carlos got separated from. I thought it was a youth trip, not an incarceration. Y'all look dressed for some military action."

The leader rolled his eyes and ignored Jesse. "Let's go, Carlos. Come with us right now." He stepped forward as if to grab Carlos with his gloved hands.

"Now hold on just a minute!" Jesse said, jumping off his barstool with surprising speed and stepping between the man and Carlos.

Jesse didn't intimidate the man. "Beat it, Gramps." The three other men stepped forward.

"Did your mama teach you to talk to your elders with such disrespect and contempt?" Jesse fired back.

"I said beat it!" The man pulled back his arm and swung at Jesse, whose eyes widened with fear as the massive fist moved toward his face. Carlos leaped from his barstool and extended his arm over Jesse's shoulder, catching the fist in his hand, halting it. The man grunted, and his pals took a step back. Jesse, mouth agape, stared at the frozen fist.

"You might wanna step aside, Jesse," Carlos said.

"Uh-huh," Jesse said, slipping out of the way, catching a glimpse of a bright yellow glow emanating from Carlos's eyes. They appeared to smoke with wisps of energy that defied explanation.

"Aw, shit, his inhibitor chip is busted," one man muttered.

"You don't hit my friends," Carlos muttered, squeezing the man's fist. The man's face contorted with pain, and when he tried to pull back, Carlos held him fast.

"Tase him!" the man shouted.

His friends reacted and reached for something at their waists.

Carlos leaped forward again and shoved the leader back, knocking him off balance and into one of the other men. The other two men retrieved their Tasers and aimed at Carlos.

"No guns, no guns!" the bartender shouted, ducking behind the bar.

One man fired, but Carlos's hand moved faster than the Taser darts. He caught them in midair. Electrical arcs danced across his hand and arm.

Carlos winced at the pain, but the current wasn't strong enough to immobilize him. An urge to push rose within him, and he followed through. The electricity that snapped and crackled along his arm shifted and traveled back over the Taser cables to the hand unit and zapped the man, who shrieked. He collapsed and convulsed under the intense electrical current, taking him out of the fight.

The second man fired his Taser, and the prongs connected with Carlos's right pectoral. Carlos grunted with pain and tightened his abs at the unusual sensation of electrical power coursing through his body.

The locals at the bar who had been watching the fight started moving back, out of the way of all the combatants.

The leader and the one he had knocked over recovered and fired their Tasers into Carlos's chest and stomach. Carlos gritted his teeth and nearly doubled over from the pain induced by the electrical assault, but he remained standing. His body shimmered with yellow motes of power that arced and traveled along his exposed skin and clothing.

The leader cautiously approached and dragged back his free arm, though he didn't swing, as though he was unsure if he should punch someone whose body teemed with the voltage of four Tasers.

Carlos straightened slowly and looked at the man with a wicked grin. "I can do this all day."

The man's eyes widened with surprise, but that didn't stop him from throwing his best hook punch.

"No!" Jesse shouted, but it was too late.

The man's fist connected with the side of Carlos's face with a loud crack—except Carlos didn't flinch. The man immediately dropped his Taser and grabbed his broken hand, screaming.

Carlos pushed one more time, and the electricity coursing through him traveled back across the three sets of Taser cables, shocking each man and knocking them to the floor.

Their bodies convulsed until Carlos pulled back, and the electricity faded and disappeared. The air smelled of ozone and the disgusting scent of burned flesh and hair, but Carlos didn't care.

"Carlos, we need to go," Jesse said, watching the four men twitch as their central nervous systems reacted to the fading voltage.

Stunned, Carlos looked at Jesse and saw his electrical reflection in the old mirror wall behind the bar. "Uh, right…. That's probably a good idea," he replied, his voice sounding dazed. He released the power coursing through him. The yellow motes of electricity dancing around him faded away.

"I'll settle up with you later, Gary," Jesse hollered to the bartender. He grabbed Carlos's arm and tugged him to the entrance.

A small arc of power snapped between them, but it felt nothing more like a static electric shock.

Jesse groaned nervously, then led Carlos to the truck.

Carlos didn't speak until they were back home. When they climbed out of the truck, he dropped to his knees as overwhelming feelings of confusion and sadness bubbled up.

"What the hell was that, Jesse?" he cried out, his voice warbling with emotion. He pulled his hands to his head. "I shouldn't be able to do that!"

Carlos began sobbing. Jesse came around the truck, knelt, and pulled Carlos into his arms.

"What the hell is wrong with me?" Carlos moaned through his sobs.

Janie poked her head out the front door, a concerned look on her face. "Jesse? What's wrong?"

"We'll be up in a minute," he hollered back. "I'll explain everything."

"Is he hurt?"

Jesse shook his head. "Not at all."

"Maybe Vanessa was right," Carlos whined.

"About which part?" Jesse asked, incredulous.

"The squad thing. She told me we were special, that we had a mission."

"Well, I don't know nothin' about no mission, but you definitely are special, son. We need to get to the bottom of this before those men come back."

Carlos looked up at him through teary eyes. "You're not scared of me? Of what I can do?"

"I don't know. Should I be? To me, you're a kind boy with a bit of an edge. I don't know if there's a mean bone in your body. You probably could've killed those men, but you didn't. That says something about your character to me."

Carlos wiped his eyes and sniffled. "I'm worried I put you in danger."

"I'm not."

"Why not?"

Jesse pulled back a bit to look into Carlos's eyes. "It's clear those men didn't expect you to have, uh, powers. Now they know you do. They're going to think twice about coming after you—and us."

Carlos took a deep breath and exhaled slowly. "I hope you're right."

"Me too. Now help an old man up, Mr. Muscles."

Carlos laughed as he stood and gently pulled Jesse up. They went inside and spoke with Janie about what had happened at the pub.

Chapter 7
There's Another One

Quinn yawned as he padded downstairs in his boxer shorts, the smell of frying eggs and coffee tantalizing his nose. When he entered the kitchen, he made a beeline for the coffeepot. "Morning, Daddio."

Daddio—his father, Aren McAlester—turned and smiled at his son with surprise. "Good morning. You're up early for a Saturday."

"Yeah. I'm going back to Virginia to see what I can find."

Daddio chuckled. "Want these eggs, then? I'll whip up another batch for myself."

"Sure," Quinn replied, still half asleep.

"Yep, great. I'm just the kitchen slave," Daddio said with a smirk.

"But you're so good at it," Quinn teased back.

"Most kids your age sleep in on Saturday or play video games."

"Most kids my age aren't superhumans." He sipped his coffee as Daddio plated his eggs.

"Touché. Is Blake going with you?"

"No. He won't have a life for months." Quinn's best friend Blake Hargreaves—now known as the superhero Helion—couldn't help because Chief Applegate had him pinned beneath her thumb and wouldn't let him out of her sight. She had unofficially sentenced him to an ungodly number of community service hours. It was the only way, everyone had agreed,

Blake could make reparation for his heinous acts as the super villain Dark Flame.

On the countertop television, Camilla Brenhurst, news reporter and superhero advocate, interviewed antisuperhero and conservative senator Orville Wilmott, who argued his position for registering and controlling the purported superheroes taking the world by storm.

"The STF expects us to believe that just because Dark Flame had a change of heart, we should accept him as Helion. After the death and destruction he caused? Absolutely not! Where is the accountability? Where are the checks and balances? How can people like you and me feel safe knowing people like him, who are more dangerous than a nuclear bomb, are free to roam the world, let alone return to high school?" The senator pointed at the camera for effect as he spoke. "If I were a parent, I'd be up in arms over the safety of my children in our schools, not to mention those who must be in the classroom with him. Who is providing oversight to ensure our children are safe?"

"Senator, is that not the purpose of the STF? To monitor and—"

Wilmott waved a dismissive hand. "The STF is a child-like organization. It has absolutely no experience in these matters whatsoever."

"Who does, Senator?" Camilla asked, pushing the gaping hole in his argument. "The STF's leadership comprises seasoned members from the Department of Homeland Security."

The senator narrowed his piercing blue eyes and made an angry grunt. "How can they guarantee he won't go rogue? Let us not forget this seventeen-year-old boy flew to Chicago and murdered the board members of a—"

"Of a recently exposed global terrorist organization, Senator."

"Well, perhaps he did the world a favor. But they should have been arrested and brought to justice."

Camilla didn't miss a beat. "And, let us not forget, Senator, that Dark Flame had been implanted with a control chip that malfunctioned and reduced his culpability. He didn't know what he was doing."

The senator scoffed. "How convenient." The program switched away from the recorded interview to the in-station broadcast.

Quinn grabbed the remote and lowered the volume. "I can't with him." He shoveled a forkful of eggs into his mouth.

Daddio frowned. "That man could negatively impact your life. We need to pay attention to what he says and does."

"But we have the support of the president."

"This president, Quinn. Presidents can change every four years. What if the next one sides with him? Or leverages antisuperheroism as an election platform and gains a cult following?"

"Do you think that would really happen?" Quinn asked, a shocked expression on his face.

"Let's hope it never does. His party sticks together, even when it makes little sense."

Quinn pushed his plate of eggs away. "Well, that's just ruined my appetite."

Daddio grunted awkwardly. "Sorry. Didn't mean to be the morning buzzkill. Go get changed into one of your supersuits. Stick some protein bars in your pocket in case you get hungry. Speaking of hungry—" He picked up the plate of uneaten eggs. "These are mine."

Quinn laughed, then headed upstairs to his room.

Carlos wiped his forehead with the back of his leather-gloved hands before splitting another quarter log with a single swing of Jesse's axe. The two halves fell to the frozen ground. A small fire behind him burned some branches that were not suitable for kindling.

He pulled off his right glove and held up his left hand, gently wiggling his fingers. He watched small yellow arcs of electricity dance between his fingers. Shaking his head, he pulled the glove back on and lined up another halved log.

After speaking with Janie and settling down yesterday afternoon, he had stacked enough wood to get Jesse and Janie through the rest of the winter and the next year too. This morning, he chopped more wood just to be alone with his thoughts and newfound powers. Of everything he had remembered so far, the powers and abilities within him still felt new.

Maybe I need to give Vanessa and this Victor Kraze guy a chance. I may not remember much about myself, but I know people shouldn't be able to do the things I did yesterday. It sounds like Victor has the answers I'm looking for. Maybe that's why Vanessa was so insistent I go with her. Maybe she can't tell Jesse and Janie the truth. That explains why she made up such an elaborate story to trick them into thinking I was simply missing.

But she didn't expect us to go to the sheriff's office, and she doesn't know how much I've already pieced together… not that it's much. I still don't know what the hell I'm doing down here.

There's no going back after yesterday. I'm different, I'm unexpected, and it's only a matter of time before someone gets hurt. What other powers do I have? What if those guys come back? What if they threaten Jesse and Janie?

Maybe I should go with Vanessa just to keep them safe. But I'd have to make her promise to leave Jesse and Janie alone.

He sighed, then swung the axe. He took a break to stack the wood after the quarters fell. When he finished, he lined up another log and raised the axe over his head. A strange whooshing sound above him made Carlos roll his eyes. He sighed and lowered the axe, believing Vanessa was about to sneak up on him again. But when he looked up, he saw a streak of bright blue moving through the overcast sky over the mountain range.

"What the hell is that?" he wondered aloud.

When it looped around, he rested the axe over his left shoulder and watched the blue streak fly over the mountain range again. It was looking for something while circling. And then it abruptly changed direction and turned toward him.

"Oh, shit, there's another one," he exclaimed, raising the axe defensively.

Blue Spekter flew southwest along the Blue Ridge Parkway, searching for hints of orgone energy in the skies near Spec, Virginia. Although the small town of Spec he sought was hard to find with his smartphone's map app, he knew he'd found it after passing through an unusually high concentration of orgone energy over three of the Blue Ridge Mountains.

Something briefly triggered his proximity sense, but he continued until the orgone concentration faded. He swung around and flew northeast between the town and the parkway until the proximity sense triggered again. He glanced down and to his left, knowing exactly where the other superhuman was. His enhanced vision focused on the person—an attractive young man holding an axe standing amidst firewood he must have been splitting and stacking.

He tapped his earcomm. "Blue Spekter to base. I found the superhuman."

"Acknowledged, Blue Spekter. Is he friend or foe?" Lieutenant Cassidy asked.

"I'm not sure yet. I'll find out soon enough."

"Roger. I'll notify Director Potter immediately."

"Great." Realizing the other superhuman was looking up at him, Blue Spekter turned and flew toward him.

Carlos took a step back as the blue streak approached, air and power rustling behind him. When he waved the axe defensively, the blue streak slowed, and Carlos saw the shape of a person form out of the blazing

69

energy. A moment later, the blue-glowing person landed about twenty feet away, their hands raised, signaling surrender. The blue glow faded away.

"Carlos?" the strange blue-clad figure said. Judging by the voice, Carlos assumed it to be a young man around his age. He wore some sort of blue bodysuit that was lightest at the neck and darkest at his feet. His gaze tracked up and down Carlos's frame. "Jesus, Carlos! When did you get so jacked?"

Carlos's eyes widened with surprise. "You know me?"

"Yeah, of course. What the heck are you doing here? You've been missing for, like, a week, dude."

"I, uh—"

The blue-suited person reached up and pulled back the cowl that hid his face. Carlos's mouth fell open when he saw the other young man was also a teenager. "I have a thousand questions, like, why are you in Virginia, and why can I sense you?"

"You can sense me?" Carlos asked, astounded. "Why can't I sense you?"

"Because I'm masking my presence. One sec." The blue-clad teen drew in a quick breath, then exhaled.

"Ow!" Carlos dropped the axe and grabbed the sides of his head at the overwhelming explosion of nearness to the other. It knocked him to his knees and sucked the wind out of him. Then the sensation pulled back from his mind, leaving him alone again. "What the hell was that?"

"I call it proximity sense. I can sense others like me. Apparently, you can too, which begs the question: Why are you like me?"

"It never felt that strong with Vanessa."

"Who's Vanessa?"

"Who are you?" Carlos spat, climbing to his feet.

They stared at one another. The blue-suited teen chuckled, then appeared surprised. "Wait, seriously? You don't know who I am? We go to the same school. You don't particularly like me."

"I don't? What school? Where?"

"Back home in Portsmouth. I'm Blue Spekter."

"Blue Spekter," Carlos muttered as memories flooded his mind. "You're... a superhero. You saved the guy on the bridge and did a bunch of other stuff. During the Christmas assembly, you fought what's-his-name. Oh my gosh, you're a kid like me. You're Quinn McAlester! You're a junior, and... and I'm a senior. Oh man, Victor doesn't like you at all."

Quinn's mouth fell open. "How the hell do you know Victor?"

"I'm not sure."

"Oh no, dude, don't." Quinn stepped closer. "You can't dangle a carrot like Nightmare and say, 'I'm not sure.' How do you know Victor?"

"Nightmare? What are you talking about? I'm telling the truth. But first answer this question: Who is my girlfriend?"

Quinn tilted his head to the side. "Everleigh. Why?"

"Huh. That checks out." Carlos sighed. "Look, I don't know how I got here. I have amnesia." He explained everything that had happened—that he had remembered and learned—since waking up in the woods Wednesday evening.

"Do you know about a control chip?" Quinn asked.

"No, but one guy at the bar yesterday said something about an inhibitor chip."

"That's new. Wait, people at the bar? Actually, never mind. We'll circle back to that one. Did they say anything?"

"Uh, they wanted me to come with them, just like Vanessa. They seemed irritated that I don't know who I am. Oh, both Vanessa and the guys at the bar said 'freeze asset one.' They seemed surprised it didn't work."

"It's a control code. It didn't work with Blake, either. I think it's supposed to shut you down or something."

Carlos gasped. "Is there a computer chip in my brain?"

Quinn nodded sheepishly. "Yeah, I think so. It's how Victor controls the superhumans he makes. He thinks it'll prevent you from betraying him or something. At least, that's what a control chip did. I don't know if an inhibitor chip is the same thing. We would have to get X-rays to find out if you have one or not. Then we gotta figure out how to get it out. Malfunctioning or not, there's no telling what it might do in the future."

"Huh. How did you even find me?"

"Remember the explosion that took out the guards you told me about?"

"Yeah."

"We have satellites that detect the energy that gives us our abilities. When you did whatever you did, it registered, and we detected it."

Carlos's eyes widened with excitement and surprise. "Wait, with everything that's going on with me, does it mean I have superpowers? Am I gonna be a superhero like you? Holy crap, will I be able to fly?"

Quinn scratched his nose. "I can't make any promises, but yeah, you have abilities. If you follow the same progression I did, they will continue to grow, and you'll discover more abilities with time."

"How long does it take?"

"Months. It depends on when Victor infused you with orgone energy."

"I don't remember any of these abilities. It's all new to me."

"Well, it takes more than abilities to become a superhero. It's one hell of a commitment that affects your life forever. Sometimes, it affects the ones you love."

"What do you mean?"

"We know Victor Kraze as the super villain Nightmare. He will not hesitate to put the ones you love in danger or kill them to get his way. Not long ago, he put my boyfriend's and parents' lives at risk after kidnapping them."

"Holy shit."

"You're not always the nicest guy at school. Kind of makes sense why Victor sought you out."

"Why would he randomly pick me out of a crowd of high school kids?"

"That, I don't know. But I'm fairly certain it wasn't random. He saw potential in you and convinced you to join his cause. Probably sold you a bunch of lies about bettering the world or something."

Carlos tried to recall meeting Victor but couldn't. "Sorry, it's not ringing a bell."

"Hey, we're being watched. Do you know that guy?" Quinn asked, pointing behind Carlos.

Carlos turned and waved at Jesse, who stood at a distance, watching them. "Yeah, that's Jesse Collins. He's the guy who found me in the barn. Come on, I'll introduce you."

Jesse chewed his lip nervously as the two boys approached.

Carlos waved. "Hey, Jesse. This is one of my classmates from back home. His name is Quinn. You might know him as Blue Spekter."

Jesse nodded. "Heard of you. Changed the world as we know it. Well, come on in and explain yourself."

Quinn and Carlos sat on the couch, and Jesse and Janie listened from their recliners.

Quinn leaned forward slightly as he spoke. "The energy that gives us our powers is called orgone. On its own, it's completely harmless, but it's all around us. An Austrian psychoanalyst named Wilhelm Reich explored its potency, but someone shut him down once its potential became known. A secret group known as The Order tried to create super-soldiers with orgone in the mid-1960s as a response to the Cold War. They worked with the CIA and experimented on American soldiers. None of them survived, or so they thought."

"My God," Janie said, covering her mouth in shock.

"One of my peers, a superheroine named Catamount, did survive and hid herself, knowing what could happen if they realized their experimentation had succeeded. She successfully sabotaged the project and brought an end to the experiments. The Order shifted their goals and focused on weather manipulation. That was in 1965."

"So, how did you get your powers?" Carlos asked, eyes sparkling with interest.

"Good question. Do you remember my best friend, Blake Hargreaves?"

"Yeah. Moody guy. There's more, but I can't place it."

73

"It'll come to you. My family, Blake, and I went camping over Labor Day weekend in Rangeley, Maine. Long story short, while exploring the woods, we stumbled across an old bunker and investigated. It led us into a deep underground cavern with a reactor that we somehow activated, and it blasted us with orgone energy. We woke up in the hospital, and that's when we met the mysterious Victor Kraze."

"So, he's a bad guy?"

"Hell yeah. But we didn't know it then. At first, he played the scientific interest card and wanted to research the effects of the energy as our powers manifested, but we were too naïve to realize he wanted to restart the human experimentation project. Victor tried to win us both over, but I didn't like him. Unfortunately, he seduced Blake, who became known as Dark Flame—the world's first super villain."

Carlos's eyes widened with recognition. "I remember him. But then he became a good guy?"

Quinn nodded. "We eventually figured out how to free him from Victor and removed the malfunctioning control chip that turned him into the world's biggest jerk."

"That sounds terrible," Janie muttered.

"It was. Victor ended up creating a small group of super-soldiers, but we defeated them over Rangeley. What we didn't know, until now, is that he had the knowledge and ability to create more. We just don't know where he did it."

Jesse cleared his throat. "You said they can manipulate the weather. Like, make it rain when it's sunny, and make it snow when it shouldn't?"

Quinn nodded. "Yes. Whenever they supercharge or use an orgone reactor, unexpected and terrible weather quickly rolls in until they're done."

"Well, there was a crazy storm that came out of nowhere on Tuesday night. Full of shrieking wind, snow, and thunder. Rolled right through the mountains in minutes."

"That's probably the night they irradiated you," Quinn said to Carlos.

"But why did I wake up in the woods Wednesday night?"

"Were there soldiers chasing you?" Quinn asked.

"Yeah. I sort of exploded, remember? Don't know how I did it."

"I figured as much."

"How did you know about it?"

"The satellites detected the energy burst because it was above ground. The reactor is probably below ground, and for whatever reason, the weather didn't trigger the satellites. It's not a perfect science. We're still learning a lot about orgone. The Order is way ahead of us."

"Whose satellites?" Jesse asked, his eyes narrowing.

"The agency I work with. The Superhuman Task Force. It's aligned with the Department of Homeland Security. We use what's already up there. I'm not really sure, though."

Jesse grunted and nodded.

"I don't know why you woke up in the woods," Quinn said. "Did you escape? Did they discard you?"

"Discard me?"

"So, it's unpleasant, but back in 1965, they discarded the failed experiments via incineration. Maybe they thought you had died, but you woke up and escaped. I don't really know. We won't know until your memories return."

"You said the reactor has to be underground?" Jesse asked.

"Well, to escape detection from the satellites, yeah. So far, we've found these reactors beneath abandoned structures. The one in Rangeley sat beneath the former home of Dr. Reich. The Order had secretly built the one in Portsmouth inside and beneath the main tower of the abandoned naval prison. Same with a reactor in Berlin, New Hampshire, only they built that one inside an old paper mill."

Jesse sat back. "The only abandoned thing around here is Iron Mine Hollow."

"What is that?" Quinn asked, leaning forward with intense interest.

"It's the old iron mine they built this town around in 1920. Very dangerous place. Wouldn't recommend you visit it, but I suspect you are a bit more suited to danger than the average person."

"Do you want to check it out?" Carlos asked.

Quinn shook his head slowly. "No. Not alone. And if Nightmare is down there, he'll be waiting for me. I'll need backup."

"I could be your backup!"

"Appreciate the offer, Carlos, but I'll need Helion and Catamount. You're still trying to remember who you are. Besides, my team needs to figure out if you have an inhibitor chip or not. And then we need to figure out how to get rid of it."

"Can't you just take it out?" Janie asked.

"I don't know yet." Quinn looked over Carlos's physique. "You seem a bit more muscular than I remember from school. That's a result of the orgone. I also don't know if your skin has hardened yet."

"Hardened?"

"Well, you might be bulletproof, like me, which means surgical knives wouldn't cut your skin."

"Bulletproof? Like Superman?"

"Yup."

"Awesome!"

"How do you remember Superman?" Jesse asked.

"I found the comics in the trunk at the foot of the bed upstairs. I was bored and read through a couple of them. Hope that was okay."

Jesse nodded, then became slightly distant. "It's fine. They belonged to my younger son. I'm keeping them for his kids. Maybe my grandkids will appreciate some vintage comics one day, though at this point, it may be my great-grandkids."

Quinn frowned. "What's your plan for getting home, Carlos?"

"My grandmother is trying to get cash from friends to pay for the bus tickets back to Portsmouth. We, uh, we don't have a lot of extra cash."

Quinn smiled. "I think I can help with that when you're ready. But first, I'd like you to take me to the scene of the crime."

"What crime?" Jesse asked, suddenly concerned.

"Sorry, meant it as a figure of speech. I'd like to examine the spot where you exploded. I'll bring you back here when we've finished."

"I'm not sure if I can find it," Carlos replied sheepishly.

"I know where it is. I hope something there will trigger your memory, possibly the path you took, and ultimately lead us to Nightmare."

"How we gonna get there?"

Quinn smiled. "You afraid of heights?"

Chapter 8
Scene of the Crime

C arlos hollered with excitement as the wind whipped through his hair. Blue Spekter held Carlos from above, his hands secured around Carlos's chest and forearms under Carlos's armpits. Although Blue Spekter flew low to avoid detection, Carlos still found it exhilarating. But when they landed in the epicenter of the charred ground, Carlos grew silent.

Blue Spekter released him, and the two boys looked around in silence. Dried blood speckled some rocks, leaves, and branches. Some plants still appeared swept back, a result of the powerful explosion Carlos had unleashed.

"Where are the bodies?" Carlos whispered nervously.

"The STF conducted its investigation and cleaned up the scene. It was pretty bloody, and they didn't want any hikers or children to stumble upon it."

"So, do you know who they were?"

"Yes. They worked for Victor Kraze."

"What did they want?"

Blue Spekter shot him an incredulous look. "You."

"Why?"

"That is the question of the hour. Do you know how you got here? How you got your powers?"

Carlos shook his head. "Honestly, I don't. Hey, can I ask you something?"

"Sure." Blue Spekter turned to face Carlos.

"Earlier, you said that I don't like you very much. Why is that?"

Blue Spekter searched for an answer. "I don't know. You're not, um... I don't know."

Carlos tilted his head. "I may not have my memories back, but I can tell you're withholding something. Spill it."

Blue Spekter sighed and pulled back his cowl. "You're not the nicest kid, Carlos. You can be a jerk when you want to."

"Oh," Carlos said with embarrassment.

Quinn pointed at Carlos. "Here's what I don't get. I can tell you care for Jesse and Janie and that you're grateful for everything they've done for you. That's not the Carlos I know from school. The reason your grandmother is scrounging for money to bring you home is, well, it's because she doesn't really have any. Money is a struggle for you and her."

"And my parents?" Carlos asked, testing Quinn's knowledge.

"I don't think they're part of your life, but I don't know the details. We're not friends. Yet."

"Okay. So, why don't I like you?"

Quinn shrugged. "You've never told me. You hang around with a group of friends like Darien James who make up the bullies' clique of the school. If I had to guess, it's because I'm Blue Spekter. Not everyone enjoys having a superhuman in their school. People fear me because of what I can do."

"But aren't you a good guy?"

"Yeah. Doesn't change the fact that people are afraid of me."

"Right. That makes sense." Carlos shoved his hands in his pockets. "That's especially true with Blake."

"Because he did horrible things when he was Dark Flame?"

"Yes. Even though he's better, some people remain terrified of him."

"That makes sense."

Quinn reached out and grabbed Carlos's shoulders. "And they're going to be terrified of you."

"But I haven't done anything!" Carlos exclaimed.

"When you remember what it was like to discover who Blue Spekter really is, you'll understand." He dropped his hands and glanced around the kill zone.

Carlos nodded at the field. "Did I kill those people?"

Quinn sighed. "I'm afraid so."

Carlos trembled, then dropped to his knees. "Oh my God."

"It was an accident, Carlos. Emotions initially trigger our powers, and I think yours accidentally activated when the soldiers threatened and frightened you."

"But what did I do?"

"From the looks of it, it's what I call an explosive blast. Normally we learn about and develop our powers with time, but I think you did it spontaneously. Your power had a pretty devastating effect."

Carlos looked at Quinn with tears in his eyes. "I killed those people?"

Quinn nodded. "I'm not gonna sugarcoat it, because the responsibility you now bear is intense."

Carlos sniffled. "This is not something I want. I don't want these powers. I want my old life back. Can Victor undo what he did to me?"

"No, and we will not ask him, understand? Besides, it might be for the best, Carlos."

"How can you say that?" Carlos shouted.

Quinn dropped to his knees and put a hand on Carlos's shoulder. "Because whatever Victor and Vanessa have planned for you would be ten thousand times worse than what you did."

Carlos sniffled and wiped tears from his cheeks.

"Victor manipulated Blake and convinced him he could save the world by bringing about some kind of new world order. I think he sold you on the same bullshit and brought you here to infuse you with orgone energy."

"Why?"

"When it's manipulated just the right way, orgone gives us our powers. Things go bad if they go wrong."

"Meaning?"

"Meaning death. I think that was the reason you ran from Victor's men. He did the same thing to you that he did to Blake."

Carlos regarded him with curiosity.

"When Victor captured Blake and me, he successfully implanted a control chip into Blake's brain. I woke up when they tried to inject me, so he never got control of me. If his men said your inhibitor chip is busted, it means you have a malfunctioning chip of some kind inside you, and we don't know what it's gonna do. That's why it's important we figure out how to remove it."

"All right." Carlos wiped his eyes and looked around. Certain trees triggered his memory. "I think I ran here from over there."

"Let's go check it out," Quinn said.

They stood and crossed the open area to a dirt road. A series of memories flashed through Carlos's mind. "There were big dogs, pickup trucks, men shouting and talking to one another on radios. There was gunfire, tree bark exploded near my head, so I jumped over a river. I think it's over there."

"This is awesome, Carlos! Let's go find it!"

They went deeper into the woods until they reached the rushing river. Carlos pointed to a cliff across the river. "There, that's where I jumped from. That's how I got here. Which means somewhere around here is the tree they shot at."

"Okay, let's forget the tree and get across the river."

Surprised, Carlos gaped at Quinn. "I don't know if I can jump across the river again."

Quinn smiled. "I'll help you. Arms up!"

Carlos raised his arms, and Quinn wrapped an arm around Carlos's torso. Then he leaped across the river and gently landed on the cliff. Carlos giggled. "I can't wait to figure out how to fly."

"Mastering flight could take a while. It was pretty quick for me, but it took Blake a while to learn."

"Can you guys do the same things?"

Quinn shook his head. "Eh, some things. There are similarities in our power sets, but there are differences too. Like, he can manipulate fire like no one else."

"What about you?"

"Originally, I could manipulate water and ice. My powers have grown, so I can do more. For example, I can manipulate electricity too."

"Interesting."

Quinn pointed to the woods behind them. "Anything trigger a memory?"

Carlos stared at the woods, but nothing came to him. "I came from that direction, but I don't understand why."

"Only one way to find out."

Carlos became uneasy. "Why are we doing this? Why are we going back... there?"

Quinn studied him for a moment. "Do you remember anything?"

"Not yet. I just don't know if I'll like what we find. I feel... anxious, even scared about going back."

"I get it. To figure out what happened, we retrace your steps."

Carlos nodded hesitantly, and the boys entered the woods. After ten minutes of walking, the woods around them thickened. "I remember this part," Carlos said, glancing around. "It was hard to run through the woods, and the branches were scraping my body."

"What were you wearing?"

"Just a pair of boxer shorts."

Quinn cursed.

"What?" Carlos asked, startled.

"It means there's an orgone reactor core around here. Dr. Madison said Victor would have the test subjects strip to their underwear prior to entering the reactor core."

"Who?"

"I'll fill you in later. Do you remember being inside a building of some sort? Or an underground cave?"

Carlos shook his head. "I woke up in the woods in my underwear. People were chasing me."

"Which means you escaped. Something happened that made them come looking for you, and they're still trying to get you back. Maybe they thought you didn't survive the infusion and dumped your body in the woods. But then somehow, they realized you had survived?" Quinn scratched his head.

Carlos stopped suddenly. "Maybe they thought I died inside the facility, and that's when I escaped. When my body went missing, they came looking, realizing I had survived."

"That's it!" Quinn said it with a smile. "Are you remembering?"

"I remember bright lights, like electricity or something. Energy flowing through me. And then waking up in the woods."

"Kind of makes sense. The infusion process is intense. When Blake and I were accidentally infused, we barely made it out of the cavern and passed out. We woke up in the hospital several days later. Except Victor was in charge of it, and, well, it's confusing."

They trekked through the woods for several more minutes until Carlos stopped and shrugged. "I'm sorry, it's all just trees to me," he admitted with a sheepish smile.

Quinn pulled out his cell phone and frowned. "Still no cell or GPS signal. That's okay. I can feel higher concentrations of orgone energy. What I'm looking for isn't far away. We should head back, though."

"To New Hampshire? I'm not ready to go home."

"I meant we should go back to Jesse and Janie's house. When do you think you will want to go home? Everyone's asking questions about your mysterious disappearance. You're gonna have to be very careful about what you tell them. You cannot tell anyone—and I mean anyone—that you have powers."

"What am I supposed to say? How do I explain where I've been? That I can't remember anything?"

"I'll work with the STF to come up with an explanation. They'll want to meet you, anyway."

"Do I have to?" Carlos asked half-heartedly.

"Absolutely. There's a lot that's about to overwhelm you. Even though the STF is a government organization, it will be your strongest ally beyond the three of us superheroes in shaping who you are now. You're not the same person anymore, Carlos. It's gonna take time to figure out what that means. The STF will help you fit into the world, and we're going to help you learn about your powers."

"I see." Carlos rubbed his chin, then nodded. "All right, I'll go home with you tomorrow."

"Cool. When your memories return, I strongly suggest that you think about leaving bad habits and bad friends behind in favor of better life choices."

"Like that Darien kid you mentioned? His name kinda rang a bell."

Quinn nodded. "Ugh, he can be such an ass. But anyway, come on. Let's fly back to the farmhouse."

Carlos giggled and eagerly raised his arms so Quinn could grab him. "I am so ready for this. How high can we fly?"

Quinn chuckled as he pulled his cowl over his face. "I can fly high enough to see the curvature of the earth. But we're not going that high today."

"Aw, man!"

"When we fly home tomorrow, I promise we'll pull a few G's." Blue Spekter paused. "Speaking of home, you need to call your grandma as soon as possible and tell her not to worry about the bus fare. Tell her someone down here generously donated the money for your bus tickets and you'll be home tomorrow afternoon."

"Will do."

Blue Spekter settled in behind Carlos. He threaded his arms under Carlos's armpits, held his chest, and slowly ascended. As the ground fell away beneath them, Blue Spekter formed a protective shield in front of them.

"Hold on to your pants, Carlos."

"What? Why?"

Without warning, Blue Spekter accelerated and swung around the Blue Ridge Mountains. Carlos screamed with terror and excitement, extending his arms like airplane wings as they flew.

Chapter 9
Unsolved Mysteries

B lue Spekter touched down on the tarmac adjacent to Hangar 227. His glowing blue eyes and body faded as he saluted the plainclothes military police guarding the building. Minutes later, the elevator doors opened, and he crossed the subterranean operations center to the conference room, where the team engaged in idle chat and enjoyed a late-morning coffee.

With the ongoing threat of Victor Kraze's maniacal schemes looming on the horizon, they needed creative solutions to find and defeat Victor and The Order once and for all. Blue Spekter chuckled at the awkward mix of assembled government and civilian resources who presently made up the STF core team: Director Potter; Captain David Prett, air force pilot and leader of a no-name secret group of data hackers; Walter, codename Trinity, and his partner Tara, codename Wonder Woman, two of Prett's non-existent hacker trio; Dr. Amy Madison, a scientific genius who formerly worked for The Order and Victor Kraze; Portsmouth police department Chief Tina Applegate; superhero Helion; and his science teacher/mentor Ron St. Germain.

When Blue Spekter closed the conference room door behind him, Director Potter cleared his throat and loosened his necktie. "All right, Quinn. Tell us what we're dealing with."

Blue Spekter pulled back his cowl and sat at the table. "It's Carlos Domínguez."

Ron's head jerked back with surprise. "Our Carlos?"

Potter shot Ron an incredulous look. "You know him?"

Quinn nodded. "Yup. I don't know how or why, but somehow Victor got him down there and infused him with orgone energy. It's fresh. The orgone bloom you detected the other night is probably when they did it. To make it worse, Carlos remembers nothing. It's like they wiped his memory or something went wrong."

Chief Applegate leaned forward, her face grim. "Are you saying another student from Portsmouth High School has superpowers?"

"Does he have a control chip?" Dr. Madison urgently asked.

Quinn shrugged. "I'm not sure. When the guys at the bar assaulted him, he said they used the words 'inhibitor chip.'"

Dr. Madison frowned, and Director Potter waved his hands in frustration. "Okay, stop. We're running ahead of ourselves and introducing too much confusion. Let's take it from the top, start to finish. Quinn, the floor is yours."

Quinn took a deep breath, then recounted his time with Carlos for the team. "And I believe he genuinely doesn't remember who he is. At school, he's an asshole. But today, he was really sweet and kind. He didn't remember his struggles, so he didn't have the usual anger or edginess he has toward everyone."

"It's like the total opposite of what the control chip did to me," Blake said, looking at Dr. Madison, who thoughtfully nodded.

"Dr. Madison, what is an inhibitor chip? Or is this a confusion of terms with control chip?" Director Potter asked.

"It's one of the microbug technologies I designed, Director," she said. "Realizing we couldn't have our army of super-soldiers rebelling or turning against us, the late Mother Superior tasked me with the design and development of a delivery system and mechanism to control superhumans. I designed the control chip to make subjects more obedient to designated authority, should they get out of hand. I designed the inhibitor chips to provide even more control by negating superhuman powers, increasing compliance, or shutting down the subject completely, depending on the chip implanted."

"Do you mean killing them?" Potter asked.

"No, of course not, but it would instantly induce a comatose-like sleep. Unfortunately, I didn't finish the design or build a prototype." Dr. Madison frowned. "If Victor's men believed Carlos's inhibitor chip malfunctioned, it's possible someone new has access to my work and successfully created one."

With a sigh, Director Potter said, "Well, that's one thing I can appreciate about Victor."

"What's that?" Dr. Madison asked.

"Like his predecessor, the late Mother Superior, even he fears that which he creates when he plays God."

"But is it malfunctioning or dormant?" Ron asked.

"Meaning?" Potter asked, one eyebrow arched.

"I think Victor's ultimate plan, before global takeover, is to either destroy Blue Spekter or win him over to the dark side, so to speak." Ron smiled at Quinn and Blake. "He's proven himself to be a mastermind and strategist. He may have intentionally released Carlos but told no one, not even his own people, so they'd naturally think apprehension is their goal, expecting no resistance. But once they saw Carlos wield his powers, they thought his inhibitor chip was busted. What if this is an Order 66 situation?"

Quinn giggled, but the adults at the table stared at Ron with blank faces.

"Then we gotta figure out how to remove the chip but without nearly killing him," Blake added, winking at Quinn.

"Order 66?" Chief Applegate asked.

"Basically, imagine he's a sleeper agent waiting to be activated," Ron answered.

"Dr. Madison, is it possible to remove his chip?" Director Potter asked.

"I honestly don't know. We should examine him prior to admitting him to this facility. A set of X-rays and possibly CAT scans will help us determine whether Victor implanted a microbug in Carlos."

"Agreed. We'll arrange something with Portsmouth Hospital. Let's agree we don't bring him to Hanger 227 until he makes his intentions known or we get that chip out."

"Understood," Quinn replied. "Could that be what's messing up his memory? So far, that we know of, nobody else lost their memory after orgone infusion."

Dr. Madison nodded. "I agree, but that was never on the list of side effects."

"What was?" Quinn asked.

"Not surviving," Dr. Madison replied flatly. "Otherwise, yourself, Blake, and Catamount are the only survivors outside of Nightmare, Vanessa, and now Carlos, excluding the super-henchmen you defeated already."

"Wouldn't their superpowers be side effects?" Applegate asked.

Dr. Madison shook her head. "The generation of superhuman abilities, though unique and unknown, was always the intended result. To date, Blake may be the only person to have experienced adverse side effects of a malfunctioning control chip. An array of powers, however, was expected."

"I see," Chief Applegate replied, frowning.

Quinn leaned forward. "Can we change gears for a moment?"

"Certainly," Potter replied. "What's on your mind?"

"How come you can't find the reactor core? It has to be in those old iron mines somewhere."

"About that," Prett said, pointing to Trinity and Tara.

Tara cleared her throat. "We reviewed the logs from the other night. We started with the biggest reading—the orgone bloom we believe Carlos triggered—and crawled backward through the logs. Hours before, there were several spikes in orgone energy that suggest weather stimulation and a possible charging event. Most importantly, the second largest spike matches readings we detect when a reactor is used to infuse someone."

"Meaning?" Potter asked.

"I believe Quinn's theory is correct," Tara said. "Victor likely infused Carlos just prior to the orgone bloom that set off the alarm."

"What if he did it a week ago?" Quinn asked. "Carlos has been missing for a week."

Trinity shook his head. "Unlikely. There's almost no unusual orgone activity for several weeks prior. What we see is consistent with collection from weather events."

"An abandoned iron mine," Quinn muttered. Heads turned and patiently waited for his continued thought. "Could The Order have hidden a reactor core in the iron mine?"

"We don't know," Director Potter replied. "The unusually high concentration of minerals in the mountains—specifically specular hematite, for which they named the town Spec—prevents our best satellite scans from penetrating the rock."

"I wonder if the high concentration of iron would interfere with the process, or if they built it differently," Ron said.

"Keep going," Director Potter said.

"Well, the three reactor cores we know about—Rangeley, Portsmouth, and Berlin—were built in a vertical fashion. Unless there's a cavern in the mines of a similar size, it may be a very different reactor core."

Director Potter shook his head. "That's speculation, Ron. Unless this will somehow be useful, I'd rather avoid it."

Ron shrugged. "We'll know when we meet Carlos and discover what his abilities are, right?"

"What about the utilities?" Trinity asked suddenly.

Tara regarded her partner with interest, and Potter folded his hands on the table. "You're thinking they've run up an electric bill?"

"Maybe. If they built the place in the mid- to late sixties, it has probably sat dormant for decades. But in the past year, say five years to be safe, it'd make sense that somewhere around it, there'd be a spike in electrical use. I'd expect a more recent spike, because Victor would have had to integrate modern tech with the antiquated tech of the sixties, like he did in Rangeley."

"And he can't power the facility with orgone energy?" Potter asked.

Trinity shook his head. "No. Orgone isn't that kind of energy."

"Too bad. Well, start crunching numbers and review the electric bills from every structure around the iron mines."

"You could start your search with the old powerhouse," Tara advised. "Somewhere around 1920, Pulaski Iron Company—PICO for short—built a small iron mining operation there. There's a dilapidated brick powerhouse adjacent to the Norfolk & Western railroad line, and—if you can find it—the remaining path for the electric cars they used to haul ore from the mine."

"I can't imagine exploring the mine would be safe," Potter said, shaking his head. "Abandoned things fall apart, especially mines. And underground, pockets of stagnant air threaten the hardiest of experts."

"Yet Victor's people could be in there, quite safe, tweaking the settings of a reactor core to make an army of super-soldiers we won't be able to stop," Quinn retorted.

Potter sighed. "I appreciate your enthusiasm to stop Victor, Quinn, but—"

"He wants you to stop him," Ron said, stroking his beard.

Heads turned in Ron's direction.

"Pardon me?" Potter said.

Quinn furrowed his eyebrows. "Why do you think Victor wants me to stop him?"

"It's not so much that he wants you to stop him, but he wants you," Ron said. "I think he's become obsessed with the one thing he can't have. He knows you're an impulsive teenager—"

"Thanks," Quinn interjected.

Ron smirked. "You're welcome. He knows you'll rush into something because of that. It's also why he turned Carlos, though Carlos was a gamble."

"You mean if Carlos had died?" Applegate asked.

Ron nodded. "Which, according to our theory, he might have. Carlos's disappearance would have become a tragic unsolved mystery, but eventually we'd forget about him, knowing nothing about this sinister plot."

"Then it behooves us to pay attention to the school's attendance rosters, doesn't it?" Applegate asked.

"Indeed," Ron said. Then he turned to Quinn. "I think Victor's obsessed with you and wants you either on his side or dead. Raising up an army of your peers is, in his twisted mind, the best way to take you out—or take you in. At least, that's my current thought."

"But why Quinn and not Blake?" Prett asked.

"Oh, he'll go after Blake next," Ron said. "He already tried to manipulate Quinn by seducing Blake. If I'm right, he's upping the ante by focusing on Quinn now. And where Quinn goes, he knows Blake will follow." Blake rolled his eyes, and Ron raised a hand. "Not as the sidekick, but as the best friend who thinks he knows Victor's devious mind. He's counting on you guys to act impulsively and irrationally."

Blake nodded, and Ron lowered his hand.

"Should we call in Catamount?" Potter asked.

"I'd sure like her help," Quinn said.

Dr. Madison sat up. "And I'd love to interview her." When Potter shot her a strange look, she added, "For scientific purposes, of course."

Quinn smiled. "So, I know what to do next." All eyes focused on him. "Besides, you know, all the stuff you have to do. Tomorrow, Blake and I retrieve Carlos and bring him back to New Hampshire."

"You want me to come with you?" Blake asked, pleasantly surprised.

Quinn grinned. "Of course, buddy."

"Do you expect trouble?" Director Potter asked.

"I'm not sure. But it can't hurt to have Blake with me if I encounter unexpected resistance."

"Understood."

"We'll bring him back to the hospital for X-rays and psychological evaluation," Quinn continued. "We need to help him regain his memory to learn what Victor is really doing and, if possible, get that chip out of his head before it's too late. Dr. Madison, that's where we need your focus right now. Someone should call Catamount—Director Potter, I assume that's you. If we're gonna move against Victor and take out another reactor core, we'll need her help."

Director Potter nodded. "I will agree to this plan under one condition."

"What's that?" Quinn asked.

"You make no move against Victor tomorrow."

"And if he provokes us?"

"That is the only circumstance I authorize you to engage in combat with him."

Quinn smiled. "Fair enough."

Carlos heard the engine switch off and the car doors close before either Jesse or Janie realized someone had arrived. He set the Batman comic he had been reading on the bed next to him and leaned over to peer out his bedroom window. Below, Sheriff Dollard and Deputy Davis were walking to the house. He watched them disappear under the porch roof, and a moment later, Carlos heard one of them knock at the door.

He sighed, then rolled off the bed and went downstairs as Janie enthusiastically welcomed the officers inside. He leaned against the doorframe, thumbs hooked in his jean pockets, and watched Janie offer Sheriff Dollard a piece of her freshly baked apple pie.

"Carlos," Deputy Davis said in greeting and announcement after noticing him.

Sheriff Dollard turned, took a step back, and stared at Carlos in disbelief. "Have you put on muscle?"

"Yeah," Carlos replied casually.

"He's been splittin' and stackin' next year's wood," Jesse chimed in.

"I see. Jesse, were you and Carlos at the Barley Shack yesterday?"

"Yep."

Dollard nodded. "Do you know what I'm about to ask you?"

"I reckon I do. But no, I didn't let him drink a beer."

Davis chuckled, and Dollard rolled his eyes. "So, is it true? The other thing?"

"Is what true exactly, Sheriff?"

Dollard frowned. "Come on, Jesse. Was he involved in a serious bar fight?"

Jesse smiled proudly. "He was, and he won. Beat up four out-of-towners who made the first move and harassed him. Shot him with one of those fancy stun guns you carry."

Davis glanced at his Taser, and Dollard shifted his stance and squared off with Carlos. "Did you know those men, Carlos?"

"No, Sheriff, I did not."

He glanced quickly at Jesse. "Beat them up, huh?"

Both Jesse and Carlos nodded.

"So, you mysteriously show up in my town. These strangers also mysteriously show up at the bar, conveniently knowing where you are. Eyewitnesses say they tased you, but you didn't go down. What kind of trouble are you in, Carlos?"

"I'm not sure. But tomorrow I'll be out of your hair."

"Oh?"

"Some friends from back home are on their way to get me. They were excited to go on a mini road trip."

Dollard narrowed his eyes as Davis spoke up. "That'll make it easier on your grandmother. She hasn't been able to scrounge up the funds for your bus tickets yet."

"Is anyone pressing charges, Sheriff?" Jesse asked.

Dollard shook his head. "No. I'm just trying to understand what happened. No one's squawkin' on record, but off–record, everyone agrees that the out-of-towners instigated the fight. They arrived, identified, and assaulted Carlos."

"That's what happened," Jesse said.

"But what it doesn't explain, Jesse, is why they were after Carlos."

"A-yup," Jesse replied with a curt nod.

Dollard frowned and scratched his forehead. "What aren't you guys telling me?"

Carlos swallowed nervously. Suddenly, Dollard's and Davis's shoulder-mounted radios squawked as dispatch reached out to summon them to the scene of a car accident.

Dollard sighed and put his hands on his hips. "Janie, I'm afraid the apple pie must wait. Duty calls."

"I understand, Sheriff."

"Carlos, good luck getting home. I'll be glad to see you and your hoodlum friends disappear from my town." Dollard shook hands with Jesse, then headed out the door with Davis on his heels.

Carlos leaned against the doorframe and sank to a seated position on the floor. "Wow, that was convenient. I really didn't wanna have to explain everything to him." He wrapped his arms around his legs and rested his chin on his left knee.

"Pish-posh, don't worry about it," Janie said. "Now there's more apple pie for you."

Carlos smiled, then looked up at his hosts. "I'm sorry if I made things awkward between you and the sheriff."

Jesse shook his head. "Bah. He doesn't like trouble in town. He'll forget about everything tomorrow evening."

"That's good news," Carlos said, smiling. Then he looked at Janie. "How about a piece of that apple pie?"

Janie chuckled. "Young man, it'll spoil your dinner!"

Carlos grinned. "No, it won't. I'm a growing boy."

They shared a quick laugh, then Jesse added, "That you are, son."

Chapter 10
An Incomplete Picture

"What's wrong, dear? You've hardly touched your dinner tonight," Janie asked as Carlos toyed with his mashed potatoes. "Aren't you excited about going home tomorrow?"

Carlos drew a breath and smiled politely. "Yeah, sorry. It's delicious, Janie. I just wish I remembered more about back home." He sat back in his seat and slouched, feeling defeated.

"Did seeing your school chum trigger any memories?" Jesse asked.

Carlos shook his head. "No, but I remember him. His story matches with what my grandmother told me, but it triggered nothing new about me. Like, why can't I remember going to school with him? Who my friends are? Or what my bedroom is like? And what's scarier, while I remember my grandmother, I remember so little about her."

"That must be so frustrating," Janie said, shaking her head.

"It's definitely not fun," Carlos replied with a faint smile. "I remember Quinn is Blue Spekter. He's not lying about that."

"A true superhero doesn't need to lie," Jesse said with a confident nod.

Carlos nodded. "He doesn't know who Vanessa is, but he definitely believes Nightmare is the devil incarnate."

"We saw that story about him on the news a few weeks ago. He's a wicked man, Carlos. They called him a terrorist. You should be wary of him," Janie said.

Jesse cleared his throat. "Yep. Funny thing is, the government thought they killed him. Apparently, they're wrong."

"I wish I remembered that, because I'd love to know how I got here." Carlos frowned and scratched his nose.

"What is it, dear?" Janie asked.

"Something Quinn said still bugs me."

"What's that?"

"He told me I didn't like him and that I hung around with a group of, well, not so nice kids."

"Hard to believe," Janie said. "It's clear to me you have a kind heart."

Carlos shrugged in disbelief. "When I spoke to my grandmother, she told me she didn't want a repeat of last year, but I don't know what I did. For all I know, I punched a kid at school, or maybe I got arrested. She kinda freaked when I said I was at the sheriff's office, so it must have been bad."

"Mmm," Jesse said, shrugging. He shoveled a mouthful of mashed potatoes and gravy into his mouth.

Janie scoffed. "Our two boys made their fair share of mistakes. But the important thing is they learned from their mistakes. Whatever happened, you've probably learned your lesson."

"What makes you think that?" Carlos asked, looking hopeful.

"Because your grandmother could have said something like, 'Why're you in trouble with the police again?' But she didn't. So, that tells me you've tried to make better choices. Keep doing that, Carlos, especially with these new gifts you have. The world will watch you, and it doesn't need another Nightmare. It needs a hero to fight alongside Blue Spekter."

"I guess so."

"Then why the long face?"

"I don't understand why I have these powers. I wish I could remember what happened, how I got here, how Victor found me, or if he chose me. None of it makes sense. Why would I leave my life to come here and do whatever I did? I don't get it."

Jesse shrugged. "Quite the conundrum. If you came here willingly, it's probably because he promised you something he knew you couldn't resist. Given how much our boys loved those comics, if someone had promised them superpowers, I bet one of them would've blindly followed too."

"Maybe," Carlos replied, unconvinced.

Jesse offered a half smile. "Sounds like your life is tough back home. Perhaps Victor simply promised you a better life."

"Maybe."

Janie smiled. "Did Quinn offer any insight into your abilities?"

"Yeah." Carlos smiled, lifted Janie's hand, and wiggled his fingers. A few arcs of yellow electricity snapped between them. Janie's eyes widened with wonder.

"Victor clearly zapped me with orgone energy. That explains how I could defeat the men at the bar. Apparently, it also explains my improved muscle tone and definition." Carlos shared what Quinn had explained about orgone energy and the likelihood of discovering new abilities with time.

"It's an amazing gift you have," Jesse said. "You must use your powers for good, Carlos. Janie is right. Whatever Victor wanted with you, put it in the past. We don't need another one of him."

"I guess so," Carlos replied with a shrug.

"I know so," Janie added, nodding and confidently smiling at him. "You are a good young man. I can't say it enough. Teenagers these days, well, the world just isn't what it was when we were young. When you need to slow down, you come on back to the little old town of Spec and visit with us."

"Stack some more wood if you want," Jesse said with a smile. "It's good for clearing your mind."

Carlos laughed. "Except for the answerless questions, my mind is pretty clear these days."

"Well, I reckon things are gonna get busy for you when you get home."

"You're gonna have to learn what it means to be a superhero," Janie said with a smile.

"Yeah, that's kind of cool," Carlos said, grinning.

"Listen to Quinn, son. He's good people too," Jesse said.

Carlos leaned forward and cleared his throat. "Um, I noticed some board games on the bookshelf in my room—Scrabble, Clue, something called Parcheesi…. Would you want to play a game after dinner?"

Janie and Jesse smiled as one. "We'd love to, Carlos," Janie replied, reaching out and gently squeezing his hand.

Chapter 11
Bring Him Home

Carlos mindlessly tossed pebbles into the field as he meandered across it, lost in his thoughts about going home. He had already thrown several large rocks that would have required heavy machinery to move, a feat that confirmed his abilities were growing. Quinn had told him to expect super strength and other powers, a notion that excited Carlos. Quinn would arrive any minute to fly him home. He was glad to put Spec behind him even though it had forever changed his life for reasons he had yet to discover.

"God dammit!" Carlos screamed, dropping the pebbles and gripping the sides of his head. He stumbled and nearly fell over, grimacing at the painful and telling sign that another superhuman was approaching. Locating them in his mind, he saw Vanessa walking toward him from the woods. "You again. What do you want?"

"I've come to see if you're ready to meet Victor Kraze." She wore tight black leather pants, a black shirt, and a black motorcycle jacket. She had pulled her red hair back into a tight bun.

Carlos scoffed. "So, I'm just supposed to accept that after Friday's incident, you're coming with an invitation? What happened to the guys Victor sent after me? They literally tried to kidnap me."

Vanessa pursed her lips and crossed her arms over her chest. "I had no control over that unfortunate incident. They got to you before I could intervene."

Carlos rolled his eyes. "Uh-huh. You want me to accompany you, acting all nice and cutesy, but those guys were assholes. What the hell kind of shitshow does Victor run? You want me to believe he's a great guy when those guys work for him? I don't think so."

"I keep trying to tell you how important you are to—"

"No, you've said nothing important," Carlos interjected angrily. "All you've told me is that Victor gave me these abilities for some greater purpose, but you won't tell me what that is. You can't tell me who I am or what I'm doing here, so why the hell would I even consider going back to Victor? It's clear to me now that I escaped something terrible, and I'm glad I did."

Vanessa sighed and picked a piece of lint off her shirt. "I'm tired of this game, Carlos. You will come with me right now," she asserted, reaching for Carlos's arm.

Carlos jerked away and raised his fists. "No! I told you to leave me alone!" Yellow electricity sparked across his knuckles.

She scoffed. "Do you seriously think you can fight me and win, Carlos?"

"I don't know, but I sure as hell can try." He opened his fingers and let electricity snap and crackle between them. He could feel it flowing through him, and he sensed greater control over what he could do with it. Combined with his newfound strength, he didn't think she could beat him.

Laughing, she said, "You're like a baby with a plastic sword. You're more of a danger to yourself than anyone else."

Carlos shook his head and dropped his hands. "You know nothing about me, so just leave me alone. I'm going home."

She stepped forward. "No, you're leaving this farm with me today, and I don't care if you're conscious or not."

Carlos's eyes illuminated with bright yellow power as he pulled his energized fists up again and took a defensive stance. "For Christ's sake, leave me alone!"

Vanessa laughed again. "Oh, please." Her eyes glowed bright teal as she scowled and pushed a hand toward Carlos. A wave of teal power surged forward and struck him square in the chest, knocking him back until he tripped and fell to the ground.

Stunned, Carlos stared at the sky, the wind knocked out of him. He let loose a low, painful groan as his body slowly recovered.

A gunshot echoed across the field, and at Vanessa's feet, a cloud of dirt and pebbles erupted into the air. Vanessa grimaced, the bullet having grazed a rock several inches from her left boot.

Carlos heard Jesse cock the gun for a second shot. "Get out of here, lady, or I put the next round in your chest," Jesse hollered across the field.

Vanessa grunted with anger. "How dare you shoot at me, you old fool!"

Shit, she's gonna kill him. He tried to get up, but he hadn't recovered from the blast that had knocked him down.

"No!" Carlos screamed, struggling to get back on his feet.

Vanessa charged at Jesse, and Carlos collapsed as intense pain surged in his brain. A high-pitched and piercing whistling sound reached his ears. Instinctively knowing where it was, he winced and saw bright blue light smash into the ground in front of Vanessa. Dirt, ice, and pebbles erupted into the air as a second bright blue explosion—originating from a bright spark of blue lightning and a loud clap of thunder—knocked Vanessa cartwheeling back twenty feet. She screamed until she hit the ground with a crack and a thud.

She shook off the disorientation and scrambled to her feet, glaring at Blue Spekter. "You!"

An orange streak flashed across the sky and landed nearby as Vanessa launched herself into the air at Blue Spekter. Helion raised his hand and cut her flight short, using his telekinesis to smash her face-first into the ground.

Vanessa wriggled on the ground, desperate to escape, but Helion pinned her down.

Blue Spekter allowed his brightly glowing blue aura to fade as he walked toward Vanessa.

"Oh my God, this Vanessa?" Helion asked, shocked.

"You know her?" Blue Spekter asked his best friend, approaching Vanessa.

"Hell yeah," Helion said. "It didn't click at the briefing yesterday because, well, I didn't think it was possible. She's the one Victor sent to flirt with and spy on me in my condo. Claimed to attend high school in Maine. All of it was lies, though. I also didn't know he transformed her into a superhuman."

Blue Spekter frowned and squatted in front of Vanessa. She writhed and struggled to break free from Helion's superior telekinetic hold. "So, when did he make you?"

"None of your damn business."

Blue Spekter smirked. "Probably when he made the other superhumans we fought. But they were muscle. You're something more. You're special to him. Why?"

"Wouldn't you like to know?" Vanessa spat.

Blue Spekter looked at Carlos, who had climbed to his feet and hobbled closer. "What does Victor want with Carlos?"

Vanessa grunted in response and continued struggling against Helion's restraining force.

"Why is Victor going after high school students from Portsmouth High?"

She only grunted in frustration again.

"Fine," Blue Spekter said. "Say nothing. We'll find him. We know he's here somewhere. It is only a matter of time before we shut him down."

"You think you've got it all figured out, don't you?" Vanessa snarled. "Well, you don't. For all your smarts and talents, you've failed to realize something critically important."

"And what's that?" Blue Spekter asked.

Her gaze pierced Blue Spekter with an evil look. "He's not the only one."

Helion gasped, and Blue Spekter's eyes widened with alarm.

Vanessa seized the moment, leaped into the sky, and rocketed away.

"Aw, crap!" Helion shouted.

Blue Spekter raised his hand. "Let her go. We'll fight another day. Right now, we need to get Carlos to the STF and then back home." Turning to Helion, he asked, "She lived in your condo building, and you never sensed her?"

Helion shook his head slowly. "Never. I didn't know."

"Damn," Blue Spekter replied. "I'm willing to bet he created her at the same time he made those other guys we fought over Rangeley."

Carlos cleared his throat. "Um, what did she mean, 'He's not the only one?'"

The two heroes looked expectantly at Carlos. He smiled back sheepishly and shrugged. "Don't look at me. If I had answers, I'd tell you."

Blue Spekter drew a reflective breath and rubbed his chin for a moment. "Vanessa knew how to use her powers. You don't, which confirms they infused you with orgone energy this week. I think that also confirms my theory that there's an active reactor core hidden here. It's probably an old one, like the one we destroyed. We have to find it before he can create another superhuman."

"I think we have time," Helion replied.

"What do you mean?"

"When you and I accidentally tripped the reactor core, we sucked all the power out of the batteries. When Victor seduced me to his cause, he went on this rant about how long it would take to collect the energy we had spent. If he's using a reactor core that was built in the early sixties, there's a good chance it doesn't have any modern orgone collection tech. This isn't Portsmouth, which means there are no buildings to hide Cloudbuster tech on."

Blue Spekter nodded. "Two great points. And with the system drained, he'll have to wait until he can collect enough to use it to stimulate the weather to get more. We still need to find it. Carlos may be the last superhuman created in Spec, but I'm willing to bet he's not the first."

"So, where could it be? It's just a bunch of mountains here."

Carlos spoke up. "Jesse said there's an abandoned iron mine somewhere in these hills. I'm willing to bet it's in there."

Blue Spekter nodded. "I agree, and I think The Order hid a reactor core deep in the iron mine. But the satellites can't penetrate the ground because of the mineral composition."

"But they could look for the access point," Carlos volunteered.

The heroes stared at him.

Surprised at the obviousness of his thoughts, Carlos couldn't help but smile. "Right? People have to work there, like the soldiers who chased me. They drive in and out, and they have to park somewhere. People walk into the woods and don't come back out for the day or something. Like a work shift, maybe. If it's in the old iron mines, it's got to be underground."

Helion chuckled. "How did we not think of that? How did the STF not consider that?"

Blue Spekter smirked. "Because they focus on orgone energy blooms. The answer is in front of them, and they don't know it. Well, we'll bring others back to Director Potter. I'm sure Captain Prett and his team can figure it out."

They stood in silence for several moments.

"Are you boys all right?" Jesse hollered from across the field. He had slung the rifle over his right shoulder.

Carlos turned and waved, then asked Blue Spekter, "What happens now?"

Blue Spekter smiled. "Are you ready to head home? Say your goodbyes and all that?"

Carlos nodded. "Yeah. I'm sure gonna miss them."

"I think the feeling is mutual, buddy. Come on."

The three boys trudged across the field to the house, making small talk along the way.

Inside, Quinn and Blake—their cowls pulled back—politely stood aside as Carlos hugged Janie, who wiped tears from her eyes. "I want you to come back and visit after you've had time to sort through this business, okay?"

"I will," Carlos replied softly, resting his forehead on her shoulder. "Thank you for the amazing food."

Janie chuckled. "Well, we have to eat, right?"

When Carlos turned to Jesse, the man became visibly distressed and awkwardly cleared his throat, quickly wiping his eyes to hide his tears. He nervously extended his hand to Carlos, who accepted. "Thank you for bringing my son back to me," Jesse sputtered through tears. Then he pulled Carlos in for a hug.

Carlos pulled away a bit and studied Jesse's face. "Back? I don't understand what you mean."

"He—" Jesse choked up with emotion.

Janie drew a deep breath. "We lost our older son years ago, when his children were toddlers. His wife, not the nicest gal, moved away, and we barely hear from her. It's been hard for us to move on, and we know it's been decades. Having you here reminded us of what it was like having Roger home when he visited. We see his brother Ray several times a year, which is nice."

"I'm sorry, I didn't know." Carlos gave Jesse another hug before the two separated.

Jesse cleared his throat and nodded. "It's all right. We didn't tell you. Our feelings bubbled up during your stay. Grief can be a funny thing." He wiped his eyes and smiled. "You need to be getting on home to your grandmother, but come visit. We'll be here."

"I will, I promise."

Jesse turned to Quinn and Blake. "You keep him safe, you hear me? Help him make the right decisions like you boys did. Keep him away from that crazy girl and her boss."

"We will, sir," Quinn replied. After shaking hands, the three boys headed outside to the front yard, while Jesse and Janie watched from the porch.

"Flying sure beats the bus," Jesse quipped, and they all shared a brief laugh.

"Ready to remember more about your life?" Blake asked, pulling on his cowl.

"Let's do this," Carlos replied. He raised his arms so Quinn could grab him.

Quinn pulled on his cowl and shook his head. "Nah. Gonna do something different today." Then he levitated.

"What do you mean?" Carlos asked, his gaze shifting between Blue Spekter and Helion.

Helion smiled, drew a deep breath, and leaped into the air. Then he reached out with his mind and gently grabbed Carlos with his telekinesis.

Carlos gasped as his body left the ground, and the three boys flew east until they found the Atlantic Ocean. They banked left and flew north, flying low over the water to avoid curious eyes from the land.

Chapter 12
Second Guesses

"All right, Carlos, last one," Dr. Madison said, smiling at him as an X-ray technician—Ray, a prematurely balding younger man with brown eyes and a thick beard—placed a heavy lead apron over his waist.

Carlos sighed and lay still on the X-ray table as a second technician—Jennifer, a pretty brunette with stunning blue eyes—set the aperture in place over his head. They had taken several X-rays of his head from different angles to, as Dr. Madison had explained, ensure the best possible view into his skull.

They cleared the room, and Jennifer said, "Clear." Something clicked, and they re-entered.

"All right. That's done. We'll give it a moment and check it out over there," Dr. Madison said, pointing to a large wall-mounted flat-screen television.

Ray removed the lead apron, and Carlos sat up, his eyes transfixed on Jennifer's curves.

Director Potter entered, hands stuffed into his pockets, and nodded to Dr. Madison. Carlos tore his eyes from Jennifer and studied the man. He looked tired. A moment later, Carlos's X-rays appeared on the television screen.

"Son of a bitch," Dr. Madison said, walking to the screen.

Carlos studied the four black-and-white images of his head and wondered what Dr. Madison was seeing.

"He's got a chip?" Potter asked.

Dr. Madison nodded and pointed at the screen. "Yes, he does. Zoom in on this black speck please, Ray."

"Sure thing." Ray tapped something on the computer, and the four images zoomed in and focused on the black speck. The momentary blurry zoom-distortion on the digital X-ray cleared as the computer autoenhanced the images.

"I don't see it," Potter said.

"It's right here, implanted directly between the cerebellum and oc-cipital lobes." She tapped the squarish black dot in three of the images. Carlos automatically spotted it on the fourth image. "This is clever. My original design attached to the cerebellum. This implementation likely explains why you can't remember things."

"Why, Doctor?" Potter asked with a sigh.

"The cerebellum controls voluntary movements such as walking, posture, balance, coordination, eye movements, and speech. In the control chip design, a verbal command would incapacitate someone by overpowering their cerebellum and inhibiting their voluntary func-tions."

"So, how does that impact his memory?" Potter asked.

"Ah. One of the key functions of the occipital lobe, or visual cortex, is vision, but it's much more complex than simply *seeing*," Dr. Madison said. "Our visual world operates with both spatial reasoning and visual memory—all controlled from the occipital lobe."

"I thought the frontal lobe processed memory?" Potter asked, squar-ing off with her.

Dr. Madison tucked her hands into her pockets. "Yes, but that area fo-cuses on concentration, analysis, judgement, problem-solving—not nec-essarily the recall of what we see or know. Also, the temporal lobe and its hippocampus are critical to forming long-term memory. Someone—perhaps a neurologist—knew what they were doing and possibly understands the interconnectedness better than me."

"And you're certain there's only one microchip in place?"

"Oh, I hadn't thought of that possibility." She quickly studied the four images of Carlos's brain. "A cursory review doesn't reveal additional chips impeding his brain functions. I suspect we're still working with the one-chip design, but it's far more advanced than the one I developed."

Potter nodded and relaxed. "When will you know if it's functioning as designed or malfunctioning?"

Dr. Madison didn't peel her gaze from the digital X-ray images. "I'm afraid I won't know that until we get it out, assuming we can without damaging it or him. Even then, you don't have the equipment I'd need to examine the chip."

"Are you saying I need surgery?" Carlos asked, miffed.

Dr. Madison tilted her head, amusement playing across her face at the notion. "That's an unlikely option, given your impenetrability."

"My what?"

"To make a long story short, your skin will become impenetrable to needles, knives, and bullets."

Carlos grinned. "That's right, Quinn said I'd become bulletproof."

"I take it you aren't yet?" Director Potter asked.

"Not as far as I know," Carlos answered, shaking his head.

Dr. Madison turned away from the X-rays. "Well, let's try to draw some blood."

Ten minutes later, an older phlebotomist named Larry affixed the elastic tourniquet to Carlos's left arm above the elbow and wiped an area of a skin over a visible blood vessel. "All right, small pinch."

"God, I hate needles," Carlos muttered, recalling a similar experience with strong aversion. He stared at the ceiling, avoiding focusing on the process.

The tip of the needle slipped under Carlos's skin.

"Holy shit," Dr. Madison said, stunned.

"What?" Potter exclaimed, jerking his hands out of his pockets and stepping back, surprised.

"That shouldn't be possible!" Dr. Madison said, pointing at the vial filling with Carlos's blood. She grabbed two more vials and set them in the phlebotomist's tray. "Draw two more, please."

"Does this mean I'm not bulletproof?" Carlos asked with a frown.

"It would seem so. At least, not yet."

"Why does this surprise you?" Potter asked.

Dr. Madison scratched her head. "Well, in hindsight, it had been a few weeks."

"What?"

"I'm sorry. When we tried to draw blood from Blake, the needle couldn't penetrate his skin. But that was several weeks after his infusion with orgone. It's only been a few days, right? Less than a week?"

Carlos shrugged. "I don't know. I think so."

"Well, you've only been missing for a week," Director Potter said. "Wait, does this mean you could surgically remove the control chip?"

Dr. Madison sighed in defeat. "A neurosurgeon might accomplish that task. I designed the microbugs for a one-way trip. We didn't expect to remove them."

"Do you know when his skin will become impervious to the scalpel?" Potter pressed.

Dr. Madison shook her head. "Monitoring Carlos may give us our best answer yet. It could be tomorrow or in two weeks. I honestly don't know. However, based on experience, it should be less than four weeks total, unless there was something different about his infusion process."

"How did Blue Spekter remove the chip from Dark Flame?" Carlos asked.

"He gambled with his best friend's life," Dr. Madison replied, frowning. "I'd like to avoid risking your life if possible."

"What did he do?"

"At the end of an intense battle, he subdued Dark Flame and then incinerated the back of his head, burning out half of his neck, skull, and brain matter."

Carlos winced. "Ouch."

"Indeed. He gambled on Dark Flame's healing factor to restore and heal the physical damage inflicted. Thankfully Blue Spekter destroyed the malfunctioning microbug, and Dark Flame made a full recovery and became Helion."

Carlos's face suddenly twisted with confusion. "Wait, did you say you designed the thing they put in my head?"

Dr. Madison awkwardly sucked air between her teeth. "Err, yes. I used to work for Victor. We can save *that* story for another day."

Carlos frowned. "Fine."

Potter cleared his throat. "Come with me, Carlos. I need to brief you before we send you home to your grandma. There are things you cannot share with her."

"What's up, Director?" Quinn asked, answering his phone.

"Are you alone, Quinn?"

"No, I'm with Keegan. Why?"

"I'm sorry to bother you, but I need to speak with you. Alone."

"Um, okay, want me to come to—"

"No. I'm outside in an unmarked car."

"What?" Quinn asked, pushing himself up from the couch. He went to the front window and spotted the telltale black SUV parked at the curb beyond the snowbank.

"Come outside, please. Front passenger seat. It'll only take about five minutes."

"Sure, one sec." Quinn hung up the call and turned to his boyfriend, who had paused the show they were watching. "Sorry, STF needs me for five minutes."

Keegan smiled and stretched on the couch. "Okay. I'll just take a quick power nap while you go save the world."

Quinn kissed Keegan, grabbed his jacket, and made his way out of the house to the SUV. When he opened the passenger door, he smiled when he saw a familiar face in the driver's seat. "Captain Prett! What are you doing here? I thought I was meeting with—"

"Hey, Quinn. Jump in. We need to talk," Captain Prett interjected, jerking a thumb toward the back seat.

"We?" Quinn repeated, peeking inside the SUV. He immediately spotted Director Potter, who nodded at him, and Director Paul Hartman from the Department of Homeland Security. "Oh, hi, guys."

"Hello, Quinn. Please get in," Prett politely instructed.

"Okay." Quinn climbed in and shut the door.

Prett pressed a button on the dashboard, and the windows darkened, preventing anyone from seeing inside the vehicle.

"That's cool."

Prett smiled, then dropped his hands into his lap, suggesting they weren't about to drive away.

"Quinn, we have a problem," Director Potter said.

"What's that?" he cheerfully asked, turning sideways in his seat to see them better.

"You mean besides the fact that Nightmare is living up to his moniker and creating superhumans at undisclosed and nearly untraceable locations?" Director Hartman asked callously.

"Apparently," Quinn replied, knowing the government didn't pay the high-strung man enough to deal with the emerging realities of superhumans in the world.

"Someone else was looking for Carlos," Potter interjected.

"Like The Order?"

"Possibly, but from within the STF."

Quinn's mouth fell open. "What?"

"We believe it's someone within Hangar 227 or the Portsmouth Police Department."

Quinn gasped, and a memory stirred. "It's not Chief Applegate, is it?"

"Unlikely. When she cut ties with Victor and The Order, she never went back. Once The Order realized she was involved with you, they sent Blake to assassinate her, but you foiled their attempts. Then Blake took down the Archimandrion Council, and they haven't come for her since."

"So, you think there's someone else?"

"Yes, but we can't know who it is," Hartman replied.

Quinn frowned. "Can't? Why not?"

"The intelligence we have from Chief Applegate and Dr. Madison suggests The Order's saboteurs and sleeper agents work alongside each other without knowledge of the others."

"Huh. So, what makes you think there's a spy?"

"Well, it's the timing of events around Carlos's discovery. Captain Prett?"

Prett cleared his throat. "Chief Applegate authorized the missing person's report on Monday of this past week. However, someone marked the report as completed on Thursday. You didn't find Carlos until Saturday, which was yesterday."

Quinn scrunched his eyebrows. "Someone? Wait, Thursday?"

"Exactly. The missing person's system audits every record change, but someone tampered with this record, attributing the Thursday change to an unassigned user."

"And does the system show who tampered with it?"

"Unfortunately, no. My team is trying to reverse engineer the hack, but there are top-notch skills at play, which suggests they've been compromising the system for some time."

"But why Thursday?"

Potter chimed in. "According to Carlos, that's when Vanessa found him. She must have reported back to Victor. That's when we think their agent impulsively completed the report before legitimate authorities—uh, you—actually found and reported Carlos as found. If Applegate hadn't noticed this and reported it to me, we might have never discovered the spy."

Quinn frowned, feeling confused. "So, you know who it is?"

Potter shook his head. "Sorry, figure of speech. We discovered the strong possibility of an Order agent covering their tracks."

"Okay, so now what?"

"We watch and wait, and we keep our mouths shut."

"Wait, you want to keep doing things as if nothing's wrong?"

"Exactly," Director Hartman interjected. "Now we have the upper hand."

Quinn shook his head. "I don't follow."

"The Order doesn't know we know. And now there are only five people who are aware of a spy in our midst: the four of us and Chief Applegate."

"What do you want me to do?"

"Tell no one of this news, not even Helion or Catamount for now. Keep your eyes and ears open for anything suspicious when you interact with STF agents or the police."

"I don't normally interact with the police."

"Fair enough. In the meantime, Captain Prett's team will work their cyber-sleuthing magic and try to figure out who successfully tampered with a system designed to be tamper-proof."

Quinn pursed his lips and drew a deep breath. His gaze shifted between the two directors in the back seat.

"Something wrong, Quinn?" Potter asked.

"You want me to just 'keep my mouth shut and my eyes and ears open.'" He made finger quotes around the last phrase.

"Correct. Is something wrong with that plan?" Hartman replied. Quinn saw Captain Prett smirk discreetly and look away to hide his face from the directors.

116

Quinn frowned. "A lot, actually. I should fly back to Spec to find the reactor. I know it's hidden in the abandoned iron mines."

"That's acres of mountainous terrain to cover. Although our satellites can't penetrate the ground because it's saturated with ferrous metals, we're actively sweeping the area for unusual activity, per Carlos's recommendation." Hartman looked at Potter, who nodded, and continued. "Victor and The Order like their abandoned underground locations because not much information exists about them, and they were abandoned before records about them were infinitely preserved on the Internet somewhere. As Tara discovered, these mines—and the town—first appeared on a U.S. geological service map in 1920, when the Pulaski Iron Company bought the land to mine the iron. But there's not much more in the records. We can't find any plans, documents, or descriptions of what it's like inside. However, we confirmed the location of the original entrance, because that's known information. Carlos's debrief also inspired us. The current staff must park somewhere and rotate in shifts, which means their cars and bodies should trigger the infrared spectrum sensors. We've got a large swath of land marked out, so it's only a matter of time before we find it."

"I can find it," Quinn replied confidently.

"Maybe. But it took you and Catamount the better part of a day to find—and sense—another reactor not so long ago."

"Yeah, but we actually found his secret reactor at Androscoggin, and I found Carlos pretty quick. He was easier to find than the town."

Hartman pressed his lips into a tight smile. "I appreciate your enthusiasm, Quinn. Let us take the first crack at this, please. I don't want you to fall into Victor's hive of potential superhumans and become overwhelmed. We find him, then we figure out how to take out the reactor together, okay?"

"What about cell phones?"

Hartman tilted his head. "What do you mean?"

"Well, they must turn on or off before they go into the mountain. They wouldn't work underground, right? So, there must be a place where cell phones reconnect at certain times—like shift changes."

Impressed, Hartman nodded. "Good idea, Quinn. Let us work on that."

Quinn sighed.

"I sense your frustration, but I also trust you know Nightmare isn't some petty criminal you can scare and stop with your abilities. He's a scheming, maniacal monster who's usually two steps ahead of us. I'd even bet us finding Carlos is part of his grand plan, but we're meant to think it an accident or an escape."

"But why?" Quinn asked.

"Like Ron said, he's obsessed with you. He's letting you know he can still get to you by taking your peers and transforming them into your enemies. I also think Nightmare took a gamble on the new inhibitor chips, but this one seemingly—or conveniently—malfunctioned in Carlos. Again, that's if we're meant to believe what we see."

"My... *peers?*"

"Carlos attends the same high school as you. Coincidence? I think not. So long as he wants to destroy you, we'll have the ability to track his movements and hopefully figure out his plan, if not his endgame. One day we might discern a way to use his obsession against him."

Quinn scrunched his face. "I'm sure you meant that as a compliment, but painting me in the crosshairs of the world's deadliest terrorist isn't unnerving at all."

Hartman nodded. "I understand."

"Are we done?" Quinn asked.

"Yes. Thank you for meeting with us. Please enjoy the rest of the day with Keegan."

"With the weight of the world on my shoulders again, sure." Quinn opened the door and stepped out.

"Quinn," Hartman called out, lowering his window.

"Yup?" Quinn replied, shutting the door.

"I'm sorry. It's my job to keep us safe and keep you grounded. I truly wish it were different. Let's talk tomorrow evening after dinner at 227."

"Yup."

Hartman nodded, then rolled up the window as Captain Prett started the SUV and drove away.

Chapter 13

Welcome Home, Carlos

"Where have you been?" Yolanda Domínguez shrieked, swatting at Carlos. She practically assaulted her almost six-foot-tall grandson on the front walk of their home in Atlantic Heights, a historic neighborhood in Portsmouth, New Hampshire. She eyed him up and down and asked, "Mijo, whose clothes are you wearing?"

"Hola, Abuela," Carlos replied sheepishly, submitting to the giant, life-threatening hug she squeezed him with. Abuela's death squeeze, he suddenly remembered, was why Vanessa's hug had irritated him back in Spec. The sight of the house behind her and the smell of Abuela's perfume through her unbuttoned winter coat triggered additional memories that confirmed he belonged here.

Lieutenant Peter Doral, the Portsmouth police officer who had driven him home at the request of Director Potter to avoid contradicting Carlos's altered story, showed his badge to Yolanda. He nodded and politely introduced himself. "Ma'am, I'm—"

Yolanda immediately let go of Carlos when she saw the badge. She clapped him on the shoulder and admonished him. "What did you do? What have you done? Why are you in trouble with the police?"

Carlos flinched. "Ow! I—"

"He's not in trouble, ma'am," Lieutenant Doral interjected forcefully, offering a pleasant smile.

"No?" Yolanda asked, suggesting both doubt and confusion.

"No. I'm Lieutenant Peter Doral. Your grandson has been working undercover with us and the FBI to expose and apprehend a notorious drug ring here in Portsmouth."

"A drug ring?" Yolanda shrieked.

"Yes, ma'am. You can be proud of your grandson. With his help, we've been able to identify and arrest several local dealers."

"Okay, but why did you disappear? Were you with him… with Hector?" Yolanda asked, once again incensed by her grandson's aloof behavior.

Carlos briefly raised an eyebrow at the name Hector.

"It was necessary for Carlos to disappear so the operation could succeed," Lieutenant Doral said. "We needed the drug ring to believe he was not a threat to their plans."

"Carlos, were you involved with this gang?"

"No, Abuela. The police sent me in with drugs to earn their trust."

"You gave my grandson drugs?" Yolanda asked angrily.

Doral shot her a quizzical expression. "Yes, but not to consume. To sell to the drug ring."

Yolanda nearly imploded and marched toward Doral. "You put my grandson in danger? You put him in with those beastly thugs and their guns?"

Doral held his ground, shook his head, and bundled his neck in his scarf against an icy breeze. "Your grandson was never in danger, ma'am. Some of the FBI's roughest and toughest undercover drug enforcement officers, mostly former military, accompanied him as members of his cadre. You wouldn't have been able to tell the real gang members from the undercover officers if you had to."

Yolanda studied him for a moment. "But why my Carlos?"

"Because we knew he could pull off the look. A hotshot Latinx high schooler with connections is a believable premise that—"

"You profiled my grandson, you white devil!"

"Excuse me?" Doral pulled his head back in shock.

"Sí, white devil. How do you like it? How do you like being discriminated against or selected because of your looks? I ought to feed you my spiciest tacos and watch you risk your life, gringo!"

"Okay, okay, Abuela," Carlos said, stepping between them and raising his hands to stop his grandmother. She grunted in anger and glared at Doral. "It's because of what happened last year, Abuela. I was the right choice for the role." Carlos dropped his hands.

Yolanda's eyes flared with anger. "No! You are a seventeen-year-old boy. You are not the right choice to risk your life for anyone, ever!"

"Ma'am," Lieutenant Doral said, but Yolanda cut him off.

"Ay, Dios mío, do not 'ma'am' me, Lieutenant! I am not some terrified immigrant you can simply disappear. I am an American citizen, and I know my rights. Carlos is a minor, and you endangered his life without my consent!"

Lieutenant Doral pinched the bridge of his nose and sighed. "The city and the county are grateful for Carlos's service. Good day." He turned and walked back to his unmarked car.

"I ought to throw my chancla at you!" Yolanda shouted.

"Please don't," Carlos pleaded, suddenly recalling—in vivid detail—many arguments they'd had over the year.

Abuela rounded on him. "I can't believe you didn't tell me. Of the people who should have known, I should have been first on your list."

"I couldn't tell you, Abuela. If anyone came to the house looking for me, they had to believe you thought I was missing. We both know you can't lie, so filing a missing person's report was the best thing you could've done, because it tipped off the corrupt officers in the department."

"I cannot lie, but you can?" Abuela asked, exasperated, as Lieutenant Doral drove away.

"Technically, I didn't lie, I—"

"You said you were in Virginia! That you remembered nothing. I called people for money! Now I look like a fool. You embarrassed me, Carlosito."

"Oh boy, look, um, I'm sorry. I actually was in Virginia. I can't tell you why yet, but I promise I'm telling you the truth about that."

Abuela huffed angrily. "Did Everleigh know?"

Carlos shook his head. "Absolutely not."

Abuela grunted, and Carlos detected a hint of satisfaction in her tone.

"Like the Lieutenant said, my involvement led to multiple arrests and the end of the drug ring that infiltrated my school. I did this to make amends for what I did last year. It's over now."

Tears rolled down Yolanda's face. "You have no concern for poor old Abuela's feelings, do you?"

"Abuela, I—"

"I thought you had died, Carlosito," Abuela said in a strained tone. She wiped tears from her face.

"But I didn't, okay? I'm here, alive and well, and the sting is done. They got the bad guys. I wasn't the bad guy this time, okay?"

Abuela extended her arms and cried.

Carlos's tears flowed, and they embraced.

"I thought my Carlosito had died."

"I'm okay, Abuela. I'm home."

They hugged for several more minutes, then she gave him a once-over. "Well, come inside. You need to change those clothes. Are you hungry? I made some arepas con queso last night."

"Yeah, I'm starving. How many did you make?"

Abuela blushed. "More than enough. I've been anxious."

"Sorry."

"It's good to have you home, Carlosito. Now, vámonos."

Inside, Carlos recognized the heavily decorated walls of Abuela's home—their home. Among the many pictures that clung to the white-and-blue walls throughout the home, the wall shrine to Our Lady of Guadalupe and the dozens of colorful crosses and crucifixes surrounding the large wooden-framed picture of this interpretation of the Virgin Mary triggered Carlos's memories. He glanced around, remembering how

Abuela had furnished the living room with older furniture and covered the pieces with colorful El Paso-styled Mexican blankets and throw pillows.

He remembered celebrating Christmas, birthdays, and other holidays with limited family and friends from the area.

"Are you okay, mijo?" Abuela asked, hesitating before stepping into the kitchen.

"Yeah, just glad to be home, that's all."

"Okay. I'll heat you some food now. Oh, and don't forget to call Everleigh. I promised I'd have you call her the minute you came home. Your mobile is on your desk. I'm surprised you didn't take it with you."

"Me too. I'll call her soon."

After stepping into his room, more memories flooded Carlos's mind as he looked around at his belongings, including his cell phone. "I remember you now. My life revolves around you," he said aloud. He picked it up and tapped at it, but the screen remained dark. Realizing the battery had drained, he plugged it into the charger on his nightstand—another moment that felt familiar. He turned away, then paused. *But why wouldn't I have brought my cell phone with me?*

He glanced around the small bedroom, noting the folded laundry on the corner of his unmade bed. He remembered painting the walls his favorite shade of dark gray-blue and the fight he'd had with Abuela over the color choice. No pictures, posters, or crosses adorned his walls, something Carlos noticed was in stark contrast to the rest of the house. Then he remembered angrily pulling all his female supermodel posters down after Abuela had thrown a fit about sin and unfettered teenage hormones having no place in her house.

A forty-inch flat-screen television sat in the center of his white desk, and a wired controller for the connected game system—an Xbox—had been left on the desk. He remembered playing video games with some of his school friends. Names like Darien, Tony, and Kyle flooded his mind, but he couldn't quite place them. Thanks to Quinn and Blake's earlier help, several school memories had resurfaced, and more things clicked for Carlos, including recent memories of his homelife with Abuela.

His phone repeatedly buzzed on the nightstand. Frowning, he stepped over a pile of clothes, sat on the bed, picked up the phone, and watched a week's worth of notifications arrive and fill his screen. Careful to leave the phone connected so it would charge, he swiped to unlock it and quickly navigated to the downloading text messages from Everleigh. Once the messages started arriving, he raised his eyebrow at several suggestive pictures, but they lost priority when hundreds of messages of concern, anger, fear, and desperation downloaded.

He stopped when a video message downloaded. Tapping the Play button, he recognized her long brown hair, fair skin, and brown eyes. She looked exhausted and worried, so Carlos figured he'd better call her right away.

"Carlos, your arepas are ready!" Abuela shouted from the foot of the stairs.

"I'll be down in a minute, Abuela. I'm on the phone with Everleigh." He tapped the FaceTime button on the phone and started the call.

"Okay. You tell her I said hi!"

Two seconds later, the phone flashed with bright light. "Oh my gosh!" an excited voice said as the phone flipped and spun in the air, showing Carlos a twirling view of the sky and snowy grass. "Carlos?" Everleigh asked, exasperated. She steadied the phone, and it focused on her face.

"Hi, Evy," he said, suddenly remembering her nickname.

Her eyes widened with shock. "Oh my gosh, it is you!" she squealed, covering her mouth with excitement. Tears ran down her face. "Where the hell have you been?"

He heard gasps and other voices—likely her friends—commenting on his unexpected return.

"I can explain everything, babe, I promise. Where are you?"

"I'm walking through Prescott Park with some friends. Can I come over?"

"Of course. Abuela made arepas con queso. Like, a lot."

"I'll be over in a few minutes. You better have a good explanation for all this! We thought you were dead!"

"I do, babe. See you soon."

Everleigh ran into Carlos's arms, nearly knocking him over. Tears flowed from her eyes as she sobbed in his embrace.

Nearby, Abuela smiled and wiped her tears with a neatly folded tissue.

"Where the heck have you been?" Everleigh whispered, her shoulders shaking with emotion. Then her hands started squeezing his muscles, and she pulled back, staring at him with bewilderment dancing in her gaze. "What the hell? You're, like, jacked now."

Abuela stepped forward with a warm smile. "Evy, I made you some arepas con queso?"

Everleigh politely smiled. "Maybe in a little bit, Abuela. I'd like to speak with Carlos first."

"Of course, dear," Abuela said, extending her arms. The two women embraced and then tenderly gazed into each other's eyes for a moment. "Our boy is home!"

"I'm so relieved," Everleigh replied.

Carlos cleared his throat. "Um, yeah. Come upstairs, I'll explain everything."

Abuela cleared her throat, then kindly but sternly spoke in Spanish. "You be a good boy and leave the door open."

"Sí, Abuela," Carlos replied. Then he took Everleigh's hand and led her to his room. She immediately looked at him with confusion, but he only smiled. "What?"

"Nothing," she said, trying to hide her confusion. When they entered his bedroom, she hugged him tightly once more, then asked, "What happened?"

He gently pulled her to the bed, and they sat on it, cross-legged, facing one another.

She shot him another strange look but patiently waited.

"Look, something big happened this past week for me. But it starts with the fact that I lost my memory."

Everleigh gasped. "What?"

"For instance, I'm clearly doing something different from what you expect. I can see it in your face."

"Ah. Kinda."

"Things come back, Evy. It just takes time. For example, I know you're my girlfriend, but I'm having a hard time remembering our relationship. I know I—"

"You don't remember us?" She pulled back in shock.

"I don't, sorry." He reached out and gently took hold of her fingertips with his.

She shot him another strange look. "But how could you forget us?"

"I don't know. That piece hasn't come back yet. I didn't remember Abuela, where I lived, or where I went to school."

Everleigh drew a deep breath, then exhaled. "Okay. I'll try to be patient, but you are kinda skeezing me out."

"Uh, why?"

"You're... nice. I kinda fell for bad-boy Carlos. You're acting like church-boy Carlos."

Carlos frowned in confusion. "I go to church? With Abuela?"

Everleigh wrinkled her nose. "Uh, no. It's an... expression. She goes to church, but you said you stopped going in eighth grade when you became an atheist."

"I'm an atheist?" Carlos asked, straightening up with interest but unsure why that surprised him.

Everleigh pulled her hands away. "Okay, I'm starting to think you're crazy."

Carlos laughed. "Not crazy, just very confused. I don't remember much."

"It's why your room has no crosses or anything religious in it. And why you painted it this dark, dreary color."

"You don't like it?" he asked, surprised.

Everleigh looked around and faked a smile. "Well, I suppose it's nice. But it's not my taste." Then she shook her head. "Honestly, it's kinda depressing."

Carlos looked around at the bare walls. "I remember taking down posters of supermodels or something and then painting my room. Did you have something to do that?"

"I don't think so. Your room was this color the first time you brought me home."

"When was that?"

"Um, three weeks after we started dating. Your grandmother wasn't home. You know, that night."

Carlos shrugged. "Actually, I don't."

She frowned. "We slept together, Carlos."

Memories of their relationship flooded his mind, and he pleasantly recalled the not-so-secret physical aspects of their relationship. "Oh, oh wow, okay, right, I remember now."

Everleigh looked at him with confusion again. "You mean you didn't remember that?"

Carlos shook his head. "Nope. But that's how I remember these days. I see something or someone says something to me that triggers and influx of memories, and then, well, most of the time, it's like they were always there. Other times, like now, I'm an observer to my own life, and the memories don't connect in my brain as mine until something triggers them. But at least now I understand why me taking your hand downstairs seems weird. I think you expected me to make out with you?"

"Well, you know I hate it when you do that in front of Abuela."

"Oh." Memories flashed through his mind. "Right. Sorry. Oh wow, apparently I'm quite a dick to her."

"Something like that."

"Am I a dick to you?"

"You have your moments, but you have your redeeming qualities. I think Abuela understands that, overall, I'm a good influence for you, but she's not thrilled about the sex part."

"A good influence," Carlos echoed, then shook his head. "Sorry, not triggering anything."

"Okay, so outside of the memory thing, where have you been?"

Carlos swallowed nervously. He wasn't supposed to tell the truth about his whereabouts and infusion with orgone energy to Abuela, but Director Potter had said nothing about his girlfriend. Conveniently, it was because Everleigh hadn't come up in the debrief, but she probably fell into the can't-say-anything-to-anyone category.

"I don't want another lie," Everleigh said.

"Okay," Carlos hesitantly replied, wondering how many times he had lied to her in the past. Trusting his gut, he lied to her one more time. "I was working with the local police and the FBI on a case. They made me leave my cell phone here, which is why I couldn't answer." He explained the short version of the drug ring bust story to her and concluded with, "Let's just say there'll be fewer drugs at our high school now."

"Oh," Everleigh said. "Why couldn't you take your phone or tell me?"

"For the same reason I couldn't tell Abuela. The situation had to be believable. I couldn't risk having someone use my phone to figure out who is important to me. I had to lie to the two most important people in my life, and I'm sorry."

"I see." She pursed her lips and huffed. "So, you can't even tell your girlfriend where you went? What you did?"

Carlos shook his head. "No."

"Or how you got amnesia?"

Carlos shook his head.

"And the police didn't tell you how you lost your memory?"

"Um—" Carlos suddenly frowned, realizing she was looking for holes in his story, or a way into the truth. "It's part of what I can't talk about."

"I see." A moment of tense silence passed between them. "And what about school tomorrow? Do you know your schedule?"

"No. The police should've alerted the principal by now. I'll get a copy of my schedule from the main office, but hopefully someone can show me around, because I don't even remember what the inside of the school looks like. Or maybe I'll remember when I get there." Carlos's stomach grumbled as the smell of frying food tantalized his nose. "Do you think we could go downstairs and eat? I'm starving."

Everleigh nodded. "Would you wanna watch a movie and snuggle later?"

"Yeah. I have no homework to do, at least that I remember."

"Do you think you wanna change out of those clothes too?"

"What's wrong with these clothes?" Carlos asked, giving himself a once-over. "Abuela didn't like them either."

"Well, when you look at what's in your closet, you'll see they're totally not your style."

"I kinda like them. They're comfortable."

"So are your skinny jeans. The baggy cut of these jeans—or are those corduroys?—make your legs look like tree trunks. Did you find those in some fresh fashion hell?"

Carlos smirked and rolled his eyes. "All right, fine, I'll change."

Everleigh flashed a mysterious smile, then lay back on the bed. "Go ahead, I won't stop you."

Carlos unbuttoned his shirt and removed it with the white undershirt he wore beneath it.

"Whoa, shut the front door. What happened to you? Oh my gosh, you're so hot now!" Everleigh gushed, fanning herself as she studied Carlos's newly developed muscular body.

"*Now* I'm so hot?" Carlos asked, feigning annoyance.

"Well, you were hot before, but this"-she waved a hand in a circle, gesturing to his torso-"is like, hot damn, boy." She leaned forward and traced her fingers across his pectorals and abdominal muscles. Though her face expressed shock and admiration, a sensation invigorated Carlos, and he stepped away. "Not now, my door's open."

"Later?" she asked, another mischievous smile dancing on her face.

"Sure, why not?"

Everleigh jumped up and over a pile of his clothes. She rummaged through his closet and picked out several items of clothing for him to wear. Under Everleigh's admiring eye, he slipped into his own stretchy skinny jeans, a black studded leather belt, and a white T-shirt that stretched over his muscles. Then they headed downstairs to eat Abuela's arepas. As they ate, Carlos carefully dodged their pointed questions, relying heavily on the story Director Potter and Lieutenant Doral had arranged.

Chapter 14
Back to School

C arlos yawned and stretched in bed. He could still smell Everleigh's perfume on his pillow, and it made him smile. He propped himself up on his elbows and looked around his dreary room. Sunlight peeked in from the edges of the curling window blinds. A glance at his alarm clock told him he had awoken several minutes early, so he reached over and switched it off. He flopped back and stretched again.

Drawing his left hand up and making a C with his thumb and forefinger, he felt the power in his body and willed a spark into existence. It snapped between his fingers, but strangely, it didn't hurt like a static electricity zap. Yellow motes danced around his hand as he played with the power in his fingers.

He looked at the slowly spinning ceiling fan above his bed, remembering how the lights had wildly flickered when he reconnected with Everleigh during the height of their excitement together. All the low-watt bulbs in the ceiling fan had popped, but they had ignored it.

He heard unusually loud footsteps trudge down the hallway to his room, so he let the spark dancing between his fingers fade. He made a mental note to ask Quinn about a correlation between their powers and arousal.

"Carlosito!" Abuela hollered through the closed door.

"I'm up."

"Madre de los Milagros!"

"You can come in."

Abuela opened the door and stepped in. "I made you a chorizo breakfast bowl," she said in Spanish.

"You did?" he asked, somehow knowing this wasn't his usual breakfast at home.

Abuela grinned. "Sí! I can be traditional and hip!"

They shared a laugh.

"Thanks. I'll be right down."

"Okay, mijo. It was nice to see Everleigh again."

"Yeah, it was," he replied with a half smile, remembering what they had done while Abuela snoozed in the living room.

"You don't seem yourself, Carlosito."

"I don't?" he asked, drawn back to the present moment.

Abuela stood at the foot of his bed after entering his room. She shook her head. "You're calm. Polite, even."

"Oh."

"Usually you're so damn impatient God himself can't move fast enough for you."

Carlos chuckled.

"And now Abuela makes you laugh. Sometimes I feel like I have to walk on eggshells around you."

"Oh. Sorry."

"And your body has changed too," Abuela said, pointing at his torso. Carlos blushed, suddenly remembering he wasn't wearing any clothing under the sheets. "You have so many muscles now. Big muscles. When did you get so big?"

"I exercise a lot more?" he replied, making up a response.

"Well, it's working. No wonder Everleigh couldn't keep her eyes off you last night."

Carlos smirked, then pushed away a dirty thought. "I dunno I saw things this week I don't want to be involved with."

"Do you mean your work with the police?"

Carlos hesitantly nodded.

"Good. Stay out of trouble and be a good boy. Now get washed up before your breakfast gets cold." She turned and walked out of his room.

"I will. Thanks." Carlos yawned again, then listened to her retreating, careful footsteps down the stairs. He rolled out of bed, grabbed a towel, and trudged to the bathroom.

Everleigh was late.

She had profusely apologized through several long text messages and blamed a malfunctioning alarm clock on her tardiness to re-introduce Carlos to the school. He decided not to wait for her and walked the quiet hallways before first period that Monday morning. A few students greeted him as he passed by, and his mind pieced together his school life.

After retrieving a copy of his schedule from the curious secretary in the main office, he sat in the cafeteria. The normally loud space brought back a slew of memories, and Carlos became confident he could navigate his high school life with almost no difficulty. His eyes darted around at familiar faces and posters on the walls, even one that showed *his* face.

"What the hell?" he muttered, staring at his image on the cork bulletin board near the cafeteria entrance. Beneath his picture were the words "Have you seen him?"

"Dude, where the hell have you been?" Darien asked, clapping Carlos on the shoulder in friendship.

Carlos somewhat remembered Darien James but didn't remember hanging out with him like Quinn had suggested. Still, when the bully approached with his familiar cronies, Tony and Kyle, a gut feeling told him to be cautious about what he said to Darien. He turned away from the bulletin board. "What are you talking about?"

Darien noticed the poster. "Oh, that. Guess you can take that down, right? You've been missing for over a week. Tempest said you didn't survive, but then you escaped or something? What the fuck, dude?"

"Who the hell is Tempest?" Carlos asked, frowning.

"Uh, are you kidding me right now?"

"No. I have amnesia."

Darien glanced over his shoulder and said, "Take five, guys."

Tony and Kyle nodded back. "Fine, gonna get breakfast. I'm starved," Kyle said.

After the two boys walked away, Darien sat and continued in a low voice. "Tempest, as in Vanessa."

"You know Vanessa Tempest?" Carlos exclaimed, eyes wide with astonishment.

"Keep your voice down," Darien spat in a harsh whisper, looking around. Then he regarded Carlos with disbelief. "Of course I know Vanessa, uh, Tempest. What's wrong with you?"

"But how do *you* know Vanessa?" Carlos asked.

"What?" Darien pulled back, stunned. "What the hell is wrong with you? Are you okay?"

"No! I'm still trying to get my memories back. Did we hang out together? Does she go to school here?"

"She doesn't go to school here, idiot."

"Uh, okay," Carlos said, watching realization spread across Darien's face.

"You know what? Forget I said anything, dude. I'm just glad you're back. How did everything go?"

"With?"

"You know. I can tell it was successful."

Failing to comprehend what Darien wanted to know about, he guessed. "Look, I've been told we hang out sometimes. I just don't remember yet. But if you're still here, it means you weren't arrested, and that's a good thing, right?"

"Arrested?" Darien asked with confusion.

"Uh, forget I said that," Carlos said, scratching his face with embarrassment.

"Whatever, dude. Let's hang out when you get your shit together. You're all weird right now. Wait, how did you get home?"

"Um, Lieutenant Doral dropped me off at my house yesterday afternoon."

"Oh," Darien replied, sounding confused. "Uh, police department Lieutenant Doral?"

"Yeah, why? Is there more than one?"

"No, I don't think so." Darien shoved his hands into his pockets.

"Okay, good. Well, I was—uh, I really can't talk about it."

"Busted again?"

"Something like that."

Awkward silence passed between them until Darien spoke up. "Well, good. Glad it worked out for you, I think."

"Yeah, me too."

"See you around, Carlos."

"Bye." Carlos watched Darien walk away, then ripped his picture down from the bulletin board and tossed it into the nearby recycling bin.

Five minutes later, Carlos winced and grabbed the side of his head when he sensed Quinn approaching.

"Sorry, you'll get used to that," Quinn said, offering a sheepish smile and a shrug.

"I hope so. Hurts like hell whenever you come near me."

"Your range will expand too. I knew you were here before I was on school grounds." Quinn sat down and let his book bag slide to the floor. "How'd it go with your grandma?"

"Good, actually. Hey, I, uh, kinda have a strange question."

Quinn laughed. "Trust me. Nothing's weird to me anymore. Shoot. Oh my God, you're nervous!"

Carlos chuckled nervously and wiped the sweat from his brow. "Yeah. So, about last night, me an' Everleigh reconnected."

"Cool. How'd that go?"

"Really well."

"Awesome. Glad she's not mad you disappeared for a week."

"The story stuck well."

"Good."

He leaned closer to Quinn. "So, uh, last night we reconnected."

Quinn pursed his lips. "Right. You said that."

Carlos drew a frustrated breath. "No, what I mean is—"

"Oh! You banged," Quinn said, a smirk on his face.

"Yeah."

Then Quinn frowned. "All right, and this is concerning why? You used protection, right?"

"Yeah, of course. That's not what I'm trying to ask."

"Then what are you trying to ask?"

"Well, while we were, you know, all the lights in my bedroom flashed. I popped three bulbs in the ceiling fan lamp over my bed."

Quinn cackled. "Yeah, that's normal for you now."

"Oh," Carlos said, relieved.

"That's gonna happen whether you're alone or with someone else. If Keegan noticed that in the beginning of our relationship, he never questioned it. But once I figured out what it was, I became terrified my dads would figure out whenever I rubbed one out. It'll sorta diminish with time, but it's been about five months since my orgone infusion, and that still happens from time to time. Kinda depends how intense the experience is."

Carlos chuckled. "I should buy lightbulbs by the case."

Quinn laughed. "Probably a good idea. We should start training too."

"Training?"

"To help you learn how to use your known powers and figure out which other ones are waiting to surface."

"Sounds cool."

"Great. I'll speak with Director Potter. We can start this week after school. The sooner you understand what's going on, the better. Oh, and one more thing."

"What's that?" Carlos asked.

"Generally, emotions trigger new powers. When something happens, think about what you're feeling. That's how you can tap into it."

"But I shunt electricity between my fingers without emotions. Like, it just happens when I think about it, and it feels completely natural."

Quinn nodded. "Yup. The rules of our powers slightly differ from person to person. Seems the only consistent one is sex and exploding light bulbs." They chuckled. "But you're right, not every power will start with an emotional response. I'm just saying, if something happens, think about what you're feeling, especially if you're not alone. We don't need people knowing you exist yet."

"Right."

"So, training? Maybe tomorrow after school?"

"Sounds like a plan."

"Great. I gotta change out some books before class. Good luck today. Find me if you need anything."

Chapter 15
It's Not a Lobotomy

"I'm going to train him," Quinn said, glancing around the conference table at Directors Potters and Hartman, Captain Prett, Chief Applegate, Dr. Madison, Blake, and Ron St. Germain.

The directors' eyes widened with horror.

"Uh, no you're not," Potter said.

"So, you'd rather have another untrained superhuman running around the streets?" Quinn asked.

Potter pursed his lips. "Uh…"

"I'm the right choice," Quinn insisted. "Carlos is in a good place. I've already connected with him, and I can reinforce virtue over vice."

"He has a juvenile record," Potter said.

"If you'd like to lock him up, be my guest," Blake chimed in.

"Hilarious," Hartman flatly replied.

"Quinn has a point," Ron said.

"I second that," Dr. Madison added.

Ron nodded at her. "Thank you."

Hartman moaned, as if doubting his decision to include a civilian on the team.

Ron ignored him. "Let's face facts. Victor will turn out superhumans whether we like it or not. Hopefully, some of his mistakes will turn out okay, like Carlos has."

"The jury's still out on young Carlos," Hartman said.

"I understand that," Ron replied. "But Nightmare has a facility—more than one, it seems—and the means to train villains and sharpen their powers in record time. He proved this to us with the battle over Rangeley. He whipped up a dozen super villains in a few weeks' time, and they subdued all three of our heroes. We need a hero facility—not an underground secret base—that can stand as a beacon of hope and serve as an academy for superheroes."

"You're going to need help," Hartman said.

All gazes turned to the director. Quinn jerked a thumb toward his best friend, but Potter shook his head. "Blake is too busy with community service."

"Don't have to remind me," Blake said, ignoring Chief Applegate's unamused gaze.

Quinn looked around. "Ana María is, well, who knows where?"

"We know how to contact her," Potter said.

"Great!" Quinn replied.

Ron smirked and abruptly changed the subject. "I know how to remove the chip from Carlos."

Dr. Madison regarded him with wide eyes. "You do?"

Ron chuckled and gestured around the table. "No offense to your intelligences, but it's amazing how you smart people don't start with the obvious and go from there."

Dr. Madison rolled her eyes. "But I've exhausted every surgical option. I would need a top-notch neurosurgeon to remove the inhibitor chip damage free."

"Why do we care about not damaging the chip?" Potter asked.

Dr. Madison shot him an indignant look. "Not the chip, Carlos!"

"Oh, right. Sorry."

Dr. Madison looked back at Ron. "But enlighten us, Ron. What is your comic book mind conjuring up? No offense to your intelligence, of course."

Quinn rolled his eyes. "Knock it off. We're on the same side."

"Harrumph." Dr. Madison fumed and glared at Ron, pursing her lips and crossing her arms over her chest.

Ron ignored her thick sarcasm. "I've looked at the facts and come up with a way to neutralize an active, dormant, or malfunctioning control chip. It's not pretty, and it comes with high risk. But I think it's the only option we have once the superhuman's skin becomes resistant to surgical instruments, or, as Dr. Madison suggested, requires skills we can't readily bring in."

Everyone nodded.

"So, here's the basic idea, and it assumes their healing factor has kicked in. The first thing to do is neutralize the chip by passing a strong electrical current through it with either Quinn's electrical powers or a TaseBolt. Quinn will place his hands or the business end of a TaseBolt at the back of the superhuman's neck or skull and, well, the high electrical current will short-circuit the chip. Any collateral damage to the surrounding skin, muscles, bones, and brain matter will heal, as we saw with Blake."

Quinn winced.

Dr. Madison scoffed. "You want to lobotomize superhumans?"

Ron ignored her. "Since the electrical shock will also stun or weaken the newfound superhuman, this is when we remove the chip with Blake's help. Using telekinesis, he can carefully detach and pull the control chip out, tearing it through muscle and skin. It's not pretty, but it works, and while it will probably hurt, the superhuman will heal, and the chip will have been removed and destroyed."

"And then they're no longer under Victor's control," Hartman happily mused.

Quinn shook his head. "I don't like it. I thought I had killed Blake when I burned out the control chip in his head. Why can't we just put him under and get a neurosurgeon? You must have secret doctors or whatnot in the government?"

"Enhanced metabolic rate," Ron replied.

"Oh, right," Quinn said.

"Would someone mind explaining that?" Potter asked.

"I can't get drunk," Quinn replied.

"You're a minor," Applegate said with a scowl.

"Minors experiment," Quinn retorted.

Applegate frowned.

"Long story short, I can drink all I want, but I can't get drunk," Quinn explained. "My body metabolizes alcohol in seconds. There's a good chance our bodies would metabolize sedatives just as fast."

Blake spoke up next. "I tried to get drunk when my parents were sloshed one night. Quinn's right. Our bodies burn off the alcohol in minutes."

"Interesting," Dr. Madison commented. "That means we couldn't knock him out and operate."

"So, we're back to lobotomizing," Potter said.

"Technically, it's not a lobotomy," Dr. Madison admitted.

"Thank you," Ron replied.

Potter dismissively waved his hand. "I don't care what we call this procedure, as I prefer to think of it as a critical extraction. But I have a question for Blake. How will you know where the chip is? It's not like you can see it."

"My telekinesis allows me to sense the world around me in a way that's hard to explain. For example, I can't see it, but I can sense the half-eaten roll of wintergreen Lifesavers in your breast pocket."

"How do you know they're wintergreen?" Potter asked incredulously.

Blake silently stared at the director's chest for a moment. "I can sense the writing on the wrapper. It's like a memory playing in my mind, but it's much clearer. There are seven left in the roll. I could pull out the middle one if I wanted to. I can even sense the specks of mint in the candy."

"Incredible," Dr. Madison gushed.

"The same thing applies to the chip. It's gonna stand out to me as neither flesh nor bone. Once I grasp it, I'll carefully unseat it by manipulating the organic matter and the chip's creepy little legs. Once it's clear, well, it'll be quick."

"Ouch," Ron said, rubbing the back of his neck.

"So, who's gonna tell Carlos?" Blake asked.

"I will," Quinn volunteered.

"Good. If Carlos is amenable, let's get it done as quickly as possible," Potter said. "I hope that post-extraction, Carlos regains his lost memories."

Heads nodded in agreement.

"Regarding training the superhumans, Ron is right. We need to connect with Catamount and start an academy of our own," Hartman said, bringing the conversation full circle.

"Why Catamount?" Quinn asked, somewhat miffed Hartman didn't select him to lead.

"Because you're a high school student who needs to finish high school," Ron answered. "If anyone understands their powers best, it's Catamount. After all, she's been living with them since 1965. How long have you had your powers, Quinn?"

"Fine," Quinn grumbled, crossing his arms over his chest.

"But she's going to need your help, Quinn," Ron added. "Yours too, Blake."

"Yeah?" Blake asked.

"I don't believe the superhero academy should adopt the traditional teacher-student classroom model you're familiar with from high school," Ron replied.

Quinn and Blake traded glances and smiled, and Potter asked what Ron had in mind.

"Right now, it makes more sense for the four of them to learn from each other," Ron said. "Catamount has the wisdom of years and the mastery of her abilities on her side. Quinn and Blake, you both have more power-wielding experience in the field than she does. All three of you share similar developmental or awareness experiences with your power sets. Carlos will benefit from your shared experiences, and together, you'll become a stronger, united team of heroes."

"Hear, hear," Hartman chimed in, rapping his knuckles on the table.

"But that's not all we'll need," Ron added, his tone slightly menacing.

"Oh?"

"We need a prison. With the new super villain Tempest on the scene—and who knows how many others Victor discreetly created—we'll need a facility to incarcerate them."

Hartman nodded. "We're working on a special prison project with a few of our international allies and a trusted scientific community. I'm sure you can imagine the challenges we face holding someone as powerful as Quinn."

"How would you hold someone like me?" Quinn asked.

"Superhumans present an opportunity for innovation, so we're exploring a variety of solutions," Hartman replied.

"Like?"

"I'm not at liberty to say much else about it," Hartman said. "If there's no other business, I recommend that we adjourn. It's a school night for you two, and I need to get back to D.C. first thing in the morning."

Heads nodded around the table.

"Good. Until we have confirmation from Catamount about the start of an academy, I trust the three of you will take Carlos under your wing and mentor him." Hartman pointed at Ron, Quinn, and Blake. "While I believe Quinn and Blake will focus on how to use his powers, Ron should focus on when to use his powers, which should be almost never. We're not ready to introduce a fourth superhero to the world. We'll need a psychological profile completed on him, and we'll—"

"You never did that to me," Quinn interjected, leaning forward. The tone of his voice conveyed his disapproval.

"How do you know we didn't?" Hartman curtly replied.

"Oh." Quinn sat back, defeated.

"We may not have sat you in front of a psychotherapist, but we have a profile on you. You too, Blake."

Blake shrugged. "I figured as much."

"Good. Then it's easy to imagine we needed thorough profiles on both of you to understand who or what the unidentified phenomenon dubbed Blue Spekter was, not to mention his counterpart later known as Dark Flame. We also profiled Catamount as well when she revealed herself to us. We'll continue to evolve what the process looks like, but I've got people building Carlos's profile as we speak."

"Why?" Quinn asked.

"To understand his background and look for indicators that could predict undesirable or dangerous behavior in the future. For example, you yourself said Carlos associates with bullies and has been mean to you at school. Through your own admission, the Carlos we met is very different. We need to understand why. If the chip altered his behavior, will its removal trigger old behaviors, or will he remain kind and amenable to our help?"

Quinn nodded. "I understand."

"Good. Well, now that we've cleared that up, let's adjourn. Quinn, let us know when Carlos is ready. We'll want to remove that chip as soon as possible."

Chapter 16
Freedom

"**I** still can't believe I let you talk me into this," Carlos said. He, Quinn, and Blake were riding the elevator to the top floor of a special wing inside Portsmouth Hospital.

"It's for the best," Quinn replied. "This way, you'll know if you're acting under your own free will or Nightmare's."

Blake scoffed. "It sucked being under his control, even though I felt free."

The elevator dinged and slowed. The doors slid open, and Carlos asked, "But I thought you said your chip had malfunctioned?"

Blake nodded. "It did, but I didn't know it." The boys made their way down the hall, past several plainclothes DHS agents. Director Potter and Dr. Madison waited at the end of the hall with several more plainclothes agents.

"Did the chip make you do bad things?"

Blake shrugged. "I don't think it made me do anything, but it eliminated my inhibitions and morality. I acted out of anger and destroyed without a second thought. I hurt people, tried to kill some, and did kill others. And the worst part? I didn't care."

"Jesus. Why aren't you in prison?"

"Well, I wasn't in control of my actions."

"But you just said you were?" Carlos asked, confusion knitting his eyebrows.

"That's the gray area. How can I be in control of my actions if something has removed my moral compass? I was under the direct influence of a malfunctioning microbug that eliminated restraint. That's why Chief Applegate has me doing so much community service. It's annoying, but—"

"Good morning, men," Dr. Madison interjected. They exchanged greetings and stepped into a large examination room. The agents closed and secured the door behind them.

"Carlos, would you kindly remove your jacket and shirt? Then please straddle this chair and rest your face and chest against the pads," Dr. Madison said, pointing to what looked like a massage chair in the center of the room.

Potter moved to a corner of the room and crossed his arms over his chest.

"Wait, am I getting a massage?" Carlos asked, somewhat excited.

"No. I believe this may be the most comfortable position for the procedure," she replied nonchalantly.

Carlos frowned. "Because it's gonna hurt, right?"

Dr. Madison offered a sympathetic smile. "Like hell."

He groaned and did as she asked, gasping when his bare torso touched the cool leather pads.

Quinn and Blake studied the X-rays displayed on the massive screens. Dr. Madison's red markup identified the microbug inside Carlos's head.

"All right, let's begin," Dr. Madison said. She rolled a sonogram machine over and tapped a few buttons. "I'll start by confirming the device is still present and intact. Blake, this will help you see where it is. After the extraction, I will confirm you removed it." Then she picked up a scalpel and sliced Carlos's left shoulder.

"Ow," Carlos shouted in surprise and anger, his eyes illuminating with bright yellow fury. An arc or two of electricity snapped across his bare back. He pushed himself up and glared at the brazen doctor. "What the hell was that for?"

Quinn frowned, and Blake took a step back, unsure of what was going on.

Dr. Madison offered a sympathetic smile and set the scalpel back on the tray. "I'm sorry. I needed to discover if your healing factor has engaged before we begin. Otherwise, you won't survive."

"Oh. Well, you could've warned me," Carlos murmured. The arcs of electricity snapping across his back disappeared, and the power glowing in his eyes faded as his shoulder healed itself.

Dr. Madison nodded. "Good. Your healing factor is active, but your skin is not impenetrable yet. Interesting. Well, this confirms we can proceed."

"Great. Anything else you gonna do that involves sharp objects?" Carlos muttered.

"No, I'm only going to place the sonogram at the base of your skull and move it around until I locate the chip. This won't hurt, but it might feel cool."

"All right," Carlos replied, leaning forward and settling his torso and head onto the massage chair. He took a deep breath, then exhaled and tried to relax.

Dr. Madison tapped a few buttons on the sonogram. "You'll feel slight pressure as I move the scanner around the back of your neck and head."

"Okay."

Dr. Madison placed the scanner against Carlos's head. After making several adjustments, she asked. "There, do you see it, Blake?"

Blake stepped behind Carlos, next to Dr. Madison. A moment passed before he said, "Yup, and I can feel it too."

"All right, Quinn. You're up."

Quinn sighed, then moved around the massage chair and stood in front of Carlos. "Sorry about this part, buddy. It's gonna hurt."

"Just do it. I want my life back."

Quinn raised his hands and placed them on the back of Carlos's head, just behind his ears. Then he looked at Dr. Madison and Blake. "Ready."

Dr. Madison pulled the sonogram scanner away.

As Quinn's eyes glowed with blue power, Carlos felt Blake's telekinetic hold settle around his body to keep him still. "What the—" Carlos uttered, but a bolt of electricity leaped from Quinn's hands through the back of Carlos's head.

"Oh, shit!" Blake exclaimed.

Quinn stopped immediately. "What's wrong?"

"Ow!" Carlos hollered.

"I don't know," Blake said, surprised. "As soon as you zapped him, I lost my focus on the chip."

Carlos slithered out of the chair, clutching the back of his head. He swore, vehemently shaking his head and backing into a corner of the room. "No way, I'm not doing that! Fuck all of you!"

Quinn turned to console Carlos, but Blake grabbed his arm. "I got this." Blake crossed the room and gestured at the floor. "Sit with me?"

Quinn and Dr. Madison pretended to occupy themselves with the X-rays while Potter stoically observed from his perch in the opposite corner.

Carlos slid down the wall, still clutching the back of his head. "The chip's not working. Why do we have to take it out?"

Blake sighed. "How do you know it's not working?"

Carlos half shrugged. "I don't."

"When Victor implanted me with a microbug, he did it in secret when I was unconscious. I had no idea until Quinn pointed it out during one of our fights."

"That sucks."

"The first time I flew, I accidentally touched the overhead electrical wires crossing the street. I think that short-circuited the microbug, and from that moment on, I started thinking and doing things I couldn't explain. Like, I didn't understand why I felt so free—nothing could stop me, not even myself. I loved it, even though I was a murderous asshole who pissed off everyone I cared about."

Carlos drew a deep breath and slowly exhaled.

"When Quinn burned the microbug out of my head, it hurt like hell, but nothing compared to the pain of hurting my friends—especially my best friend, Quinn. He believed in me when no one else would, and he knew that if the chip could come out, I'd come back to him—and I did."

"I didn't know that," Carlos said sheepishly, nervously clearing his throat.

"What we don't know, Carlos, is whether your chip is broken or simply dormant, waiting for a specific activation code to turn you into the next Dark Flame," Blake said. "You know what I did at the Christmas assembly. Trust me, you don't wanna be that guy. I was out of control, even though I believed I was in control."

"Wow."

"And remember, you are not quite yourself right now—you're too nice. You can be a real dick when you want to."

Carlos smirked. "Like you?"

Blake chuckled. "Oh yeah. So, we're gonna stick by you, and not give up. We're gonna help get that thing out of your head."

"But you lost your sense of it," Carlos whined.

Blake nodded. "Quinn's power is intense, and it caught me off guard."

"It hurts."

"I know. Maybe he can grab your shoulders instead. And maybe that will move the direct current away from my telekinetic sense. Let's ask him if he can dial it down too, okay?"

Carlos took another deep breath and exhaled as he nodded. After Carlos sat in the massage chair and relaxed, Dr. Madison confirmed the position of the chip once more.

"He's all yours," she said to Blake and Quinn.

The superheroes got into position, and Quinn grabbed Carlos's shoulders. "Just enough power to lock up your muscles, okay?" Quinn asked.

"Uh-huh," Carlos replied anxiously.

With his eyes glowing bright blue, Quinn looked at Blake.

Carlos grunted as his body tensed when Quinn passed a current between his hands. Small arcs of power snapped across Carlos's bare back.

"Much better," Blake said as he held Carlos in place and reached into Carlos's head to grab the microbug.

Carlos groaned as Blake carefully detached each leg of the microbug from where it had implanted directly between his cerebellum and occipital lobe. When Carlos felt the last leg of the microbug detach, Blake gently pulled it away from Carlos's brain matter.

"It's free, and I'm moving it away from his brain," Blake said.

Dr. Madison spoke up. "Like a Band-Aid, Blake. Be merciful."

Blake drew a quick breath. A few seconds later, Carlos felt the back of his neck tear just before Blake said, "Got it."

Carlos screamed, and his body jerked violently against Blake's telekinetic restraint.

Quinn immediately stopped zapping him. "It's okay, Carlos, it's done." Quinn stepped back, and Blake released his telekinetic hold.

Carlos, still screaming and writhing in agony, pulled his head up and jumped back from the chair. His eyes blazed with yellow power as electricity arced and snapped across his face and torso. An arc leaped from his right hand and connected with a metal rod in the ceiling.

"Quinn!" Potter hollered with alarm.

"On it!" Quinn shouted back.

Blake jumped back as energy arced around and cascaded from Carlos.

Quinn drew a deep breath and raised his hands, then erected a powerful blue force field around Carlos. A second later, Carlos exploded with power, but Quinn contained the furious blast and absorbed the reactive orgone energy.

"Holy shit, you're powerful for a new guy," Quinn said, shaking his fingertips. A few motes of power flashed around his hands.

Carlos collapsed to his hands and knees, his shoulders heaving as he recovered.

Blake stared at the microbug in his palm, then grimaced. "Nasty little thing." A second later, his hand burst into flame, and he incinerated the microbug.

"Hey!" Dr. Madison exclaimed, then sighed. "I was hoping to study that."

Blake shrugged sheepishly. "Oops, sorry. Next time."

"Carlos, how do you feel?" Potter asked.

Carlos rolled to a seated position on the floor and stretched his neck by tilting his head from side to side. "A little more like myself, I think?"

"How does your head feel?" Blake asked.

"It hurts. No thanks to you two," Carlos spat.

The angry tone in his voice made Dr. Madison raise her eyebrow.

Carlos suddenly straightened up. "Uh, at least, it did. Now it doesn't."

"That's your healing factor," Dr. Madison said. "The injury you sustained from the extraction process has already healed."

"Oh. Cool."

Potter stepped forward. "Carlos, do you remember how you met Victor Kraze?"

Carlos shook his head after a moment. "No."

Potter frowned.

Carlos furrowed his eyebrows and looked at Dr. Madison. "I thought you said my brain had healed?"

Dr. Madison nodded. "Given the back of your neck healed, and you feel no pain, I assume your brain has also healed, at least physically."

"Physically?"

"Mental trauma takes patience and time. That is not my diagnosis, but perhaps your healed brain cells will prompt your memories' expedient return."

Potter sighed in frustration. "The minute you remember anything, report it. Quinn, give him my number. We need intel about what Victor is planning."

"You're just letting him go?" Dr. Madison incredulously asked.

"Do we need to keep him?" Potter asked.

"Uhhh–"

"He's not your scientific play toy, Doctor."

Dr. Madison's expression hardened, and she straightened up. "That's not what I meant. We just pulled an incredibly sophisticated device out of his brain, and we're not sure what's going to happen next."

Potter drew a deep breath. "You're right, and I'm sorry. I haven't slept well. Many eyes above me are watching this."

"Tell those eyes to chill out," Carlos said sarcastically.

Potter smirked. "If only it were that easy."

Blake spoke next. "Despite my trip through the orgone reactor core after Quinn extracted the microbug from my head, I turned out okay. I think it's safe to assume Carlos will be okay as well. What if Quinn and I check in on Carlos for the next few days?"

"Doctor?" Potter asked expectantly.

Dr. Madison nodded. "I would appreciate that. Carlos, if anything seems wrong, I want you to call me. Quinn, Blake, if you notice anything, please report it immediately."

"We can do that," Quinn replied with a smile.

Potter clapped his hands. "Great, it's settled. Now go on, get out of here. Go do your homework or whatever you do on a school night."

Chapter 17
The Family Business

Three days later, Carlos lay on his bed, absentmindedly tossing a red squishy ball into the air above him. "Why the hell was I in Virginia?" he wondered aloud, struggling to piece together memories that slowly surfaced.

"Carlosito!" Abuela hollered from the bottom of the stairs.

"What?" he snapped, jumping in surprise.

"Dinner!"

He sighed. "I'll be right down." Abuela had demolished the grocery budget by preparing his favorite meals each night. Her cooking was impeccable, but her relentless doting irritated him. Dismissing the thought, he rolled off the bed and went downstairs.

"Jesus, Abuela," Carlos muttered when he saw the incredible feast she had cooked for him that night.

"Don't take the Lord's name in vain in this house, young man," she spat in Spanish.

"It's a lot," he replied with annoyance, pointing at the festive spread on the table.

Abuela frowned at him. "Why are you so testy with me, mijo? I cooked you all this good food."

"There's enough here for four people."

"You're a growing boy. Have you seen yourself in the mirror? Look at all the muscles you have. Now come, eat. Eat!"

Carlos sighed and sat down in his usual seat.

Unfazed, Abuela set her hands on her hips and stared at him. "Why have you been so testy these past few days? What is wrong?"

"Nothing."

"Nothing?" Abuela echoed with exaggerated disbelief. "People without problems are happy, Carlosito. You look miserable, like you did before you disappeared."

He scowled at her. "What's that supposed to mean?"

"You came home a kind boy on Sunday. You were polite to me, but now you're back to your rude, impatient old self. I don't like it one bit. I want my nice grandson back. What happened this week? What aren't you telling me?"

"Nothing," Carlos insisted, his right knee bouncing with nervous irritation.

"Then why aren't you happy?" She leaned forward with concern and crossed her arms over her chest.

He shot her an angry look. "I'm just not, okay? How many times must I remind you I still don't have all my memories?"

She stood tall, pressing her lips together. "Ah. Is it related to the thing you did with the police?"

"No."

"Is it Everleigh?"

Carlos shook his head. "No. I don't want to talk about it."

Abuela frowned. "But why not?"

"Because I don't know what to talk about," he yelled, nearly jumping out of his seat. "I don't remember what I was like before Sunday. People tell me I was an asshole, but I thought I was a nice kid. I don't know who to be, or who they expect me to be, or what you want from me."

Abuela's expression softened, and she dropped her hands. "Carlosito, I want you to be happy. I know we have had our challenges over the years.

155

Your life changed overnight when you were only five years old, and so did mine. I didn't think I would raise you, but here we are."

Carlos glared at her. "What, so *you're* not happy I'm here?"

"Oh, mijo, I'm so happy to have you here. Maybe a little too happy, and that bothers you, I think. That's why I made you good food this week, to celebrate. I thought I had lost you, mijo, and you're back. God answered my prayers. How could I not celebrate?"

"Will you tell me about my life? About what happened?"

Abuela nodded and sat at the table. "Okay, I will. Um, where do you want to start?"

Carlos scoffed. "Probably with what happened when I was five years old. Maybe it explains why I'm so angry all the time."

Abuela drew a deep breath and exhaled slowly, then smiled and nodded at him. "You never told me why you feel so much anger. But I'll tell you what I think. If you remember more, will you tell me how you truly feel?"

"Yeah, sure."

Abuela leaned forward and folded her hands together on the table. "When you were a little boy, I told you that your father had died of cancer. But that was a lie."

"What?" Carlos sat back, astonished.

"Carlosito, five-year-olds don't understand the way the world works, so it was necessary to protect you from the truth."

"Okay," Carlos said begrudgingly.

"When you were twelve, your uncle Hector started coming around a bit more, and that scared me."

"Why?"

Abuela hesitated before answering. "Because he wanted to recruit you into the family business."

"Still not seeing why that's a bad thing," Carlos said.

Abuela clutched her heart for a moment, her eyes brimming with emotion. "Oh, mijo. That's when I told you the truth about your parents. Your mother's maiden name was Rodriguez, and you know she was

Hector's sister. But the family business is the affair that brought you down this week, the very thing that you worked with that policeman to stop."

"Brought me down?" Carlos tilted his head to the side. "Wait, when you say the 'family business'—are we drug dealers?"

"I am not. And I don't think you are. But your mother Gracinda and her brother Hector Rodriguez belonged to a drug cartel—Las Navajas—that is, a family business your late abuelo Ernesto hid from me until they killed him, God bless his soul." She made the sign of the cross and kissed her hand. "When your mother realized she was pregnant with you, she tried to leave Las Navajas to protect you. Hector and his friends did not take kindly to what they decreed was betrayal and planned to murder her in the hospital while she rested and kidnap you."

"What?" Carlos asked as memories of his past reformed in his mind.

"But God had a plan, and he watched over you. Your father Enrique, while sitting with your sleeping mother, startled the murderer. The police report said they fought, but just before security arrived, the murderer killed your mother."

Carlos cursed, and Abuela smirked. "I'll let that one go. Once security apprehended the murderer, they found Enrique injured and Gracinda dead."

"This is Hector, your son? My uncle?"

"I'm sorry, mijo, but it's true. And he's your estranged uncle. We don't want him around here."

"Wait, he's here? How did he find us? How did Dad die?"

"Hector's thugs found and murdered him when you were five, but you were with me that day, so I fled with you."

"He murdered my father?"

"Not Hector, someone else. But I know Hector and Las Navajas were behind it. We lived in motels for several years, and eventually we ended up here."

"How did we survive?"

"I worked for the motels and cleaned the rooms. They gave me less pay, but it put a roof over our heads."

"When did Hector find us in New Hampshire?"

"About two years ago. But you were no longer the child he could take and brainwash, so he left you alone—or so I thought."

More memories resurfaced in Carlos's mind. "Is this related to what happened last year?"

Abuela nodded. "It has everything to do with what happened a year ago. Hector beguiled you, and you hung around his people, disobeying my rules to keep you safe. The police arrested you in a drug bust, but the court had mercy on you because you had no drugs on your person or in your system."

A memory flashed, and Carlos drew a deep breath. "But Hector works for the state. How can he be a drug lord?"

"Hector lives two lives and has always kept his nose clean. He sends people he trusts to do his dirty work. For whatever reason, they don't talk if the police arrest them. They are loyal to him, even if it means going to prison."

"Hector didn't fall from the bridge," Carlos said suddenly, remembering how Blue Spekter had saved Hector.

"Huh?"

"Never mind."

"Okay." Abuela regarded him with curiosity.

Carlos's eyes lit up as more memories flashed across his mind and filled in the gaps. "Oh my gosh, that's why I hate Blue Spekter!"

Abuela frowned. "We don't hate people, Carlosito. It's not the Christian thing to do. But what does this have to do with Blue Spekter?"

"He saved Hector after he fell off the bridge, right?"

"Sí, Carlosito."

"And I'm mad at Blue Spekter now because Hector is still alive?"

"Are you asking me or telling me, Carlosito? Because I don't know the answer to that question."

158

He reflected for a moment before answering. "I think I'm telling you. Hector was a brutal bully. He would find me after school and harass me, often in front of my friends. He always wanted me to do jobs for him or come meet some people to work for—"

"Which you did," Abuela interjected, sounding displeased.

"Right, but that was only to—"

A moment of silence passed.

"To what, mijo?"

"Infiltrate."

"Huh? What is this word?"

Carlos stared at the food on the table as his stomach growled. *I'm not ready to tell you how Hector forced me to open the doors to his drugs at school.*

"Abuela, do you think we could take a break from talking about this? It's kind of heavy, and as much as I've lost my appetite, I'm starving."

"Of course, mijo," Abuela replied, offering a polite smile.

They quietly prepared their plates. As they ate, Carlos listened as Abuela talked about the latest gossip from church, the hippie customers at the market she worked at, and whatever else she could fill the silence with. Despite the shocking revelation and the memories that had returned, a smile crept on his face as she spoke. Abuela saw it and winked at him, unable to hide her own joy.

"My parents aren't home. Do you want to fool around?" Everleigh asked.

"Not really," Carlos replied with a quiet sigh. When he had picked up his phone, he had wanted to call Quinn, but Everleigh had called first.

"Excuse me?"

"I'm not in the mood, that's all."

"Well, get in the mood."

"No."

Everleigh scoffed. "I offer you a night full of endless sex, and you say no?"

"I've got a lot on my mind. Memories are coming back. I don't think I could focus tonight."

"Funny, *that's* never been your issue."

"Thanks for the vote of confidence, but my answer is still no. I need to think and talk to someone."

"Well, you're talking to me," Everleigh replied hopefully.

Carlos scoffed. "You're not who I need to speak with."

"Wow. I see how it is. Rude much?"

"That's not how I meant it, and you know it."

"I am your girlfriend, Carlos. Sometimes I wonder if you actually remember that."

"I do, but it doesn't mean you get to boss me around. That's not the way it's gonna be."

"Hmmm. Is my bad boy back? You're turning me on, Carlos."

"Apparently. Look, Evy, if you don't mind, I got stuff to do. I need to talk to the police about my family."

"Oh, you're turning me on, Carlos. What am I gonna do with myself in this big house?" There was something odd—and edgy—about Everleigh's tone.

"I'm sure you'll figure something out. Goodbye." Carlos disconnected the call and stared at his phone. *Did I just turn down sex? Man, what the hell is wrong with me?*

Chapter 18
Competing Priorities

"Hey, man. What's up?" Quinn asked. His voice sounded tired on the other end of the phone.

"Uh, hi. I need a favor," Carlos replied, nervously clearing his throat. He lay on his side on his bed, propping his torso up with his left elbow as he stared at the phone on his pillow in speakerphone mode.

"Okay. How are you feeling?"

"Fine, thanks. Uh, can you take me back to Virginia?"

"Why? Did you remember something?" Quinn's voice sounded hopeful.

"No, but I need to look for answers."

Quinn hesitated. "You want to find the reactor core, right?"

"Yeah."

"Look outside your window."

"What?" A bright flash of blue light behind the closed window shade suggested Quinn had flown to his house. Carlos sat up in surprise, then frowned. "Stalking me now?"

"You know we're not supposed to go back to Spec, right? Victor is counting on that. It's a trap. Can I come in?"

"I'll come outside. I could use a walk, anyway."

Quinn laughed. "Okay, but there's no way in hell I'm bringing you to Victor right now."

"You don't have to tell Director Potter," Carlos said, pulling on a sweatshirt.

"Are you kidding me? I can't go behind his back right now. Do you know how long it took me to earn the man's trust?"

Carlos sighed and crept down the stairs, whispering into the phone. "Look, I'm gonna go back with or without you. I need to know what happened. I've remembered so much, but I can't remember how or why I got involved with him."

"We'd need to take Blake with us. Catamount too."

Frustrated, Carlos slipped into his winter boots. He grabbed his jacket, opened the front door, and quietly closed it behind him. He pocketed his phone and glared at Quinn. "Aren't you the strongest of all of us? Why can't you take down Victor?"

Quinn pocketed his phone. "What about Vanessa?"

"She didn't seem to be a problem for you, either. Why the hell aren't you wearing a coat? It's freezing out," Carlos said, pulling on his winter coat.

"And what if there are other superhumans? Why should we assume you're the only one? I'll teach you how to keep yourself warm when you need to."

"Oh, okay."

"Come on, let's walk." Carlos nodded, and the two boys wandered through the neighborhood. "If we go, I need to tell Director Potter."

"Call it a training exercise, then. I don't really care. Look, I don't especially want to ask for your help, but I need it."

Quinn shot him an incredulous look. "Dude, what's gotten into you? Are you feeling okay?"

Carlos sighed. "Apparently I'm a bit too much like myself, or what people remember me to be."

"What does that mean?"

"I snapped at Abuela, and she made a snide comment. I spoke with Everleigh, who, well, let's just say I don't know if I screwed things up for good or not."

"Uh, okay. So, you're back to being Carlos the jackass?"

"Excuse me?" Carlos said, clenching his hands into fists.

Quinn pointed at Carlos's fists. "See what I mean? I told you before that you seemed different. You, well, you were nice to me when I found you chopping wood."

Carlos consciously relaxed and shook his hands. "What's that supposed to mean?"

"You have a short temper, and you're quick to strike. It's old news to hear Carlos was involved in yet another fight somewhere in town."

"Are you—" Carlos abruptly stopped as memories flowed through his mind, and he recalled several scraps around town with troublemakers and other teenagers. "Oh, right." To prove his loyalty to the family business, Hector had made Carlos beat up any dealers at school or in town who were late with payments. Within a month, he had earned Hector's trust. Hector then had given him an entourage of street muscle who followed him around the seacoast and intimidated delinquents within their dealer network. He also had intercepted and beat up rival gangs who tried to move in on their territory.

"Carlos, are you there?" Quinn had stopped and now stared at him.

"Yeah, sorry. A ton of memories just flooded back. I had something to do, and you fucked it up, okay?"

Quinn jerked his head back in surprise. "Me? How?"

Carlos grimaced and slowly rounded on him. "Today I remembered why I hate you, Quinn." Carlos drew a deep breath and exhaled as anger faded into sorrow, even remorse.

"Uh, okay. Why do you hate me?" Quinn asked, stunned and wide-eyed.

"Hector didn't fall, Quinn."

"Who's Hector? Oh, you mean the guy who fell from the bridge?"

"He was pushed."

Quinn stared at him for a moment, mouth agape. "What?"

Carlos shrugged and started walking.

Quinn watched him go for a moment, then caught up to him.

Carlos cleared his throat, then shared what he had remembered and confirmed with Abuela at dinner. "After I had earned my uncle's trust, I started selling drugs to earn a cut of the money because I needed to pay someone to push my uncle from the bridge."

"Holy crap, Carlos! Why didn't you just call the police and turn him in?" Quinn sounded shocked and alarmed.

"Are you kidding me?" Carlos spat. "The police listen to you because you're white. They might have listened to me, but if they didn't, my uncle would have found and come after me and Abuela."

"But—"

"He murdered my parents, Quinn. He murdered his only sister and tried to kidnap me. You need to understand something in my world: retribution. He would have come after us without a second thought. What would the police have done except call the coroner when they found my body?"

"Who the hell did you get to push him?"

"Someone from a rival gang I paid off. It was supposed to look like an accident, and, well, I guess it did. Since he didn't die, there's no crime. Leave it alone."

"Have you ever heard of conspiracy to commit murder?"

"I said leave it alone," Carlos snapped.

"This is insane, Carlos. You're a teenager. You're supposed to be plotting your next high school sports victory or something fun, not the gruesome death of your evil uncle."

"And that's why I hated you and your perfect picket-fence life."

Quinn ignored the snide comment. "What did Hector do after? That was back in what, early October?"

"I don't remember yet, but when Abuela and I picked up the conversation, she told me he had disappeared. She thinks his near-death experience put him in the public spotlight and forced him to go underground after the media plastered his face on the news and Internet as part of your story."

"Do *you* know where he is?"

"No. Abuela thinks he moved away, but she doesn't know."

"So, uh, do you have any plans to hurt him?"

"Hell yeah. I want to hunt his ass down and hurt him real bad."

"Carlos, you don't wanna be the first person in the superhuman prison."

Carlos shrugged but said nothing.

Quinn sighed. "Retribution is their way, Carlos. It doesn't have to be yours. Rise higher, do the right thing. He can't hurt you now."

"He'll come for me, and when he realizes he can't hurt me, he'll kill Abuela. I'm certain of it."

"You think he'd kill his own mother?" Quinn asked, mouth agape.

"Yes. You told me Victor Kraze would 'not hesitate to put the ones you love in danger or kill them to get his way.' So will Hector. They're the same. I—" Memories slammed into Carlos's mind, and he suddenly remembered the key piece of information everybody wanted. "Oh my God!"

"What?" Quinn asked, jumping back.

Carlos turned and grabbed Quinn's shoulders with excitement. "I remember how I met Victor Kraze! I remember how I got involved with him."

"How?" Quinn excitedly asked.

Carlos saw the conspicuous black SUV with the blacked-out windows parked across the street. This marked the third day in a row he had seen it that week. Unconvinced it was the police or a rival gang, he walked to the driver's door, slowly reaching for the concealed gun holstered against his backside.

The window slid down, and the driver nodded at him.

Carlos hesitated, for she was beautiful. Her most prominent feature was the striking frizzy, wavy, and long red hair that fell around her shoulders. Her wide green eyes watched him with wonder and excitement. The scent of a light, flowery perfume hit Carlos's nose.

"Why are you wherever I am this week?" Carlos asked.

She smiled at him. "I'm just the driver, kid. The boss wants to speak with you."

He briefly shifted his gaze to the window behind her. "Who you with?"

"Not Las Navajas or your rival druggie gangs, if that's what you mean." She briefly tilted her head toward the back seat. "He only wants to talk to you."

Carlos drew a deep breath and looked around. "I don't want any funny business."

"There won't be any," she replied.

Carlos stepped to the back driver-side door and cautiously opened it.

The man inside smiled at him. "Hello, Carlos. I'd love a few minutes of your time." He wore a black suit, a white shirt, and a skinny black tie. His medium-length black hair was parted on the left and styled with a shiny hair gel. Although the man had shaved, Carlos could see the stubble of a mustache, soul patch, and chin-strap beard.

"What do you want?"

"I'd rather not discuss that with the door open. Would you come inside?"

"So you can kidnap me? Do you work for Hector?"

The man chuckled. "My name is Victor Kraze, and I absolutely do not work for your uncle or any of the petty gangs around town."

"Your name's familiar."

"I'm sure it is. I'd like to offer you an opportunity."

"I've heard that before," Carlos muttered.

"What if I told you I had the power to help you eliminate Las Navajas, to hurt Hector as he hurt you? What if the same opportunity allowed you to shut down the drug rings terrorizing the city?"

Carlos slid into the back seat and shut the door. "I'm listening."

Victor smiled. "Now, I'm going to tell you something shocking, but I promise I'm not here to hurt you. I'm here to help you, give you a gift. All I ask in return is that once you deal with your uncle, you come work for me."

"What's your business exactly?"

"That's a good question. Here comes the scary part. Remember, I'm not here to hurt you."

"All right."

Victor's eyes illuminated and glowed red.

"Oh, shit!" Carlos exclaimed, pulling the gun from his waistband and aiming at Victor. "You're that super-freak, Nightmare!" The revolver shook in Carlos's hand.

Amused and unfazed, Victor tilted his head and looked at the gun. "I prefer the word super *villain*, and yes, I am. I'm not here to hurt you, Carlos. I'm here to offer you superpowers. Besides, we both know that gun won't hurt me."

Carlos looked at the gun, shrugged, and lowered it. "Why me?"

"You have shown a tenacity others have not. You are driven, motivated, and you go after what you want. Not only that, you're patient and calculating. You knew you couldn't take down your uncle yourself, and you know what he'll do if he finds out you plotted against him. Yet you acted without fear and arranged his assassination in the shadows. I need people like you in my organization."

"How do you know all that?"

Victor smiled. "I do my homework, and I don't approach someone without knowing a great deal about their motivations. I want you on my team, Carlos, and I'm willing to do what it takes to get you there."

"Who is this group you work for?"

"They work for me. I'll tell you more, but I need to know if you're in or out. If you say yes, we're driving to Virginia tonight. If you say no, walk away. I trust you won't say anything, given you know what I can do."

Carlos scoffed. "What, I'm supposed to decide my future in two seconds while you threaten me if I say no?"

"Yes. Think about it. If you worked for me, you would be better than Blue Spekter or Helion. After dealing with your uncle, you'll help me build a better world."

"How?"

"By doing what must be done—taking out the bad guys before bad things happen. Imagine if we could have prevented—"

"Does Blue Spekter work for you?"

"No, and he is a threat to me and my organization. The media has painted him as the good guy, the superhero, but he only wants to help those in power keep their power. After all, he saved your uncle when we both know he should've died for his horrible crimes."

It was Carlos's turn to tilt his head. "That's a bit of a stretch. The man fell, and he saved him. End of story. Blue Spekter doesn't know the truth."

"I'll give you that," Victor conceded. "However, doesn't wish to punish those who must be punished. He'd rather let a failed justice system deal with criminals. You and I both know some dogs need to be put down. We can do that together, you and I, starting with your uncle."

Carlos nodded. "I'm in."

"Oh?" Victor asked, surprised.

"Like you said, I'm methodical and calculating. This gives me the advantage I need."

"All right, then. We'll leave in an hour so—"

"I'm ready now."

"Uh—"

"Let's go, Victor."

Victor raised his eyebrows in surprise and shrugged. "All right, Vanessa, you heard the young man. Let's gas up and head to Virginia. We should be there tonight."

Quinn stopped and stared at Carlos, ignoring the frigid breeze that blew between them. "You got into a car with a complete stranger, who you knew was the planet's number-one enemy, on the promise he'd give you superpowers?"

Carlos chuckled. "Yeah. That seems crazy in hindsight, huh?"

Quinn nodded, wide-eyed, and the boys continued walking. "Do you remember anything else about what happened?"

"A little. Vanessa and Victor traded driving hours, and we chatted about whatever. I asked Vanessa why she worked with Victor. She said she was in it for the long game, to make the world a better place, to do all the things people talked about but never did. They were very good salespeople for their cause. They got me hook, line, and sinker."

"Sounds familiar."

"Once we got to Spec, Victor asked to blindfold me so I wouldn't know how to get in and out of the facility."

"Dammit," Quinn muttered.

"But once we were inside and I heard a door close behind us, he removed the blindfold."

"What did it look like inside?"

"I could tell we were underground, like in a cave or mine, I guess. There were wires and lights anchored along the rock and concrete walls, and we eventually made our way to a massive chamber with more wires and weird… stuff."

"Hexagonal panels?" Quinn asked.

"Yes!" Carlos replied, clapping his hands together as the full picture recreated itself in his mind. "He had me strip down to my boxers and stand on some special platform. There was a countdown, flashes of light, and then I could barely stand. Next thing I knew, I—" Carlos hesitated. "Uh, there's a gap here."

"You woke up somewhere?"

Carlos snapped his fingers. "Yes, that's right. I woke up on the metal table, and I was still in my boxers. It was cold. I heard voices... oh, it was Victor and Vanessa. They thought I had died, and Victor ordered her to incinerate my body. That's when I got up and ran. I remember scrambling over wet rocks to get out of the cave."

"Did you exit through the main entrance?"

"No. I remember squeezing through a wicked tight crevice in the rocks. And then I... well, I ran for my life through the woods once I realized people were chasing me. But I didn't know who or why. Eventually I did that explosion thing, and then I found the barn. Jesse found me the next morning."

"And imagine Victor's surprise when he discovered you had escaped," Quinn murmured. He looked at Carlos. "Do you remember when they put the microbug in your ear?"

"Oh, that. Yeah, I remember. Someone rushed in after the flashing lights stopped in the cavern thingy and put something against my ear. It felt weird, like a bug was crawling into me. Some muscled dude held me down, and I couldn't stop it. I guess I blacked out, cuz I remember nothing else."

The boys walked in silence for a few moments.

"You have some tough choices in front of you, Carlos."

"Knew you were gonna say that."

"You escaped, but Blake went there. He one-hundred-percent bought Victor's bullshit and went straight to the dark side. I told Blake I would be the one to stop him if I had to. Please don't put me in that position again."

"I'll try not to."

"Director Potter will flip his shit when he finds out Victor was in town less than two weeks ago. I'm willing to bet it wasn't his first time, either. You need to tell Potter all of this."

"Okay." They had circled the block and now stood in front of Carlos's house again.

"Speaking of Potter, I told him I would train you."

"You did? I mean, you will? That's awesome," Carlos replied, his face lighting up.

"I'll teach you how to use your powers and work on my team. But we operate on the side of justice, not false promises of grandeur from Victor."

Carlos gasped. "You want to make me a Guardian?"

Quinn chuckled. "Whoa, slow down, buddy. Let's take it one step at a time, okay?"

Carlos smiled awkwardly, unable to hide his excitement. "Fine."

"Potter wants to start a superhero academy of sorts, where we train, learn to work together, and hone our superpowers."

"That sounds awesome."

"I'm glad you're interested. Now, let me talk with Potter about Spec. I know you want to go back, but I need you to understand how dangerous that will be. You remembered a lot tonight. Maybe more memories will come your way over the next few days."

"Okay."

"I need you to promise me one thing."

"What?" Carlos asked, turning to face Quinn.

Quinn put his hands on Carlos's shoulders and looked him in the eye. "That you won't go after your uncle. But specifically, that you won't kill him."

Carlos frowned. "Given I don't know where he is, that shouldn't be a problem."

"Good. Let me help you bring him to justice. There's nothing I want more than to take care of the bad guys, but there's a right way to do it. You wanna be a Guardian? You gotta do it my way—our way."

"Fine. I'll try it your way."

The boys shook hands, and then Carlos watched Quinn leap into the air and fly away. He sighed, wondering if he would ever gain the ability of flight.

Chapter 19
Lost

The next day after school, Carlos meandered through town and made his way to one of his uncle's popular haunts on Islington Street. Hidden behind a building, he peeked at the corner store. Seeing nothing out of place, he promptly ignored his agreement with Quinn and marched across the mostly empty parking lot.

With the improved clarity of his enhanced vision, he saw through the window and watched Dario—the on-duty enforcer—tap the cashier next to him, alerting him to Carlos's presence.

Unafraid, Carlos marched inside and took stock of the plainclothes gang members throughout the store. To the untrained eye, they looked like shoppers, but Carlos knew they were Las Navajas members protecting the business.

"You gotta lotta nerve coming back here," Dario mumbled in a low voice.

Carlos ignored him and focused on the cashier, who slowly moved to retrieve a weapon from under the counter. "You won't need that," Carlos said, eyeing the man. "Just tell me where he is."

"And who might that be?" Dario asked, puffing out his chest.

"Hector."

Dario shrugged. "Haven't seen him."

"Since when?"

"A while."

Carlos took a step forward. "Why are you treating me like the enemy?"

Dario crossed his burly arms over his chest. "Why'd you go to the cops, ese?"

"I didn't go to the cops," Carlos spat, becoming annoyed. He felt power simmering inside him.

Dario slowly shook his head. "Not what I heard, ese."

Carlos jerked his thumb toward the back of the store. "Is he back there or not?"

Dario stepped forward. "You ain't going nowhere until you fess up."

Carlos noticed the reflections of four gang members in the security mirrors making their way toward the front of the store. He casually glanced around and offered a cocky smile. "Come on, guys, it's me."

"Don't care, ese. Time to leave while you can," Dario said.

Carlos shook his head. "Not until I get what I want. Where is Hector?"

"I told you he's not here," Dario replied angrily.

Carlos scoffed. "You expect me to think he'd walk away from his cash flow?"

"Didn't say that."

Carlos smirked. "Now we're getting somewhere. You know what, I'll go check the back room myself."

"You will not! Grab him!" Dario nearly screamed.

Two of the men lunged at Carlos. He summoned just enough electrical power to shock them without giving away his superpowered nature. When they made contact, he threw up his arms and swatted them away, and the men hollered in shock and backed away, wringing their hands and arms.

Carlos snickered and jerked a thumb to the back. "I'm going to look for Hector. Stay out of my way."

The other gang members reached for their concealed weapons and looked around, but they relented because there were customers in the store. Seizing the moment, Carlos hurried past one of the startled gang members he had zapped.

"Follow him," Dario barked, and the four gang members obeyed.

Carlos burst through the old double-swinging doors at the back of the store. He hurried through the small maze of stock shelves to the dealer's secret back room where Hector's office would be. Some gang members along the way stared at him until they recognized him and jumped out of their seats to pursue him. Pushing through the next set of doors, he marched to the center of the room and looked around at the various tables for money counting and drug repackaging. The attentive overseers monitoring the room aimed their submachine guns at him as his gaze landed on Hector's darkened office window.

"Where is Hector?" he barked as the gang members caught up and grabbed him. One of them set a cocked gun against the back of his skull. They tried to pull him back, but Carlos used his super strength to stand fast.

"I want Hector. Where is he?"

Everyone at the tables froze in awe of the spectacle, and one overseer shouted, "You are not welcome here."

"Why not? I was last week."

"You went to the cops. The only reason you're not dead is because you're Hector's nephew."

Carlos sighed and rolled his eyes.

An angry Dario pushed through the crowd. "I told you he wasn't here, ese."

"Fine. I believe you. Tell me why everyone thinks I went to the cops?"

"You were seen getting out of a car with a cop at your house after your little hiatus. Only now we know what the hiatus was for."

"What was it for?"

"You took down a drug ring in town."

Carlos scoffed. "Do you recall any drug rings that were taken down while I was gone?"

"No, we just assumed it was this one."

"Yet here you are," Carlos said, pointing out the obvious flaw in Dario's logic. "Was anyone arrested?"

"Uh... no."

"That's right, Dario. That's because I wasn't talking Las Navajas business, okay? It was something completely different."

"What, then?"

"It's none of your damn business, Dario. If I was gonna snitch on a family, it sure as hell wouldn't be ours. It'd be somebody else's."

Dario grimaced.

Carlos shook off the hands holding him, and they relented and let go. "It's one thing for you to see the police dropping me off. It's another to think you know my business. Who told you?"

"What?" Dario's tough exterior faltered for a moment.

Carlos took a step forward. "Who told you I was with the police? Only a few people were told that story, so who told you?"

Dario regained his composure and smirked. "If you ain't the snitch, then maybe there's a snitch on you."

Carlos curled his fingers into fists and fumed. "I'm done here. If Hector shows up, tell him his nephew is looking for him."

Carlos walked out of the store and immediately sensed and saw Tempest. She batted her eyelashes, smiled, and waved at him while leaning against a black Land Rover. She hugged herself through her winter coat for warmth and smirked. "Well, that seemed like a colossal waste of time to me, hon."

"What do you want, Vanessa?" Carlos asked, feeling and sounding defeated.

"You have powers. At least, you had them. Did the government chop your balls off?"

"No," Carlos replied defensively.

"Did Quinn?"

"No," Carlos echoed with an impatient sigh.

"You have powers, Carlos. You should have taken what you wanted from those jerks."

Carlos clenched his jaw for a moment. "What do you think I want?"

"The location of your evil uncle Hector."

Carlos's eyes widened with surprise. "How do you know that?"

"Do you think we recruited you without checking your background?"

"Recruited me?" Carlos echoed.

"Don't you remember?" Vanessa asked, somewhat surprised.

Carlos shook his head. "Not everything has come back, but I—" He stopped speaking as memories flooded his mind. Then, for the first time, he regarded Vanessa with new recognition. "You were chatting with me *before* that day with Victor in the SUV."

Vanessa nodded.

"It was you, me, and someone else. You were recruiting me. Where—who—is the other guy?"

"That's not important right now. Do you remember why we recruited you?"

"You thought I could help better the world."

"Exactly," Vanessa replied with a big smile. "It's our mandate to catch and punish people like Uncle Hector. But he's a small fish compared to the killer sharks we need to take care of."

"Isn't that what Quinn wants?" Carlos asked, testing her.

Vanessa scoffed. "You're funny. He wants to rely on antiquated forms of legislation and justice that exist only to keep corruption in place. It's one reason they haven't thrown Hector in prison. His lawyers have always found loopholes whenever the police arrested him in the past. You have the power to take care of him."

Carlos gasped. "You mean kill him?"

Vanessa rolled her eyes. "Yes, Carlos. That's what you signed up for. The justice system has failed this country, and criminals are everywhere. They flourish because prison is no longer a threat to global organizations that have learned how to cheat the system."

Carlos shook his head. "I will not kill my uncle."

Vanessa raised her arms in exasperation. "After everything he did to your family? To your parents? Don't you think it's only right and fair to avenge their deaths by killing murderers? Not to mention how many other people he's injured or killed?" She lowered her arms.

Carlos took a step back and shook his head. "I don't know."

"How many people have died because of your family's drug business?"

"How should I know?"

"I'll tell you," she said. "Hundreds."

Carlos shrugged. "Wouldn't surprise me. He's an unforgiving bastard."

"We need to stop people like Hector."

"Carlos?" Everleigh inquired, approaching the shop from the side parking lot.

Carlos's jaw dropped in shock as he reeled around and stared at his girlfriend with confusion. "Hi, Evy. Uh, what are you doing here?"

She pointed to the shop. "Picking up a few things for my parents. Why are you here?"

"Everleigh!" Vanessa interjected enthusiastically, stepping forward and extending her hand. "It's so nice to meet you. Carlos has told me so much about you."

Carlos's face fell as Vanessa spoke.

Everleigh bristled and reluctantly shook Vanessa's hand. "Has he, now?" she responded cautiously, glaring at Carlos. "Funny, he hasn't mentioned *you* yet."

"No? Well, I'm sure it's, you know, what happened while he was gone."

"She was with you?" Everleigh asked pointedly, incensed.

"Uh, not really," Carlos replied, fumbling.

Everleigh glared at him. "I see."

Carlos cursed under his breath. "It's not like that, Evy."

"A pleasure to meet you, Vanessa," Everleigh said sarcastically. Then she turned to Carlos and waved her finger in his face. "When I get out, you better be gone."

"Can't we talk about this?"

"I'm not in the mood!" Everleigh shouted. Then she grunted in anger and stormed off to the corner store.

They watched her depart in silence. When the door closed behind Everleigh, Carlos rounded on Vanessa. "Why the hell did you do that?"

"I did you a favor," she replied smartly.

"Are you kidding me? You probably just broke us up."

"Good. Carlos, that girl is a distraction who can't be trusted."

"She can't be trusted? You're the one secretly recruiting teenagers for some secret organization and giving them superpowers. *You* can't be trusted," Carlos retorted.

Vanessa shot him a patronizing look. "Come now, everything I've told you has been true. Mostly. The only two things I made up was being your girlfriend on the youth group trip, but that benefited Jesse and Janie." She tilted her head and scratched her chin with feigned innocence. "I wonder how they are these days."

"If you hurt them—"

"We haven't, but Victor wants the dividends from his investment in you," Vanessa said in a sweet but menacing tone. She pointed in Everleigh's direction. "When you figure it out, you'll thank me. Trust me."

"Figure what out?"

"You'll see." Vanessa winked at him, then climbed into the Land Rover and drove off, leaving Carlos with more questions than answers.

Chapter 20
Sniff to Smell, Reach to Feel

T he outdated mercury vapor lighting inside the empty warehouse flickered as the building's power grid reacted to the intense electrical arcs snapping around Carlos's hand.

"That was great, Carlos," Ana María said with an approving smile. "All right, let's try that again, and try to focus your energy. Remember, let the energy you feel flow through you. It's as much part of you as your hand or nose. When you want to touch something, you reach out to feel. When you want to smell something, you sniff." She raised a hand and held her open palm toward Carlos. "Strike my palm with an arc of power."

"Okay," Carlos responded, bouncing on the balls of his feet like a boxer. "Sniff to smell, reach to feel."

"Good luck," Blake added sarcastically, hands tucked into his jeans pockets.

Carlos smirked. A super-heated arc of raw electricity snapped from his hand and connected squarely with Blake's chest. Several stray arcs scorched the worn concrete floor and metal beams of the empty warehouse they practiced in.

Both Quinn and Ana María—the superheroine Catamount—shielded their eyes from the brightness of Carlos's powerful arc.

Blake howled in pain as he fell back, his body convulsing with Carlos's high voltage. Smoke rose from his singed shirt and the blackened concrete. "O-o-o-w!" Blake stuttered.

Quinn snorted a quick laugh and clapped his hands. "Okay, *that* was funny."

"You try being the target for once," Blake muttered, wincing as he climbed to his feet.

Ana María lazily suppressed a grin. "I admit, I'm amused, but you won't be laughing when Nightmare's goons attack you with their finely tuned, merciless abilities."

"What do you want us to do, beat each other up or something?" Carlos asked.

"Dammit! That's another ruined sweatshirt," Blake whined, pulling his burned clothing away from his chest.

"That's what Victor's thugs do," Quinn interjected.

"What do you mean?" Carlos asked.

"When Ana María and I went looking for Dr. Madison, we saw Victor and his superhumans practicing all kinds of combat, from normal martial arts to superpowered offensive and defensive maneuvers," Quinn replied. "I learned how to grow and control my powers by sparring with Ana María."

"And Victor set me up with a trainer too," Blake admitted. "I thought it was foolish, given I had powers, but I still learned from him."

Quinn nodded and spoke again. "That's what the superhero academy idea is about, a response to Victor's very effective super villain training program."

Carlos shrugged and scratched his nose, noticing how intently Ana María observed him for the third time that night. "Well, Vanessa didn't put up much of a fight back in Spec. You guys stopped her, and fast. If the rest of his thugs are like her, we'll—"

"I think she let us defeat her," Quinn said. "She's not called Tempest because she's dainty. She's got a good poker face, that's all."

Ana María stepped forward. "Regardless, we must be ready for whatever Victor throws at us."

"So, you're taking the job?" Quinn asked, smiling.

Ana María smiled back. "I'm strongly considering it."

"Great," Quinn replied.

"I wouldn't be alone, of course," Ana María said. "There would be support from the STF, and we must learn from each other. I may be, uh, older, but I don't know everything. Together, we're stronger. Separated, we're weak, and Victor knows this. We should expect Victor will do everything he can to win back Carlos."

"Well, he hasn't done an outstanding job," Carlos said with a laugh. "Vanessa wasn't very convincing."

"How can Victor win him back?" Blake asked. "We removed the inhibitor chip from Carlos's brain. There's no way he can force Carlos back to his side."

Ana María shook her head. "We must never underestimate Victor. If we do, we hand him victory."

Carlos chuckled. "That's funny."

Quinn, Blake, and Ana María stared at him.

"You know, Victor, victory. It just... uh, never mind." He shoved his hands into his jeans pockets, embarrassed.

Ana María raised her hand. "Again."

"Hey, Ana María?" Carlos asked.

"Yes?"

"You keep staring at me. Why?"

Ana María shrugged. "You look very familiar, but I can't place it."

"Oh." Carlos assumed a fighting stance, curled his fingers like claws, and snapped another bright arc of power toward her.

"Again!" Ana María insisted.

With a wicked grin, he shouted, "Unlimited power," and blasted her with multiple arcs of powerful lightning that leaped from his fingertips.

Blake and Quinn shielded their eyes, and Ana María squinted against the intensity.

"Damn, dude, that's so bright," Blake said.

"I think I figured out your superhero name," Quinn said, lowering his hands.

"What, Sidious?" Blake asked.

"No."

"Bolt?" Carlos asked.

"Nope," Quinn replied.

"How about Zapper Dude, or just Zaps for short?" Blake said with a smirk.

"Definitely not," Carlos answered, shaking his head.

Quinn grinned. "Arcbright."

"Oh, I like that," Ana María said.

Carlos nodded slowly. "It's different. I like it too."

"Clearly, your dominant power is electricity manipulation," Quinn said. "One day you might even transmute, like Blake does with fire and I do with water. Wield that well with your other powers, and you'll be a formidable hero villains will have to deal with."

"And let's not forget electricity tends to be our key weakness, except for him," Blake added, jerking a thumb toward Quinn.

"Wait, *you're* immune to electricity, and I'm zapping *her*?" Carlos asked, pointing at Ana María.

Quinn shrugged. "She didn't ask me to be the punching bag today."

"But you're more than welcome to take over," Ana María said with a smirk. "Carlos, how about it?"

A mischievous grin crossed Carlos's face. "Seriously?"

Quinn hardened his expression. "Careful what you ask for, punk."

"Think fast!" Carlos snapped his hands toward Quinn. Several bright arcs of white-hot electricity seared the air between them and connected with Quinn's body, scorching his clothing. But Quinn remained unfazed, and Carlos pulled back in surprise.

"That all you got?" Quinn taunted.

Carlos drew a deep breath, then leaped forward and unleashed the full power of his electrical barrage against Quinn, who simply raised his right hand and caught electrical arcs with his fingertips. The electrical orgone energy collected there, growing into a ball of power.

"Whoa," Blake said, stepping back.

Carlos stopped zapping Quinn and stared in wonderment. "How are you doing that?"

"To me, it's all orgone energy. Here, catch." Quinn threw the crackling ball of electricity at Carlos, but he didn't know how to catch it. It exploded across his body, arcs of power snapping at the ceiling and floor.

Carlos stuttered a laugh as his body convulsed. "Wow, that tickles." The electrical energy dissipated, and his clothing smoked.

"Tickles?" Blake asked sarcastically. He shot Ana María a curious look.

"Interesting. Even I can't absorb electrical energy like the two of you." She pointed at Quinn and Carlos. "I wonder how many of Victor's people are immune to electricity?"

"None, I hope," Quinn said.

"Why does it matter?" Carlos asked, once again feeling Ana María's intent gaze.

"We thought electricity was our weakness," Quinn said. "That's why they developed those TaseBolts."

"Those things hurt a lot," Blake added.

"And while they stopped us both in the beginning, they don't hurt me anymore," Quinn said.

"You mean I'm unstoppable?" Carlos asked with a wicked and excited grin.

Quinn shook his head. "Not at all. Humans might not stop you, but we can."

"How?" Carlos asked

"We can hurt each other badly, and if we interfere with the healing factor, it pretty much shuts us down." Quinn explained how, in a weakened state, Blake as Dark Flame had impaled him with rebar through the torso. The rebar had prevented him from healing and using his powers to stop Dark Flame. "The STF knows this, and so does Victor."

Carlos winced. "Yikes."

"Victor also has some kind of mind-warping power that can mess you up if you get close enough to him. I call it the parallax effect," Quinn said.

"What does it do?" Carlos asked.

"It completely changes your perception," Quinn replied. "One minute you're fighting him, the next minute you're dancing on Mars in a tutu on a checkered floor. He can make you see whatever he wants. It's weird, but that's when he can getcha."

"All right, boys, I don't know how you got here, but I have an SUV parked out front," Ana María said. "It's probably covered in a foot of snow in this storm."

"I flew, and I have a dinner date with Ravone in a bit," Blake said.

"Me too," Quinn added. "But not the Ravone part."

"I walked, and I don't have a date either," Carlos replied with a smirk.

"Then I suggest we all get on with our evenings," Ana María said. "Next time we meet, bring your supersuits, or you'll burn through your wardrobe in weeks."

"I don't have one," Carlos whined.

"We'll work on that," Quinn said.

"Cool," Carlos replied, grinning.

"I did something you won't like," Carlos admitted, trudging through the heavy snow in downtown Portsmouth. It was relatively quiet, as most folks—except the young—refused to brave the treacherous conditions of the nor'easter.

Quinn shot him a concerned look. "And what would that be, Arcbright? That really is a cool name, by the way."

Carlos chuckled nervously. "Yeah. I... uh, since I can't go back to Spec, I went looking for Hector."

"Ah. Did you find him?" Carlos could tell Quinn was trying not to frown.

Carlos shook his head. "I found trouble and a mystery."

Quinn raised a curious eyebrow. "Is your secret safe?"

"Yes," Carlos muttered with annoyance. "Hector wasn't around, and his thugs wouldn't tell me anything. They insisted I had gone to the police and thought I was a rat. That was kind of weird, but not the weirdest part."

"What's the weirdest part? Wait, how did they know you went to the police?"

"I'm not sure. Lieutenant Doral, you, my abuela, and Everleigh are the only ones who know. Maybe Blake, if you told him. But it's not even a true story! Somebody must have seen me with Lieutenant Doral when he dropped me off at my house."

"Interesting."

"And confusing. Anyway, when I left the store, Vanessa was waiting for me outside."

"Vanessa was in Portsmouth?" Quinn asked, shocked.

"Yeah, but it gets weirder."

"It does?" Quinn asked, stepping around a pile of icy slush. "I didn't tell Blake, by the way."

"Okay. Well, Everleigh showed up, claiming she was shopping for her family or something."

Quinn shrugged. "What's wrong with that?"

"Only everything. Everleigh's family has money. Trust me, they don't shop at the corner store."

"Good point." They stopped at an intersection and pressed the Crossing button.

"And then Vanessa introduced herself and basically broke us up."

"So, is that the weirdest part?"

Carlos frowned. "No. Everleigh showing up is the weirdest part. Her family shops at Whole Foods or Fresh Market and pays way more than they should for food."

"Oh." Quinn pointed at the coffee shop diagonally across the intersection. "You wanna grab a hot chocolate or something? We can talk about Spec."

"Sure."

The revving of an engine distracted them, and the boys turned and watched in horror as a speeding beige sedan lost control on the icy, snowy road and spun sideways into the empty intersection.

Quinn swore, then dashed into the intersection to stop the car, but he slid on an icy patch. He grunted when he fell against the right rear fender of the sedan, causing it to spin around and slide across the intersection into a utility pole. With a loud crack, the utility pole shattered, and three snow-laden transformers topping it broke free from their brackets and dangled from wires.

Carlos's mouth fell open in shock. In less than two seconds, the otherwise quiet and slush-covered intersection had become a mess of arcing wires and sparking traffic lights that exploded with electricity as they fell across the intersection. A few panicked pedestrians screamed and ran from the intersection, slipping and sliding while trying to avoid electrocution.

A wire snapped, and one transformer fell. Righting himself, Quinn hurried over and caught it. "Carlos! Help me!" Quinn shouted, electricity cascading over his body.

"What? How?" Carlos shouted, nervously looking both ways before stepping into the intersection. Dancing live wires and sparking fallen traffic lights littered the intersection.

"Just do something!" Quinn shouted. Bright blue power blazed from his eyes and shimmered around him as he looked for a place to set the transformer.

Above, another set of overhead wires twanged and snapped. Carlos strained to see them against the dark sky, obscured by heavy, falling snow. Just then, the second transformer broke free, and Carlos's eyes and body ignited with bright yellow motes as he zipped toward it, sliding to a stop as the massive transformer fell into his arms.

"Nice catch," Quinn said with a smile.

Carlos smirked. He knew the transformer should be heavy, but to his surprise, it felt light. Then it exploded and knocked both boys to the slushy ground. Above them, the third transformer exploded into a ball of flame and fell on top of Quinn. Behind them, a woman screamed.

"Now what?" Carlos whined. He turned and saw a dangling traffic light break free and swing toward a mother and her two small children.

"I'll be fine, go help them!" Quinn shouted.

"Right!" *I need to get there now*, he thought.

With a bright, dizzying flash, Carlos suddenly stood in front of the mother, but the transformer was no longer in his hands. *What the hell?*

"Look out," she shouted, pointing behind him, but it was too late.

The traffic light slammed into Carlos's back and made him stumble forward. Catching his balance, he glanced over his shoulder, then pointed up the street and spoke to the mother.

"Ma'am, you need to leave now!"

"No argument there," the mother answered, grabbing her kids. "Thank you for saving us, Helion."

"Oh, uh—" He stopped talking as she fled up the street. Shrugging, Carlos stooped to pick up the live wires. *Now what?* Electricity coursed through him, and he felt its raw, untamed power begging for him to control it.

He heard Quinn grunt and watched him push the busted transformer off him. Standing, Quinn shot Carlos a brief glance and pointed to the beige sedan. "We need to help them."

Several wires lay draped across the beige sedan, trapping the driver.

Go there now, Carlos willed.

With a bright flash, he vanished and reappeared across the intersection near Quinn.

"Did you just teleport?" Quinn asked, stunned.

Shaken himself, Carlos shook his head. "I don't think so, but I think I can travel with the current through the wires."

"That's awesome!" Quinn replied, powering down his glowing blue eyes and body.

"This makes no sense," Carlos said, frowning at the sedan. "Why didn't the power go out?"

Quinn pointed at the utility pole diagonally across the intersection. "I bet that last transformer is keeping this section of the grid powered up."

"Not for long," Carlos replied, pointing his hand at it.

"No, wait!"

But it was too late. A powerful arc of hot white electricity erupted from Carlos's hand and connected with the last transformer. Sparks sizzled across the canister, and then the intersection went dark and quiet.

"What did you do?" Quinn asked, exasperated. "It's freezing out. People need to heat their homes!"

Carlos shot him an incredulous look. "Uh, Quinn? What would the utility company do? Leave the power on as ordinary humans picked up electrical wires and replaced three busted transformers?"

Quinn looked around, then sighed. "You're right. They have to fix the transformers. You didn't have to blow that up, though."

"I didn't. I think I just turned it off.... I'm not really sure."

"What do you mean?"

Carlos let the power fade from his eyes and body. "I can feel the electrical current, where it goes, and what it wants to do, and I can tell it what to do as well. In return, I get a sense of what could happen. Somehow, I just knew which path would blow up the transformer, so I took the other path. I think it has an off switch."

"Huh. I can't do that."

Carlos grinned. "Cool."

Quinn smiled back. "Come on, let's go check out the reckless driver. Someone's responsible for this mess, and it's not us."

Red, white, and blue lights flashed in the darkness as emergency vehicles arrived at the intersection. Quinn and Carlos walked to the beige sedan and pulled the wires off. One of the fallen traffic lights had crushed the hood of the car, and the wounded driver couldn't open his door.

Quinn tapped on the passenger window and pointed down, but the driver shouted the window wasn't working.

"Can you unlock the door?" Quinn shouted back, tugging on the locked handle.

The driver nodded, and a moment later, the locks clicked.

Quinn pulled open the door and leaned into the car. "Buddy, you got some explaining to—Kyle?"

"Ugh," Kyle grunted, leaning back on the headrest.

Carlos leaned forward and stared at their stunned classmate in disbelief. Deployed airbags surrounded Kyle.

"Are you hurt?" Quinn angrily asked.

"Pretty sure I broke my left arm," Kyle groaned, wincing in pain.

"Good," Carlos replied angrily. "I hope it hurts, given this little stunt you pulled off—or failed at. Do you know how many people you could have killed, including yourself?"

An upset police officer and EMT approached the car. "What the hell are you two doing here?" the officer shouted, nervously hopping over the now-dead electrical wires. "You need to lea—"

"I'm Blue Spekter," Quinn interjected, making his eyes briefly glow blue.

"Oh," the officer said, stopping short and looking at Carlos. "What about him?"

"He's with me." Quinn pointed into the car. "Kyle here needs help."

"Friend of yours?" the officer asked, suddenly intrigued.

"No, but we're classmates."

"I see. I'm Officer Murphy."

Quinn stood. "Nice to meet you. Kyle thinks he broke his left arm."

"He's lucky this mess didn't kill him."

"Yup."

The paramedics and firefighters wriggled into place as Quinn, Carlos, and Officer Murphy stepped back. Murphy looked around at the intersection, shining his flashlight at the electrical carnage across the intersection. The big, heavy snowflakes scattered most of the bright light. "Jesus, what a mess. You mind explaining what happened here?"

Quinn took a deep breath and recounted the story to the officer. When he finished, Murphy stared at Carlos. "So, you're like him?"

Carlos nodded, briefly illuminating his eyes yellow. "Call me Arcbright."

Murphy shook his head and looked at Quinn sheepishly. "Chief Applegate won't like this."

"She already knows. Besides, it's not like we can do anything about it now except—"

"Except make sure you're on our side, Arcbright," Murphy interjected.

"I am."

"Good. Why don't you two get home? This storm will only get worse through the night. We know how to reach you if we have more questions."

"Thanks," Quinn replied, shaking hands with Murphy.

Carlos awkwardly did the same, and the two boys headed away from the accident. "So, how often does that happen?" Carlos asked as they trudged through the snow.

"Car accidents, or being present for them? Cuz car accidents happen all the time."

"True. Being around for them, I guess."

"It's rare. I usually show up after something happens and try to sort it out. I guess that mom and her kids were lucky we were around to save them."

Carlos shook his head. "What was she thinking, standing there like that when the wires and transformers were falling everywhere?"

Quinn chuckled. "That, my friend, is the unanswerable question. Why do people stand around and gawk in the face of danger?"

"Curiosity, I guess."

"Look, we'll keep training you, and I'll help you find Hector. But returning to Spec, well, I can't take you back to Spec to find Victor. Not yet, anyway. Like I said, we'd need Helion and Catamount. We both know returning to Spec is a trap."

Carlos sighed, then nodded. "I know, I know. I'll wait."

"Thanks. I'm sure it's difficult. Just remember, Victor wins if he divides us. If he can separate us, he can manipulate us."

"He could do that anyway," Carlos replied.

"True. But strength in numbers, and all that."

"I get it." Carlos smirked and pointed up the street. "They still have power. How about we get that hot chocolate?"

Quinn nodded. "Let's do it."

Chapter 21
Low Blow

T he nor'easter that ravaged New England that night had become thundersnow near the seacoast, and the sky flashed with positive-charged lightning. As Carlos trudged home through the slushy snow, he felt electrical energy surging through the night with each flash, and he wondered if Quinn felt this when he sensed the potency of orgone energy around him.

Entering the Atlantic Heights neighborhood, his soggy, iced-over sneakers and cold feet made him regret turning down Quinn's offer to fly him home. But he had wanted some time alone before Abuela assaulted him with worry and concern about why he was out in such a terrible storm.

He sighed, feeling sullen about the day's unexpected turn of events. His already convoluted life had become more complicated by the unintentional revelation of a new superhuman to those who had witnessed the daring intersection rescue.

When he turned onto his street, he winced in pain and cradled his head in both hands, slipping but not falling on the unplowed road. It would take him some time to get used to the proximity sense of another superhuman, but he immediately became concerned and wondered who was at his house. Supposedly Quinn had flown home, Blake had a date—a crazy idea in this weather—and Ana María had driven home.

So, who was in his neighborhood?

Panic gripped him as he continued forward until he sensed and saw Tempest standing in front of his house. He didn't want another visit from her, but he almost breathed a sigh of relief that Nightmare hadn't come for him. Curling his hand into fists, he hollered, "What the hell do you want?"

"Oh, hi, Carlos," she replied innocently with an annoying, cutesy wave.

"What do you want?" he repeated, becoming cross.

"I figured you'd come home after training with those false heroes, so I came to offer you one last chance to return with me to The Order. We made you, after all. It's only fitting you hold up your end of the deal."

Carlos shook his head. "No way in hell. Wait, how did you know I was coming home?"

Vanessa smirked. "Did you think there was only one implant?"

Carlos's mouth fell open and his eyes widened at the idea of something else inside his body.

Vanessa shook her head and tutted. "You're always going to be one of us, Carlos."

"No, you can't make me do anything I don't want to."

Vanessa shot a glance at his house. "Oh, I think your grandmother could be a persuasive force in your decision-making process, don't you agree?"

Carlos's body tensed, and he narrowed his eyes. "What does that mean?"

"The choice is yours if you want her to live a happy life. At least, whatever's left of it. Know what I mean?" She smiled and batted her eyelashes. Then her face hardened. "Do what The Order asks of you, Carlos." Then her face softened, and she smiled again and shrugged. "If not, unfortunately, accidents happen."

Carlos took a step forward. "If you hurt my abuela—"

"Carlos!" Vanessa said with feigned shock, grasping her chest. "I would do no such thing!"

Confused, Carlos narrowed his eyes. "Huh?"

She shrugged again and briefly opened her hands in front of her. "But someone else might. One never knows what Uncle Hector will do."

"You leave him out of this!" Carlos screamed, advancing on Vanessa.

She raised her hands in surrender. "I said nothing untrue. You're the one poking around in your uncle's affairs. We both know he could choose violence so you get the message."

"What message?" Carlos roared, his shoulders heaving with anger.

"That you leave him alone, or someone you love gets hurt, since he can't hurt you."

Carlos seethed with anger, drew a deep breath, and glared at Vanessa. He felt hot, raw power bubbling up inside him.

She offered another sickeningly sweet smile. "That's why you'll do what Nightmare wants, all right? Besides, if I wanted to… encourage your compliance and force you to return to Spec to work for The Order, I would tell you how I plan to torture and kill Janie and Jesse—"

"No!" Carlos shouted, his eyes igniting with bright yellow fury as electricity and fire erupted across his body. He drew back his right arm and lunged forward, but Vanessa ignited an aura of teal and blocked his punch with her mind, sidestepping as Carlos slipped and tumbled forward.

"Oooh, you have a temper! I love—"

Carlos turned and silenced her with a powerful arc of white-hot lightning that connected with her face. The unexpected blast sent her reeling until she tripped and fell into the snow.

"Ow," Vanessa uttered with an irritated laugh, clutching her scorched face. "Didn't expect that. Nice one."

Carlos closed the space between them and crouched over her, ready to strike again. "Leave them alone! Those people are nothing but kindness!"

"Get off me!" Vanessa grimaced and kneed him hard in the groin.

Carlos coughed a sharp, agonized gasp, and his breath stuck in his throat. He fell into the snow, clutching himself. His body trembled as excruciating pain radiated through his lower abdomen.

Vanessa climbed to her feet and dusted off the snow. "That's the last time you talk back to me, you ungrate—" She paused and looked up at the snowstorm, mouth agape. A split second later, something crashed into her. The force flattened her, and snow erupted like a volcano around them.

Carlos struggled to focus, but tears blurred his vision. Someone bathed in bright orange light shouted at them. "What the hell do you want?" The blurry and bright orange-yellow figure moved and stood above Vanessa, ready to fight. She gasped for air and raised her hands defensively—or was she surrendering?

"Better yet, don't answer." The figure reached down and grabbed her by the coat collar, then shot straight up into the air. Carlos did his best to follow the bright orange-yellow light, but the radiating pain and falling snow obscured his vision.

Carlos's super hearing heard the familiar voice say, "Tell Victor to leave us alone, or else." Then he saw the blurry, bright light spin and flash several times before tossing Vanessa away.

At least, that's what he thought he saw. He winced as another wave of pain roiled through him.

"Hey, buddy, you okay?" the orange-yellow-glowing figure suddenly said, softly landing next to Carlos. Carlos only grunted as the figure—whom he now recognized as Blake—squatted next to him. "Oh, she got you in the nuts, ouch."

"Yeah," Carlos grunted.

Strong arms wrapped around his body and hoisted him up. "Come on, I'll take you back to my place to recover."

"What... about your... date?" Carlos painfully huffed as Blake ascended into the sky and crossed the river.

"Netflix and chill, man. I can be late."

"Thanks," Carlos replied.

Thirty minutes later, Carlos had recovered enough to change out of his cold, wet clothes and put on some of Blake's dry clothing. Quinn had arrived at the behest of Blake, and the two heroes patiently waited for Carlos to explain what had happened.

"Sorry I'm screwing up your date nights," Carlos mumbled.

Quinn and Blake exchanged smiles. "We're both dating special people," Quinn said. "They get it."

"She was waiting for me," Carlos finally said. "She threatened to hurt Abuela, and when I still wouldn't listen, she threatened to kill Jesse and Janie. We started fighting, and then she nailed me in the nuts."

"Ouch, a ball buster," Quinn said, instinctively moving his hands to cover his groin. "Now you understand firsthand what I meant by 'we can hurt each other.'"

"Yeah, no shit," Carlos said. Then he looked at Blake. "How did you know?"

"I was on the balcony of my condo, ready to fly to Ravone's house. I saw the unusually bright flashes of light in your neighborhood and knew something was up. And when I flew over, I sensed you two before you sensed me." He jerked a thumb at Quinn. "Then I borrowed from his playbook and came at her before she could figure it out."

Quinn gasped and sat back, visibly disturbed.

"What's wrong?" Carlos asked.

"He's going after loved ones again. It's something Mr. St. Germain said could happen when all this superhero stuff started, and it's something Nightmare actually did to me. Now he's doing it again. He's predictable, but not in a way I like."

"Smells like desperation," Blake muttered. "I'd like to think it means he's afraid of us."

"Wouldn't that be nice?" Quinn replied with a small smile.

"So, are we going to help them?" Carlos asked.

Quinn shook his head. "We can't go to Spec without checking in. For all we know, this is a trap. Can you call them? You must have their number, right?"

"Yeah," Carlos answered with a nod. He fished his phone from his pocket and called the elderly couple's landline. He put the call on speakerphone so Quinn and Blake could listen in.

On the third ring, Janie answered. "Hello?"

"Hi, Janie, it's Carlos."

"Carlos! How wonderful to hear your voice. How are you doing? Are you happy to be home? Oh, it's late. Are you all right, dear?"

"Yeah, it's great to be home, and I'm doing fine. Learning about, well, you know, stuff."

"That's wonderful, dear."

"Listen, I'm just checking in. Has Vanessa been harassing you?"

"No, dear. We haven't seen her since the day you left. Why, is something wrong?"

"I don't think so, but if she shows up, promise you'll call me? My friends can help."

"I see. Well, if she shows up, I'll give you a ring."

"We're going to come visit, if that's okay. There are a few things we need to check out. I don't know when, but it should be soon."

"Well, if you boys need a place to stay, you know there are plenty of empty bedrooms upstairs."

"Thanks, Janie. Say hi to Jesse for me."

"I will. He's passed out in his recliner. He'll be sorry to have missed your call, but he'll be glad to know you're coming around these parts soon."

"Great. Have a good night, Janie."

"You too, Carlos. Good night."

"Bye." Carlos disconnected the call and shrugged. "I don't think they're in danger right now. She sounded perfectly normal to me. Maybe Vanessa was bluffing?"

"Or threatening," Blake mused.

"Or it's a deception," Quinn added, nervous worry crossing his face once more.

"What do you mean?" Carlos asked.

"What if Vanessa *wants* us to go back to Spec? That leaves your grandmother undefended. And if we stay here, that leaves Jesse and Janie defenseless."

"So, we split up," Blake said. "Ana María can stay nearby to protect Carlos's abuela. The three of us can check Spec."

Quinn nodded. "Only after we check in with Potter tomorrow."

"Tomorrow?" Carlos echoed, concerned.

"You said yourself Janie sounds safe. So, they're good. I'm also fairly certain Vanessa won't start something with the three of us here in Portsmouth."

"How can you be so sure?" Carlos asked.

Quinn tapped the side of his head. "Nightmare is waging a psychological war against you. He believes he can convince you to join him, so he'll weaponize the people you love to get what he wants."

"How do you know this?"

"He kidnapped my dads and Keegan because he thought the idea of losing them would make me crumble before him. Instead, I listened to my best friend and Ana María. We worked with Director Potter and planned a daring rescue."

Carlos shot Blake a strange look. "But I thought you were the bad guy back then?"

"Uh, well… this was after I resurrected."

"You what?" Carlos exclaimed, sitting upright.

"Long story."

Quinn chuckled and continued. "My point is, Victor wanted me to rush in and rescue them. I'm glad I didn't, because he had a small army of superhumans waiting for us when we attacked. If I had gone alone, they would've overwhelmed me and put one of those chips in my head, and now I'd be working for the bad guy."

"Wow."

"So, first thing tomorrow morning, we meet with Director Potter and tell him what we know. I may lead the Guardians, but I don't have the experience he does. I—we—need his help to plan because when you face facts, we're teenagers fighting a maniacal super villain. We need all the help we can get. That's what the STF is for."

"What am I supposed to do in the meantime?" Carlos asked, perturbed.

"Go home. Protect your grandmother. Go to bed."

Carlos sighed. "I'm tired of being told to sit on the sidelines and wait."

"Carlos, you—"

"Blake, you saw I zapped her good, right?" Carlos interjected.

Blake shook his head. "No. I saw you writhing on the ground, holding your junk after she nailed you in the nuts."

Annoyed, Carlos stood and crossed the room. "It was a stupid mistake. I'll be ready next time." He leaned against the balcony window and folded his arms over his chest.

"That's the whole point, Carlos," Quinn said. "Stupid mistakes can cost us our lives because when we're injured, we're vulnerable until our healing factor kicks in. Can't say anyone has kicked me in the nuts recently, but the pain must have prevented you from healing."

Carlos turned. "I thought we were invulnerable."

"We are to humans. But remember, we are not invulnerable to each other. Imagine if Vanessa had managed to re-chip you while you were down?"

"Oh! That reminds me," Carlos said, returning to his seat. "She said she could track me. Could there be another chip in me somewhere?"

Quinn and Blake stared at each other, mouths agape. "Never thought about that," Quinn admitted. "Tomorrow, we get you scanned and talk with Director Potter. We need a plan."

Chapter 22
Double Tagged

Director Potter narrowed his eyes. "What exactly do you hope to accomplish by returning to Spec?"

Carlos sighed.

Their conversation hadn't gone well. At Potter's instruction, Carlos, Quinn, and Blake had reconvened at Portsmouth Hospital so Victor wouldn't learn the location of STF headquarters. As soon as Carlos entered the room, Dr. Madison had curtly instructed him to strip down to his underwear so they could scan him for a tracking device.

Two medics in lab coats conducted a series of tests and full-body scans to determine the veracity of Vanessa's insinuation, slowly checking and rechecking every square inch of his nearly nude body. He shivered in the cool hospital air, absentmindedly watching the handheld metal detector slowly move over his right arm.

He shifted his gaze back to the director. "Why don't you know what he's doing? Are you afraid of him?"

Potter's right eyebrow twitched. "Yes, I'm terrified of him. We don't know what he's doing or how many superhumans he has created and trained. I only have three—maybe four—superhumans to defend the country. Hell, the planet. So, I hope you can understand why throwing you directly into the mouth of danger seems foolhardy to us."

"Sounds like you need a mole," Carlos muttered.

"That option is on the table."

"You know I'm the perfect candidate for that, right?"

Potter shook his head. "That option is *not* on the table."

"Why not?" Carlos asked, frowning.

"What happens if Victor insists upon inserting a functional control chip?"

"Oh, right," Carlos said.

One medic's scanner rapidly beeped, and everyone's eyes shifted to the flashing red light on the device.

"No way," Carlos muttered, twisting around to look at his backside.

Blake chuckled and stepped forward, then squatted several feet behind Carlos.

"What are you doing?" Carlos nervously asked, looking over his shoulder at Blake.

"Oh yeah," Blake said, surprised. "There it is."

"What, a tracker?"

Blake looked at Quinn, then tilted his head toward Carlos.

Quinn stepped forward with a big smile. "Hey, buddy, how are you doing?"

Carlos turned to face Quinn. "I'm f—"

Quinn touched Carlos's shoulder, sending a short blast of electricity through his body. Surprised, Carlos momentarily tensed and weakened. Then Blake telekinetically ripped the tracker from Carlos's buttocks.

Carlos howled in pain and grabbed his behind, leaping and hopping across the room. He swore multiple times in anger and glared at Blake, who held a GPS tracking device in the palm of his hand.

"Don't smash it, please," Dr. Madison said, her hands clasped as she begged. "I'd like to study it."

"Sure thing." Blake extended his hand and the bloody device to Dr. Madison, who sighed and pulled on a set of exam gloves before taking the device from Blake.

"You could've warned me," Carlos exclaimed.

Quinn shrugged. "You're already healing."

"We'll also replace your phone in case Victor tampered with your current phone," Potter said.

Carlos smirked and rubbed his sore behind. "Can I get the latest model?"

"I'll see what I can do."

"Thanks."

Potter pointed to the medics. "Keep scanning him for redundant tracking devices."

"Yes, sir," a medic replied.

Blake smirked. "You know, I could probe him with my telekinesis. I can differentiate metal from skin, muscle, and bone."

"You will not probe me," Carlos replied emphatically.

"It's just a word. I can scan you, if you like that word better."

"Fine."

"Proceed," Potter said.

"Okay," Blake replied. He stepped forward, closed his eyes, and extended his left hand toward Carlos.

The medics stepped back and waited.

"I feel nothing," Carlos said.

Blake shushed him.

"Sorry."

Several long minutes passed before Blake finally shook his head. "There's nothing else."

"That's good to know. Continue scanning," Potter directed the medics. "I'll feel better having this cross-checked. It's nothing personal, Blake."

Blake nodded.

Carlos rolled his eyes. "And in the meantime, I'm freezing my ass off in this cold room."

"You'll heal and survive," Potter said with a mischievous smirk. "Now, it's time we discuss a reconnaissance mission in Spec."

"Finally," Carlos muttered.

"Your patience is commendable, Carlos. I had hoped Victor would forget about you, but I don't believe he will. I think you're right: he wants his investment back."

"He won't get me back."

Potter laughed, shook his head, and gestured wildly with his hands. "Forgive me, but a total stranger revealed as the world's number-one enemy convinced you to get into a car with him and drive to Virginia in less than fifteen minutes."

Embarrassed, Carlos lowered his eyes.

"I hope you understand why an unsupervised visit is a horrible idea."

Carlos leveled his gaze at the director. "It was a stupid decision made on a bad day."

Potter tapped an imaginary surface with his right index finger, punctuating each word. "Cannot. Happen. Again."

"It won't."

Potter drew a quick breath, then relaxed. "When you're finished up here, go home and rest up. Tomorrow, Quinn and Blake will bring you to operations at STF headquarters."

"We will?" Quinn blurted out, surprised.

"Yes. Now that Victor can't track him, I'm not worried about a security breach."

"Wait, so you trust me?" Carlos asked, frowning.

"I have little choice, right?" Potter fired back.

Confused, Carlos only stared back.

Potter straightened to his full height and squared off with Carlos. "I am not stupid, son. You three super-teens are gods among mere mortals. Right now, you only listen to me out of respect for authority, not because I can overpower you. So, I must extend the olive branch and a willingness to work with you. It is I who must earn your trust and respect, but you must earn mine as well." Potter softened his stance. "I truly hope and expect that you will listen to your super-peers and make the right choices that define what kind of man—what kind of hero—you will be."

"Okay," Carlos replied with a small nod.

"It's only a matter of time until someone betrays the STF or discovers the location of our secret headquarters. Don't be the guy who helps Victor. See you soon."

Carlos watched Potter leave, then looked at Quinn, who winked at him.

With a laugh and a shrug, Blake said, "Wonderful talk, as always. Wanna get lunch when this is done?"

One medic laughed, and Dr. Madison rolled her eyes.

"Burger Bar?" Carlos asked.

"Yes, please," Quinn said.

Chapter 23
Ambushed

"Carlosito, I think your friends are outside," Abuela said. She watched the street casually, peering at the outside world from behind the yellowed window sheers hanging in the tiny living room. She liked to know who did what in the neighborhood.

"What?" Carlos replied incredulously from the couch, lowering the Xbox controller and pulling the headset's left ear cup away from his ear. "But I'm playing online with them right now."

"What's going on?" Quinn asked in the headset.

"He's getting his butt kicked," Blake teased, shooting at Carlos's avatar in the game.

"Dammit," Carlos uttered when his character died.

"Your friends are—ay, Dios mío!" Abuela replied, suddenly clutching her chest.

Carlos's super hearing heard the slamming of multiple car doors, angry voices, and many guns cocking. He threw the controller and tore off the headset, then bolted from the couch and put himself between Abuela and the window.

"He's inside," Dario shouted, then aimed an assault rifle at the front window. "Uncle Hector sends his love, ese!" The twenty gang members with him opened fire.

Abuela screamed as Carlos grabbed and spun her away from the window.

"Move!" he shouted. Glass and wood exploded as bullets zipped through the air, obliterating the window. Carlos felt bullets tear through the muscles of his arms and sink deep into the flesh of his thighs and buttocks. He doubled over in pain and took his grandmother down with him—hoping she hadn't been hit—and they crashed through the coffee table.

Terrified and shaken, Abuela cursed in Spanish and covered her head, switching to hastily repeated prayers to Our Lady of Guadalupe.

Carlos shuddered in agony as pain radiated through his body. His left arm throbbed, and when he tried to move it, he screamed, realizing it was broken. He felt the power surging behind his eyes as he looked around, desperately gripping his thigh with his right hand where one or more bullets had struck him. His gaze landed on his phone, and he tore his right hand away from his thigh to grab it from the carpet. He desperately tried to unlock the phone, but his shaking thumb only streaked blood and sweat across the unresponsive screen.

Another volley of gunfire tore through the house, forcing them both to shield their faces from spraying debris. When the gunfire subsided, Carlos pulled the phone close to his face. He frowned at the copper bullet mashed into the display, which explained why he couldn't unlock it.

"Carlos? You okay, man? What's going on? Is that the game?"

The headset! Carlos's right hand and arm blindly—and painfully—searched the couch cushions for the headset.

Abuela's prayers had become whimpers of terror, but Carlos didn't have time to check on her. He needed Quinn to save them.

"You and that whore better be dead, ese," Dario shouted. Several of the men with him laughed, then opened fire again.

Another spray of bullets tore through the house, and they instinctively protected their heads again. When the gunfire stopped, Carlos earnestly searched the couch again until he found the headset. He quickly pulled it toward him and fumbled to set it over his head with one hand.

"Carlos?" Quinn asked.

"Quinn!" Carlos shouted, wincing in pain as his wounds itched and the bullets in his body burned. "Get over here! They're shooting at me!"

"What? Who is?" Quinn asked, sounding confused.

"It's Las Navajas, and they shot me in real life. Get over here!" More gunfire shredded the walls.

"Oh, shit! You mean that's not the game? Where are you?"

"My house."

"Hang on."

Quinn looked at Blake, who stared back in shock. "It has to be his uncle."

"Who?" Blake asked.

"No time to explain. Come on!"

The two heroes ran to the balcony of Blake's condo and leaped from it, igniting their powers and dashing across the river to Carlos's neighborhood. The sound of gunfire reached their ears, and they turned toward the commotion. In seconds, a fully illuminated blue Quinn spun and landed between the gang members and what remained of the living room window.

They stopped shooting in surprise.

Blake landed next to him, blazing orange.

"Oh goody, we'll take out you freaks too," one of the angry men shouted just before they swung their rifles around and opened fire on the heroes.

The bullets harmlessly bounced off their bodies but tore holes in their clothing.

When the gang stopped shooting, Quinn and Blake sighed and pointed to their destroyed clothing. "They're never going to learn, will they?" Blake asked.

"Nope," Quinn replied with a grin.

"Hey, assholes!" Carlos shouted from the front door.

Carlos's itchy and trembling left arm relaxed as an uncomfortable popping sound and sensation left him wiggling his fingers in surprise. *Did my broken arm just heal itself?*

He pushed himself to a seated position, and a moment later, he felt a strange squishing sensation as his body pushed five bullets from his thighs and buttocks. They silently bounced on the carpet, each stained red with his blood.

No freaking way!

"Mijo, your eyes," Abuela whispered with wonder.

"I have superpowers, Abuela," Carlos admitted.

"You're not hurt?" she asked with wonder, pointing to the blood smeared in several places.

"No, I'll be okay."

"Mijo, God has blessed you!"

"Well, err, I'm not sure he had anything to do with it, but—"

"You need to be a good boy, mijo."

"Yup," he replied. "I'll be right back. Stay here."

"Okay," she replied, still shaken.

"Wait, are you hurt?"

They both looked over her body but saw no bleeding wounds. She wiggled her arms, legs, fingers, and toes. "I think I'm okay, mijo."

Carlos smiled. "Okay, good. Be right back. Stay down." He leaped across the living room, opened the bullet-riddled front door, and stepped outside. "Hey, assholes!"

Everyone turned and stared at him, for his eyes glowed bright yellow.

"What the hell?" Dario said, taking a step back.

Carlos felt the power surging through the overhead electrical wires and immediately tapped into it.

"Carlos, carefully consider your next move," Quinn cautioned in a low voice Carlos's super hearing would detect.

With a bright flash, Carlos pulled raw power from the grid and, more of out of theatricality and wonderment than menace, let several arcs fly between his hands and the wires.

Several gang members gasped or swore in horror, but Carlos let a bolt surge through the gang—all except Dario. The other gang members' bodies twisted and convulsed for a moment, then collapsed. Their assault rifles clattered on the pavement, and the sudden sound of approaching police sirens echoed through the neighborhood.

"Carlos!" Quinn shouted, his face aghast.

"Relax, I tased them."

Relief washed over Quinn's face as his blue glow dissipated.

"That was kinda awesome," Blake said, crossing his arms over his chest as his orange glow faded.

Carlos took a step toward Dario, whose lips quivered with fear. "Not so tough, are you, big man?" Carlos said.

"Don't hurt me," Dario pleaded.

Carlos scoffed and grabbed the bigger man by the collar. "You expect mercy when you tried to kill me and Abuela?"

Tears ran down Dario's face. "I'm sorry, I was only following orders."

"Whose orders?"

"Hector's."

"So, he's paying attention. Good. Why are you here, Dario? Why does Hector want me dead?"

"To send a message to everyone that Hector and Las Navajas are untouchable, even by the police."

"What do the police have to do with this?"

Dario scoffed. "You should know. You're the one who keeps squawking to them."

Confused, Carlos let Dario go. "No, I don't. I haven't been to them once about you guys."

"You were with them the week you disappeared, taking down a drug ring."

"That again?" Carlos said.

Quinn and Blake shot each other a concerned glance.

"We just can't figure out which ring you helped them with," Dario said with a shrug.

Carlos glared at him. "I told you there are only a handful of people who know that cover story. Who told you?"

"Cover story?" Dario echoed, surprised. Then he offered an exaggerated, mischievous shrug. "Well, I told you that if you ain't the snitch, maybe there's a snitch on you." Dario smirked. "Besides, it's way more fun to let you figure it out on your own."

Carlos rolled his eyes. "Fine. So, where is he?"

"Who?"

"You know who. Hector."

"I don't know."

Carlos grabbed Dario by the throat and hoisted him to his feet. "Tell me where Hector is!"

Dario gasped and sputtered. "I don't know, I swear. He only communicates with me by telephone."

Carlos scoffed. "You expect me to believe that?"

"I swear it's true." Dario shook with fear, and tears ran down his face.

"Whatever. Night night." Carlos raised his other hand and threw a bolt at Dario, knocking him to the ground and into unconsciousness. The three boys watched Dario's body twitch involuntarily.

"Tell me again who knows that cover story?" Quinn said with a frown.

"Uh, well, Lieutenant Doral, you, my abuela, Agent Potter now, and maybe Blake."

Blake shook his head. "I know about a cover story, but I don't know the details."

"Oh, and Everleigh," Carlos said.

Quinn pursed his lips, remaining silent as several police cruisers pulled up.

"What?" Carlos said, realizing Quinn had figured something out.

Quinn shoved his hands into his pockets. "Do you think Everleigh—"

"No!" Carlos interjected, tightening a shaking fist. "Don't even say that."

Quinn quickly raised his hands in a gesture of surrender. "Hear me out."

Carlos took a deep breath and scowled. "Fine."

"You guys do this?" one of the police officers asked, rushing with several others to handcuff the unconscious gang members.

"Yeah," Blake replied.

"It's, like, the whole Las Navajas gang! It's Christmas day! Thanks, guys! We need to talk about that, though." He pointed to the front of Carlos's house.

Abuela peeked from the front door, cautiously watching everything and everyone.

"Sure," Quinn said with a half-hearted nod. He turned back to Carlos. "What if they're using Everleigh to watch you?"

Carlos's shoulders slumped, but he pushed the rising doubt back down. "Why?"

"Trust me, the STF and Lieutenant Doral didn't run to Dario and the gang. I sure as hell didn't, and I'm willing to bet your abuela didn't either. Who does that leave?"

Carlos slowly nodded.

"Blake didn't know, and you also told Everleigh. You also caught Everleigh at the family store, and that shook you up. What if she was checking in?"

Carlos shook his head. "No. That's impossible."

"Whatever remains, however improbable, must be true," Blake said, shoving his hands into his pockets and poking his index finger through a bullet hole.

"She... we... you know."

Quinn nodded. "I hope I'm wrong, but hearing Dario's comments, it sounds like the snitch is someone close to you. Someone you'd least expect to betray you."

Carlos shook his head and stepped back. He angrily waved his hands in front of them. "Then it's any one of you, the STF, or the police. Hell, it could be the team who made up the cover story, for all I know."

Quinn shook his head. "It's not us, and you know it. We have nothing to gain by outing you to Hector. Hell, we didn't even know you were involved with Las Navajas until recently."

Blake cleared his throat. "There's one way to test this theory, guys."

Tears ran down Carlos's face. "What's that?"

"We ask her together."

Chapter 24
Paper and Glass

"You sure about this?" Quinn asked as they climbed out of his blue Subaru WRX STI Limited.

Carlos nodded. "Blake's right. It's the only way to find out."

"What if she lies?"

"I'll know."

Blake chuckled. "Right, cuz you can tell she's been lying to you for how long now?"

Carlos didn't answer.

The three boys walked up to the house in silence, noting how manicured the snow-covered grounds looked. Steam rose from the surrounding snow, but they didn't notice. The boys ascended the front steps, and Carlos knocked on the front door of Everleigh Sanders's home. The trio impatiently waited in the cold until Mr. Sanders opened the door. Upon seeing Carlos and the superheroes, he welcomed them into the spacious, white marble-floored foyer and made small talk until Everleigh effortlessly glided down the grand staircase.

"Well, I'll leave you to it, then," Mr. Sanders said, smiling at Everleigh before disappearing into the grand house.

She giggled, then ran to Carlos. When he didn't react as she tried to hug him, she pulled back in confusion. "What's wrong, babe?"

Tears ran down his face. "I know, Evy."

She cocked her head to one side and asked playfully, "Know what?"

"That you've been snitching on me to Hector's men."

Everleigh's mouth fell agape for a moment before the tears flowed, but Carlos didn't fall for it.

"They paying you?"

She nodded. "I'm so sorry."

Carlos choked down his emotions. "When did it start?" The waver in his voice betrayed hurt and embarrassment.

Everleigh wrapped her arms around her body and cleared her throat. "Um, from the beginning."

Carlos's eyes bulged with horror. "So, *everything* has been a sham? We're a sham?"

She shook her head. "Not everything. I actually have feelings for you."

Blake scoffed, then turned and ran his finger inside the frame of a family photo on the wall.

Quinn drew a deep breath and sighed.

Carlos didn't care to hide his emotions and wiped his eyes. "We're done. However much Hector paid you, I hope it was worth it."

Everleigh wiped her eyes. "I'm sorry."

"Not as sorry as I am." Carlos shrugged. "Whatever. Come on, I'm done here."

The three boys left the house, and when they approached the WRX, Carlos stopped and tucked his hands into his pockets.

"What's up?" Quinn asked, turning toward him.

"I think it's time I look for my uncle."

"You mean hunt him down?" Blake asked solemnly.

"Yeah. He paid a teenage girl to fake date and sleep with me. I'm willing to bet that's far from the worst thing he's ever done."

"Let us help you," Quinn implored.

Carlos shook his head. "No, I got this."

"But we can bring him to justice together and—"

"Sorry, I don't have time for your nice-nice sense of justice," Carlos said, scowling. "There are people I gotta go through to find him. You'll only slow me down. I'll take him out myself, so you don't have to get involved. It's easier that way."

"Are you talking about killing him?" Quinn asked.

Carlos looked away. "Go away, Quinn."

"Excuse me?"

"Go away," Carlos said flatly. He narrowed his eyes, discreetly extended his fingers, and zapped them both.

Blake yipped as the raw power coursed through him and made his hair stand on end. Quinn grimaced but absorbed the power, glaring at Carlos. Blake nervously shifted his stance. "Quinn, what are you—"

Suddenly, Quinn leaped forward, grabbed Carlos, and launched into the air.

"Oh, shit." Blake pocketed his hands and watched as they rapidly ascended into the air.

Thousands of feet up, Quinn halted his ascent, his outstretched right hand holding Carlos by his neck.

"What the hell are you doing?" Carlos wheezed, struggling for air. His hands frantically swatted at Quinn's arms.

"Look around," Quinn barked, slowly rotating so Carlos could drink in the spectacular and terrifying view. "This world is cardboard to me. To us."

Carlos desperately flailed his arms and legs, still struggling for air. "Dude, what—"

"I talk, you listen," Quinn said, shaking him. Carlos whimpered, then nodded, his hands grasping at Quinn's arm. "We're at thirty thousand feet, give or take. The air is rather thin up here, so shut up and don't fight me."

"Yeah, okay," Carlos huffed.

Quinn's eyes illuminated with bright blue power. "I've been so careful with my powers, always taking care not to hurt anyone or break anything, acting like the fragile world I live in is made of paper and glass."

Carlos gasped at the hand tightening around his throat. He furiously swatted at Quinn's arm to no avail. Desperate, he blasted Quinn with electrical energy, but Quinn merely absorbed it into himself. The yellow power briefly mixed with Quinn's brightly glowing blue eyes.

Unfazed, Quinn continued. "I was too afraid to lose control because I didn't want to hurt anyone. I was terrified someone would die because of something I did, and I wanted to bury my powers in the sand. Nightmare changed that for me."

Carlos, suddenly afraid, stared wide-eyed into Quinn's blue-glowing eyes. His hands clung to Quinn's arm, and his legs fell slack. Quinn's grip on his neck was tight, but it wasn't lethal.

Quinn frowned. "But you think you can take the world on, don't you, tough guy?"

"I... I don't know."

"I need you to hear me right now. What you did down there, using your powers against us in anger? That's a definite no-no. Never do that again."

"It was just a joke, man. Lighten up?"

"A joke? So, you like a good joke, eh? How about I use my powers against you?"

Carlos paled with fear. "Oh God, no, please don't—"

Quinn let him go.

Gravity pulled on Carlos, who flailed as he fell and shrieked. He panicked, hyperventilating, struggling for a decent breath of air. The one power he hadn't learned was flight, and he didn't know how long he had until he splattered on the ground, which came fast.

"Fly, dammit!" Carlos shouted, desperate to slow his descent. Seconds ticked by, but he could not move through the air in any direction but down. The wind rustled past him, stinging his eyes and blurring his vision with tears that were quickly wicked away. Buildings and roads on the ground became recognizable, and he saw Blake staring up at him with his enhanced vision, shaking his head, arms crossed over his chest.

Carlos cursed as the ground rushed toward him. He closed his eyes, winced, and covered his face with his arms, hoping he wouldn't die. Suddenly, he no longer heard or felt the wind. Cracking an eye open, he saw the pavement several inches beneath him.

"What?"

An unusual but familiar sensation washed over him as his body righted itself and Quinn landed in front of him. Carlos breathed heavily with relief and warily regarded Quinn.

Quinn shoved his hands in his pockets.

Carlos noticed Blake turning his hand and realized Blake had used telekinesis to arrest his descent and set him down. When Carlos's feet touched the ground, Blake lowered his hand, and the strange sensation faded from Carlos's body.

Quinn cleared his throat. "I hope you learned something about who you are in the world today. I will not stop you from hunting your uncle. But if, starting today, you don't make the right choices, you'll give me the rare chance to show you just how powerful I really am. Are we clear?"

Blake pursed his lips and awkwardly stared at the ground.

Carlos rubbed his neck and nodded. "Crystal."

"Good. I'm sorry I had to do that," Quinn said.

"You're *sorry?*" Carlos replied sarcastically.

"Words weren't working. You seem to think having powers lets you become the bigger bully. That couldn't be farther from the truth."

"He ever do that to you?" Carlos asked Blake.

Blake smirked. "Nope. But I only tried to kill him, uh, twice. You're just being a dick. Those rescued from Victor must understand the immense responsibility we have, whether or not we want it."

Quinn chuckled. "You sound like Ron."

Blake smiled. "Yeah, I was thinking the same thing."

"But you can do anything, guys, *anything*," Carlos said. "Why listen to the rules?"

"Does Hector?" Quinn asked.

Carlos drew a breath, then exhaled, shaking his head. "No. And that makes him a terrible man."

Blake offered a faint smile. "Doing whatever the hell you want leads to a very lonely and angry place. As Dark Flame, I did whatever the hell I felt like. I hurt and murdered people, Carlos. Did that make me happy or help me become a better person?"

Carlos swallowed and stared at the ground. "Probably not. Especially the murder part."

"Definitely not," Blake said, correcting him.

Carlos drew a deep breath. "Fine. I get it. I'll play by your rules."

"Our rules, Carlos," Quinn corrected. "We live by these rules for the same reason you wouldn't slap your grandmother across the face—because it's the right choice."

"And she'd murder me, superpowers or not," Carlos replied with a smile. The three boys nodded and regarded one another in silence for a moment. Carlos clapped his hands together. "Well, okay. This is my moment: I'm choosing to be a superhero. I just hope my actions back my words when push comes to shove."

Quinn smiled. "I know you have it in you."

"Me too," Blake said, clapping Carlos on the shoulder.

"But, uh, I think I'm gonna need your help," Carlos said.

"Yeah?" Blake asked.

"I'll leave Victor alone until we can face him together, but I want you to help me find Hector and bring him to justice. Actual law-and-order justice, not excruciating death by my hand. He has to pay for what he did to our house, not to mention everything else he does."

"Good," Quinn said. "You got your uncle's phone number?"

"Uh, yeah, why?" Carlos asked, shooting Quinn a confused look. Blake also raised an interested eyebrow.

Quinn smirked. "I think I know how to find him."

Chapter 25
Strike!

"I can't believe you guys hid this base in town all these years," Carlos exclaimed as he walked through the underground operations center of Hangar 227 to a set of glass-walled conference rooms.

Quinn laughed. "I think I said the same thing when I first arrived."

"Ow," Carlos said, grabbing the side of his head. Then he looked at Quinn with alarm. "There's another superhuman down here!"

"Relax, it's Ana María," Blake said.

"Oh, duh," Carlos said.

"You'll figure out how to tell us apart. We each have a slightly different sensation."

"I have you and Quinn figured out, but she's still new to me."

"Right."

Ahead of them, Captain Prett stepped out of hacker central, a dedicated high-tech surveillance room for his team. He waved and shook hands with Quinn. When they entered the room, Quinn quickly introduced Carlos to the rest of the highly skilled hacker team—Trinity (Walter), Wonder Woman (Tara), and Goodbutt (Chris)—sitting at their multimonitor stations. Nearby, Ana María quietly worked at her own station. She glanced at Carlos and did a double take, carefully studying his features. Carlos nodded to her, and she returned the gesture.

Captain Prett tapped a button near the open door. The clear glass windows between them and the operations center became opaque. No one could see in or out. The door automatically closed and became opaque as well. "Not that what we're looking for is incredibly confidential, but they don't need to know that." He gestured at the crew working in the main operations area. "So, you're the new guy, eh?" Prett asked in his charming southern drawl.

"Yeah," Carlos answered. "Thanks for helping me out with this."

"Don't thank me yet," Prett replied with a wide smile. "Do you have a phone number for me?"

"Sure." Carlos handed Captain Prett a slip of paper, who passed it on to Wonder Woman, or Tara.

She took it and set it on her desk, eyeing the paper as her fingers worked the keyboard. "Shouldn't take long."

"I'm not sure how this is going to help," Carlos admitted, shoving his hands into his pockets.

Goodbutt grabbed a cell phone from his desk and waved it in the air. "They gave us GPS and made it fun, but they really gave us all tracking devices."

"Your uncle's phone location is coming up," Tara replied.

"That fast?" Carlos watched a circle appear on a map over Portsmouth, New Hampshire. "Huh. That's weird."

The map zoomed in as the circle shrank and became a blue dot on Court Street, in the Haymarket Square neighborhood. Tara pointed at the screen. "That's where he is. At least, where his phone is."

"I don't get it. Abuela thought he moved away after Blue Spekter rescued him from the bridge fall. He wanted to leave the public eye."

"Sometimes the best place to hide is right under everyone's nose," Prett said.

"Wait, can you track anyone?" Carlos asked, astonished.

"So long as they have a phone, yes," Tara said with a pleasant smile.

"He could be visiting—maybe he lives somewhere else?" Trinity offered. "We can monitor the phone and track his movements for a few days."

"He doesn't have a few days," Carlos replied. "We're going if that's where he is."

Just then, a terminal klaxon sounded. All the hackers turned toward the unmanned station, and Trinity rolled his chair over to it. "Orgone activity detected in Spec."

"How do you know that?" Quinn asked.

Trinity grinned. "We placed some new orgone surveillance equipment we're field-testing around the town. A couple of them just triggered, which means—"

"Where exactly?" Carlos asked, but before anyone could answer, his cell phone rang in his pocket. He fished for it and mumbled an apology. His eyes widened when he saw the caller ID.

Unfazed, Trinity continued. "These three are around—"

"Hello?" Carlos interjected loudly, answering the phone and raising his index finger to silence Trinity.

"Carlos, she's here!" Janie screamed into the phone.

Carlos quickly pulled it away from his ear and tapped the Speakerphone button. "Who's there?"

"That crazy redheaded woman," Janie said, her voice panicked. Everyone in the conference room stared at the phone in Carlos's hand. "The one who said she was your girlfriend. She's shooting fire out of her hands at the trees, and she already set the barn on fire! Jesse's trying to free Mabel, but"—Janie's voice became shrill with terror—"oh my goodness, she's hit Jesse! He was only trying to free the sheep!"

"Hector can wait. We need to help them," Ana María said, rising from her workstation as Janie cried and hyperventilated. Ana María dashed to Carlos and grabbed the phone out of his hand.

"Janie, listen to me. You need to hide in the basement. Can you do that for me?" Ana María asked. Then she pointed at Quinn and Blake. "Go get changed," she whispered.

The door opened, and Director Potter stepped inside. Captain Prett quietly filled him in.

Quinn and Blake headed to the locker room to change.

"I don't have a basement," Janie shrieked as Ana María handed Carlos his phone back. The frightened woman cried over the speaker.

"I'll be right back," Ana María said. "Tell her to hide in the bathtub and pull a blanket over her head."

"Where are you going?" Carlos whispered.

"To change. Then we're going to rescue your friends."

"This is a trap," Director Potter said sternly, rubbing the bridge of his nose.

"Obviously," Ana María spat back, then rushed out of the room.

"Janie, can you go to the bathroom and hide in the bathtub?" Carlos asked.

"I think so, but the phone won't reach in there."

"That's okay. We're on our way. We're coming to save you," Carlos replied earnestly.

"Thank you, Ethan," Janie said, absentmindedly using his temporary name.

"Go hide. We'll see you in a few minutes."

"Okay."

Carlos winced at the clicking sounds of several failed attempts to hang the phone up. Carlos ended the call and turned to the director. "Why is this a trap?"

"Victor knows how to get to you, Carlos. He's using Tempest to attack Janie and Jesse because he knows that will draw you out to protect them. I assume he thinks you can fly, and I hope he doesn't expect you to show up with three superheroes."

"We're four," Carlos corrected him. "I'm Arcbright."

Potter's left eyebrow went up for a moment before he recomposed himself. "That remains to be seen, Carlos," Potter replied, intentionally using his civilian name.

Carlos frowned.

"It would seem Victor desperately wants his investment back. Whatever he saw in you, he thinks you'll see reason—his reason—and return to him."

"But why?" Carlos whined.

"I don't know, and we don't have time to discuss it right now," Potter replied. He pointed to the door as Quinn and Blake returned as Blue Spekter and Helion.

"Catamount's almost ready," Blue Spekter said. "What's the plan?"

"I'm here," she replied, appearing behind the boys.

"You've fought Tempest before," Potter said, crossing his arms over his chest. "You tell me."

Blue Spekter pursed his lips and looked at Helion, but Catamount spoke up. "You two stop Tempest. Carlos and I will rescue Jesse and stay in the house with Janie."

"I don't need a babysitter," Carlos grumbled.

Potter's eyes bugged out, but Captain Prett spoke first, his southern drawl cutting through the tension. "Son, you must learn to work as a team. My team is successful because we know our strengths and weaknesses, and we dole out tasks according to our strengths."

Catamount chimed in. "While we all have superpowers, we've got more experience than you, and—"

"Unless we reverse the trap," Blue Spekter interjected, and everyone turned toward him. "If you think she's not expecting us, then we give her Carlos."

"How the hell do you know that?" Potter asked, startled.

Blue Spekter tapped his left ear. "Super hearing, remember? We heard the entire conversation from the locker room."

Potter smirked. "Go on."

"The three of us hide our presence and bring Carlos to the farm. Catamount checks on Jesse, but we don't reveal ourselves right away. We'll coordinate through our earcomms and triangulate around her. She won't expect it. Then, Carlos, you go back to the house and stay out of the fight. If Tempest shows up with reinforcements, well, you did too."

"I like it," Catamount said.

"Agreed," Potter said. "Now get out of here. Time is ticking."

Carlos looked down at his T-shirt and jeans. "I don't have a supersuit."

Blue Spekter chuckled. "Stay out of any fires, and don't burn off your clothes."

The icy wind rushed past Carlos's ears as the four superheroes flew to Spec at speeds Carlos never thought possible. The ground beneath them whizzed by in a blur, and the three other superheroes hid their powered nature from Tempest and had also turned invisible. Blue Spekter decelerated as they approached the small town of Spec.

"Oh, that's not good," Blue Spekter muttered as the sound of sirens from approaching fire trucks reached their ears.

Carlos's heart sank when he saw the dark columns of billowing smoke rising against the unusually gray and overcast winter sky.

"I see the field, and I see Tempest," Blue Spekter said, his invisible head just above Carlos.

"Where? Oh, there," Carlos replied, spotting the villain setting trees on fire near the burning red barn he had previously taken shelter in. "Why is she setting everything on fire?"

"Vanessa probably heard Janie calling you, and she's being annoying while waiting for you to show up." Blue Spekter drastically slowed and whispered, "I'm gonna set you down in the field. Make it look like you're landing on your own two feet, okay?"

"Sure."

"I'll take left point," Helion whispered in their earcomms.

"I'll take right, near that burning copse of trees," Catamount added.

Carlos's body suddenly tingled with potential energy, and he shuddered.

"There's a ton of orgone energy in the air. Can you feel it?" Blue Spekter asked. "Everyone, be careful."

Tempest turned when she sensed Carlos and grinned wickedly. "There you are."

Carlos grimaced. "What the hell do you think you're doing?" he shouted, bringing his legs down as Blue Spekter set him down about twenty feet away and let go.

Tempest, wearing a dark, skintight supersuit with teal lines, teetered her hands and shoulders. "Well, I didn't think you'd answer your phone, so here we are."

"If you hurt Jesse, I'll—"

"Please, the old man was foolish to come out here."

"Where is he?"

Tempest nodded at the house. "I let him crawl back to his mousy wife with his tail between his legs."

Feeling momentary relief, Carlos balled his hands into fists. "You didn't have to burn the barn down."

"Didn't I, though?" Tempest said, flashing a bright smile at Carlos. She wore no mask and didn't bother hiding her easily recognizable red hair.

"What about the sheep?"

"Crispy," Tempest replied with a wicked grin.

Enraged, Carlos felt raw power bubble up inside him. His eyes ignited with bright yellow fury as he raised his hands, poised to strike.

Tempest sneered, then waved her hand across the space between them. A powerful gust of wind surprised Carlos and hurled him sixty feet through the air. He landed on his back with a thud and moaned, the wind momentarily knocked out of him.

Tempest dashed toward him, her eyes glowing with teal energy. She stood over him, shook her head, and tutted. "You were always going to join us, Carlos. Stop fighting me. I can teach you how to control that wonderful temper of yours and put it to good use."

"Never," Carlos wheezed as his body quickly healed. He pushed himself to his feet and lunged at Tempest, zapping her with a powerful arc of white-hot lightning that harmlessly connected with something that dissipated the energy.

Tempest chuckled. "Cute, but I expected that."

"She has force fields, like me," Blue Spekter announced quietly through their earcomms.

Tempest rushed Carlos, clutched his throat, and squeezed.

Carlos choked and gasped, desperately clawing at her arms.

She ascended into the gathering storm around them, where the winds picked up and swirled violently. Lightning flashed, and cracks of angry thunder rumbled across the valley.

"You think I need fire to destroy this place?" Tempest asked scornfully, her face twisted with anger. "I am the oncoming storm that—"

"Oh brother," Helion said over their earcomms.

Tempest paused, tilted her head, and smirked. "So, you're not alone, huh? Brought your little friends because they thought little newbie Carlos was too weak to handle me? Pathetic."

Carlos gurgled a response, struggling to breathe.

"How about a taste of your own medicine?" The winds whipped and twisted around them fiercely, and then Tempest tossed him away. A moment later, a lightning strike sliced through the air—and Carlos.

Tempest looked around and shouted, "Come out, come out, wherever you are!"

"Wait, please," Carlos whispered, slowly ascending from the ground, controlling the powerful lightning bolt that arced and flashed, jumping from hand to hand as it snapped, gathering strength.

Tempest's jaw dropped when she saw him rising, unexpectedly wielding the electrical energy in her storm.

"What the hell is that?" Helion shouted, becoming visible and present in everyone's mind as his attention and focus shifted away from hiding.

"What? I don't see anything," Blue Spekter shouted.

"It's gonna hit him!" Helion leaped toward Carlos, but something streaked through the air and collided with Helion, resulting in a massive, blinding explosion.

"Blake!" Blue Spekter shouted in their earcomms, launching himself into the air to catch Helion.

A second white-hot streak collided with Carlos, who grunted and lost control of the electrical energy he wielded. He wasn't ready for the concussive blast of the explosion or the intense double pop when both eardrums ruptured. Screaming with pain and surprise, Carlos gulped in an unhealthy mix of smoke tinged with something that smelled like rocket fuel and electrified storm air as he tumbled head over heels away from the mysterious explosion. Then he slammed into the ground, forming a small crater. Dirt and snow rained down around him.

"Were those missiles?" Catamount asked, as Tempest ramped up the storm's intensity.

Their earcomms crackled, struggling for signal clarity in the whipping winds around them, and Director Potter relayed new information to them. "Guardians! We've detected multiple surface-to-air missiles launched in your vicinity."

"No shit," Blue Spekter interjected, turning his head as he heard a strange whistling sound to his right—just before a missile smashed into his chest and exploded.

"I think they're targeting us with lasers when we take flight," Catamount said. "All three boys are down. I sense whoever is doing this, but I can't find them."

"It's an ambush," Potter replied flatly. "Catamount, can you see where the missiles came from?"

"Negative. The storm is too strong, and it's erasing the exhaust trails. I'm not even sure how they're hitting their targets with this wind."

"Understood, Catamount. Can you take out Tempest and evade any missiles they throw at you?" Potter asked.

"I'll try. They may not have realized I came with the boys."

"Be careful."

Catamount checked her surroundings, then clenched her teeth and leaped toward Tempest, maintaining an awareness of where she thought the missiles were coming from. Several missiles streaked across the turbulent sky from a different direction but harmlessly exploded upon the force field she summoned.

"Oh, hey, girlfriend," Tempest shouted, sensing and noticing Catamount. "I brought a friend. Hope you don't mind."

Suddenly, a new, fast-moving presence exploded in Catamount's mind and collided with her, sending red and crimson fireworks into the surrounding storm. "Nightmare is here!" Catamount shouted, hoping Director Potter would hear, seconds before she smashed into the ground. Snow and dirt erupted into the air.

The black-clad masked figure stood over her. "Not Nightmare. My name is Wrath."

Chapter 26

Deimos

E verything hurt.

Even breathing hurt.

The smell of burnt flesh filled Carlos's nostrils, and he choked, coughed, and then spit blood into the air.

Do I have my fingers? Do I have my toes?

He groaned and pushed through the pain as he clenched his hands into fists and felt all his fingers.

Thank goodness.

He cried out as his body healed itself. Broken bones in his rib cage realigned themselves with popping sounds, and his broken left femur snapped into position. The tibia and fibula of his right leg did the same.

He winced and coughed up more blood. He wiped his mouth with the back of his forearm and noticed his bare arm.

Where the heck is my T-shirt?

Something in his mind screamed at him, but the excruciating pain blocked everything out.

"Hurts, doesn't it?" Tempest asked, squatting next to him, her voice barely audible over the constant ringing in his ears.

"Ugh." He tried to move, to get away, but his still-healing limbs were useless.

"You will heal and be one of us again."

"I said no," he angrily mumbled.

Tempest shrugged. "You have no choice this time. We made sure of that." She smiled at him and stood, capping something metal in her hands before pocketing it.

"What is that?" he asked, panicked.

"Oh, this?" she innocently asked, proffering what appeared to be an EpiPen.

"What did you do to me?" he cried out, struggling to get up. Pain spiked in the parts of his body that hadn't healed yet.

"I gave you a gift, Carlos. The gift of forgetting."

"No, not again!" Carlos screamed.

"When the control chip activates and overloads your brain's limbic system, you'll forget these false heroes and remember your place among us as Deimos."

"Quinn! She chipped me," Carlos shouted with tears running down his face. When no one responded, he shouted his message again.

"Received, Arcbright," Potter replied. "I'll let them know."

"Oh, your friends will be too late, assuming they survived the missiles."

"I survived," Carlos replied.

Tempest gave him a patronizing smile. "Yeah. We hit you with the baby missile."

Carlos frowned. A moment later, his vision swam, and his head felt funny. "No!" He shook his head and tightened his fists.

"Huh. Guess your chip is activating. Great!"

"You have no right," he shouted, losing himself to an unknown, overwhelming force.

"Fight it if you can, Arcbright," Potter said in his earcomm.

Mostly healed, Carlos grabbed the sides of his head, sensing another for the first time. "Get out of my head." Nausea overcame him, and he fell back. His vision swam, but in his mind, he clearly saw himself reflected in a mirror but empty, devoid of happiness, and full of rage.

Carlos gasped as the other took over.

Deimos blinked and sat up. Noticing the woman next to him, he nodded with recognition. "Tempest."

"Deimos."

"What happened?" Smoke and wind whipped around them, obscuring the view of the burning farm at the edge of the field.

She crouched next to him and spoke with urgent concern in her voice. "Enemies of The Order known as the Guardians attacked us and knocked us to the ground. You hit your head pretty hard."

"Why did they attack us?"

"They're looking for the reactor core, and Nightmare sent us to discourage them." She extended her hand, and he took it, then hoisted himself up.

"Who knocked me out?"

"Blue Spekter."

Deimos narrowed his eyes. "Right."

"Helion and Catamount are here too, but we've got a friend helping us today."

"All right."

A bright blue-glowing force pushed through smokey wind, and Deimos clenched his jaw. "Arcbright, are you okay?"

"Arcbright?" Tempest repeated, sneering at the superhero name.

"Get lost," Blue Spekter said, unleashing a powerful blast of blue energy from his eyes that hit Tempest squarely in the solar plexus and sent her reeling.

"Hey!" Deimos shouted, leaping to his feet, balling his hands into fists, and shifting into a fighting stance.

"Dude, what're you doing?" Blue Spekter asked, surprised.

"You won't find what you're looking for!" Deimos sneered, then leaped into the air, eyes and body electrifying with power as he hurled himself back down and crashed into Blue Spekter. Yellow and blue energy exploded between them as Blue Spekter fell back. Deimos moved to straddle his body, arms pulled back and ready to pummel the hero.

"Arcbright! What the heck?" Blue Spekter shouted, raising his hands defensively.

"There is no Arcbright, only Deimos."

"What the heck is a Deimos?" Blue Spekter asked, confused.

Blue Spekter's earcomm crackled with another voice. "Quinn, Tempest put a control chip into him. You should assume he's hostile now."

Having no memory of his earcomm, Deimos twisted his neck, confused, searching for the source of the voice. "Who is that?"

Blue Spekter gasped and stared at Deimos. "Carlos, do you know who I am?"

Deimos sneered at him. "You're Blue Spekter, my enemy. Enemies of The Order must die!"

"Cuz I haven't heard that before," Blue Spekter replied with an annoyed eye roll.

Deimos grimaced, then pulled back his right arm.

Helion shot across the space between them, knocking Deimos off Blue Spekter and into the sky. Orange and yellow sparks erupted when they collided.

Grunting, Deimos desperately smacked the new foe, but he couldn't break Helion's iron grip.

"Where did she stick you?" Helion shouted, eyes burning with orange fury as they flew through the forest, crashing into trees and flattening a path through the forest beyond the field until Helion abruptly shot up into the sky.

"Let me go!" Deimos shouted.

Helion smirked. "For someone who can't fly, that was a stupid thing to say." Then he let Deimos go and telekinetically pushed him down.

Deimos cartwheeled through the air, struggling to control his descent. But just as he snagged an electrical current in the air, he crashed into the ground on his left side, snapping his arm and shattering his hip. He cried out as momentum rolled him onto his back. His breath caught in his throat, his body paralyzed from the incredible pain surging through him.

A bright yellow-orange light, dripping with dazzles of power, descended upon him. Helion stood over him but said nothing. Unable to move, Deimos watched Blue Spekter land next to him. "You got the message?"

"Yeah, I'm trying to find the chip," Helion replied.

"This one's different. It's made him super hostile against us. Like it's telling him what to do."

Suddenly, both superheroes froze and looked at the stormy sky to Deimos's right.

"Where is Catamount?" Blue Spekter asked.

"And who is that?" Helion added, the glow of his powers fading away.

"That would be Wrath," Deimos answered, a wicked grin on his face despite the painful popping of his healing bones.

"Catamount, do you need backup?" Blue Spekter asked. Only the churning wind and thunder answered him. "Catamount, do you need backup?" he impatiently repeated.

The sound of something crashing nearby reached their ears, sending tremors through the ground. They watched the sky at the far side of the field briefly illuminate with red and pink hues.

"Ouch." Catamount squinted at the black-clad masked figure standing over her. Unlike the Guardians and Tempest, this villain completely obscured his face with a mask. The lenses over his eyes barely hid the bright red glow of his eyes.

"Wrath, huh?" she asked with a smirk, using her powers to push herself up to her feet until they were standing face to face, inches apart. "I guess Nightmare is too afraid to face us himself."

Wrath grunted, then let a fist fly at Catamount's face, but she didn't flinch or move. A loud crack echoed across the field as red sparks exploded between them. He stepped back, shocked. He shook out his hand, wincing behind the mask.

Catamount shot him a scornful look. "It's not polite to hit a lady, Wrath."

"How mediev—"

Catamount spun and let her heel silence the snarky comment. It smashed into Wrath's jaw and whirled him into sprays of twirling crimson motes. Using her momentum, Catamount landed another kick and let loose a volley of punches. Wrath grunted with each hit, stepping back as she advanced on him. Catamount finished with a powerful roundhouse kick to his gut that knocked him through the air until he crashed fifty feet away.

Snarling, Wrath jumped to his feet and touched the side of his head, retracting the dark lenses and revealing his brightly glowing eyes. Twins beams of raw energy lanced through the air, hitting Catamount's torso.

Catamount briefly leaned back as the powerful onslaught connected with her, then stood tall and smirked, absorbing the energy as if it were a gentle breeze. She saw Wrath's head pull back slightly in surprise.

Then he drew a deep breath and increased the power of his attack, adding hot, fiery beams of red energy from his hands. The dirt and snow on either side of the converging beams blew away in response to the raw power. The converging energy Catamount didn't absorb dissipated into the air.

Confused, Wrath halted his assault, his eyes sparkling with red energy until the dark lenses slid back into place.

Catamount didn't wait. She dashed toward him, leaped into the air, pulled back her right hand, and pummeled him into the ground. Dirt and snow exploded with red-and-pink geysers of energy, leaving a six-foot-wide-by-two-feet-deep crater around Wrath's body.

He grunted, but Catamount didn't give him the chance to recover. She jumped into the crater and bent over, grabbed his right arm, and flung him west.

"Catamount, do you need backup?" Blue Spekter impatiently repeated, his voice crackling in her earcomm.

"I'm fine. How are you?"

Blue Spekter sighed. "Arcbright is a bad guy now with a bad guy name—Deimos."

"I see."

"Can you knock out Tempest? We need this stupid weather cleared, but we can't sense her."

"I see her. Stand by."

Catamount clenched her teeth, then leaped at the unsuspecting villain. Tempest looked down casually as Catamount crashed into her gut, folding the teal-glowing villain in half. They rapidly descended, and Catamount slung Tempest into the ground.

"You think it's that easy?" Tempest asked, her eyes sizzling with power. A lightning strike seared through the air above Catamount and connected, blackening the frozen field at her feet. The heroine didn't flinch.

"What? How?" Tempest uttered, shocked.

"I've been around a lot longer than you, honey."

"Well, there's only one place for you, Granny. Enjoy your stay at Shady Pines!"

Catamount's body succumbed to an immense force that propelled her straight up into the sky. Several bolts of lightning connected with her until she reached the apex of her journey above the storm clouds.

"Oh, shit." Catamount looked to her left as Wrath crashed into her and dove, hurling her into the crater he had once occupied. She grunted when she landed, a spray of dirt exploding around them as the crater deepened.

"How does the cold, hard ground feel, bitch?" he snarled, clenching his fists as he stood over her sore body.

"Why do I feel like we're outnumbered here?" Helion asked, frowning. He watched the ground spray settle around Catamount and Wrath.

Tempest, hovering thirty feet above the field, turned toward them and gently swirled her outstretched arms. Behind her, a wicked and fast-moving dark gray twister formed and crossed the field, stopping to gather strength around Tempest, who hovered in its eye.

"Uh, what do you suppose she's gonna do with that?" Blue Spekter asked.

"I have no clue, but I have an idea," Helion answered.

Blue Spekter shot Helion a quizzical look, then shrugged. "Go. I'll keep Carlos down."

Helion walked toward Tempest, who laughed maniacally as he approached.

"I number your days, Guardians," she shouted with a taunting, sing-song voice. She raised her hands to channel lightning into the churning air around her. "Up, up, and away, Blakey-poo." She moved her arms forward, and the growing twister approached Blake, churning up dead hay, dirt, and snow.

Helion stopped, put his hands on his hips, and stared at her. He waited for the right moment.

"Uh, what are you doing?" Blue Spekter nervously asked through his earcomm.

"Firestorm." The edge of the raging twister reached Helion, and his eyes ignited with fury and power as he extended his arms and super-heated his body. As the winds overcame him, Helion's body transmuted into a living, fiery flame. Twirling debris in the cyclone rapidly ignited, fueled by the wind and chaotic energy of the intense lightning in the storm. Fire exploded from the ground and raged upward in seconds.

Tempest shrieked in protest, but it was too late. The flash fire consumed the twister and encircled her, now fueled by her own powers. Scorched and injured, Tempest fell and slammed into the ground. The remaining foul weather she had created cleared, revealing the bright overcast weather of the day.

Helion reverted to his human form, noting how parts of his supersuit had burned away during the attack. "Dammit." He grabbed a scrap of fabric resting on his left shoulder, then shoved it into what remained of the waistband that barely covered his privates.

"That's a good look," Blue Spekter teased.

"Funny," Helion replied, staring at Tempest's scarred body to make sure she didn't get up. Her supersuit had not protected her from his powerful flames, and he let his gaze linger on her slender—albeit twisted—nude form.

"I could use your help, pervert," Blue Spekter said.

"Yeah, yeah."

Catamount glowered at Wrath, but she decided to not give him any satisfaction. "A little colder than I expected, actually. Tell me, how does this feel?"

Twin beams of raw pink energy lanced through the air from her eyes this time and tore into Wrath's torso.

Stunned, he grunted as her immense power flung him back, arms and legs flailing as he tumbled through the air.

Catamount willed herself to her feet, keeping her eyes and energy beams focused on Wrath until he smashed into a sizable oak tree that collapsed on top of him. She smirked with pleasure as the energy beams fizzled out. She looked around and saw Tempest, her clothing burned away, lying twisted and motionless on the ground.

Blue Spekter and Helion stood near Carlos, who was also on the ground, but she didn't know how Jesse and Janie had fared.

She took a deep breath, then spoke. "Catamount checking in. Both Tempest and Wrath are down."

"What about Carlos?" Potter asked.

She looked at the boys, and when Blue Spekter shook his head, she answered with, "Still not himself."

"Extract him immediately," Potter replied. "Leave the other two for another day. Don't bring Deimos back to base, though. I'll find another suitable location for you to remove his new chip."

"But we could take them prisoner," Blue Spekter argued, stunned by the director's decision.

Catamount walked toward them, and Potter continued speaking. "And we'd have no way to secure them, Blue. It's a tough decision, but it's best we wait for the right time. Rescuing Carlos is our top priority."

"We should check on the old couple," Helion said.

"All right," Potter said. "Catamount, stay there and coordinate with emergency services. I held them back so they wouldn't get hurt. Then please go check on the elderly couple who live there. Blue Spekter and Helion, fly Deimos north before he or his friends recover."

"Understood," Blue Spekter half-heartedly replied.

"It's the right decision," Catamount said.

"I know, it just sucks."

Chapter 27
Fight Back!

At fifteen thousand feet, Deimos felt the frigid air whip through his hair and watched the world pass by beneath him. Blue Spekter was carrying him back to New Hampshire, the hero's arms tucked beneath Deimos's arms and wrapped around his chest. Helion flew with them, but Deimos ignored both heroes. Instead, he absorbed new information the chip fed him, including the mental experience of flight and other powers he hadn't learned from the Guardians yet, such as invisibility.

The chip also informed him of his directives as a servant of The Order, the most important of which was the elimination of the Guardians.

Through the STF earcomm they had apparently forgotten about, he learned their destination was an old farm field in the middle of nowhere that would serve as a safe place to remove the chip in his head, but Deimos had other plans. He closed his eyes and drew a deep breath, sensing the orgone in the surrounding air.

"Whatever you're doing, knock it off," Blue Spekter said, giving him a little shake.

"Nah. The trip's been fun, but I have other plans," Deimos replied.

"Don't—"

A snap of lightning erupted from Deimos and crashed into Helion, who yelped and cartwheeled away from them, succumbing to gravity.

"—be a dick," Blue Spekter said, releasing Deimos.

Deimos fell, but he rolled onto his back, tucked his hands behind his head, and crossed his legs at the ankles. He smiled at Blue Spekter and felt the air around him and used his newfound knowledge to will himself forward. "Thanks, but I think I got this."

Blue Spekter's mouth fell open with surprise when Deimos rocketed away, turning west.

Deimos glanced over his shoulder and saw the orange glow disappear when Helion hit the ground. Then he saw the surprised and angry Blue Spekter change direction and rapidly close the distance between them. While Deimos knew how to fly, the chip couldn't give him the mastery or speed Blue Spekter had. "Shit."

"Do you really wanna live like a slave?" Blue Spekter shouted.

Deimos abruptly decelerated and spun around. "I am not a slave," he shouted back, extending his arm and unleashing a powerful blast of electricity at Blue Spekter, who skillfully rolled and spun out of the way.

The high-pitched whistling sound of something streaking through the air distracted Deimos. He looked to his left, confused. Suddenly, an orange burst of energy exploded and collided with him, sending motes of orange and yellow power into the air as Helion collided with him and dove. Momentarily panicked, Deimos smacked wildly at Helion's body, but the hero flew faster until they crashed into the cold ground below them in the middle of a snow-covered forest. Small rocks, dirt, snow, and pine branches exploded into the surrounding air.

Waves of excruciating pain surged through Deimos, and he gasped, wide-eyed, unable to inhale the oxygen his body suddenly craved. Blood rolled down his face from his open mouth. Helion had used him as an impact shield and scrambled to restrain him, pressing his right knee into Deimos's broken chest.

"Hurts, doesn't it?" Helion muttered, glaring at Deimos.

Deimos uttered a faint, wheezing cry. He couldn't fight back despite the chip's incessant instructions to destroy Helion or die trying.

Deimos watched Helion look around until Blue Spekter landed next to them. "We gotta get the chip out of his head."

"Working on it," Helion responded impatiently. "Over there, get me that stick, please."

"A stick? Why?" Blue Spekter asked.

"Remember the rebar incident?"

Blue Spekter winced at the painful memory and rubbed his chest. "Ouch."

"We need to keep Lightning Fingers from healing so I can extract the chip."

"Right." Blue Spekter looked around and spotted a solid branch. He picked it up and handed it to Helion. "This ought to do."

Helion took the stick and used telekinesis to whittle one end into a sharp point.

"Are you sure we should do this? It seems... unethical."

Helion rolled his eyes. "You worry about the ethics while I make sure this vicious bastard doesn't recover and kill us?"

"Uh—"

Helion impaled Deimos through the chest with the stick-turned-spear.

Deimos uttered a gurgled scream, spraying blood into the air.

"Jesus," Blue Spekter exclaimed, horrified at the sight.

"It's not the battlefield decision I would have made," Potter said in their earcomms, "but I'm not on the battlefield, am I? You need to trust each other and save Arcbright if you can."

"Trust one another, yes," Blue Spekter said. "But torturing him? That's unacceptable. Crimes are still crimes. If we can't follow the rules, how are we any better than them?"

"He's going to heal when I'm finished, Blue," Helion argued. "I just can't have him squirming around while I detach the chip from his brain matter. He'll be fine."

Blue Spekter pouted. "This is what Nightmare's goons did to us at Rangeley."

242

Helion shot his best friend an annoyed look. "Carlos wanted us to remove the first chip, and we did. This is no different. Besides, until we find a better way to—"

"Oh, shit," Blue Spekter said. Both heroes froze as their proximity sense triggered.

A split second later, Wrath flew between them, unleashing a powerful blast of energy that knocked the unsuspecting heroes down.

Deimos felt a set of powerful arms grab him tightly.

"You don't need this," Wrath uttered, yanking the stick from Deimos's bloody body.

Deimos wailed with discomfort at the sensation, but his healing factor kicked in, and broken bones popped back into place as his muscles and flesh healed too.

Wrath ascended and flew away from the momentarily stunned heroes.

"You saved me," Deimos said, gasping and coughing as his healing lungs expelled fluid that dripped from the corners of his mouth.

"You got careless."

"Didn't see you winning either," Deimos spat back.

"Touché."

"Ugh, everything hurts," Deimos complained.

"You'll get used to it. Stop whining."

"Easy for you to say," Deimos replied sharply as his sternum popped back into place. "Ouch."

Wrath glanced over his shoulder. "Ugh, those two just won't give up."

"What do you mean?" Deimos asked. Suddenly, the proximity sense of Blue Spekter and Helion flooded his mind.

"You better have healed enough to fight. I'm not your goddamn babysitting service," Wrath grumbled.

Deimos mentally checked his body, wiggling his fingers and toes. "I think I'm ready. You can let me go."

"You can fly?"

"Apparently so."

243

Wrath let go hesitantly, but Deimos caught himself and extended his arms forward. "I got this."

"Cool. We have orders to pull back, not engage the false heroes."

"They're not gonna stop until they get me back."

"You will not let that happen."

"How?"

"This won't be your last battle with them, so remember this simple strategy. Always start with the weaker one, which usually is Helion, then Catamount, and then fight Blue Spekter. Never engage *him* first or alone if he's got friends, because you'll never win."

"Makes sense. I just—" Deimos abruptly stopped speaking, and his eyes went wide with surprise.

Wrath glanced at him, and suddenly Deimos was gone, yanked back by some invisible force.

"What the hell?" Wrath shouted. Deimos watched Wrath spin around midflight, ready to chase after him. A blinding blue flash caused Deimos to squint, and he barely saw Wrath raise a hand to shield his eyes. Deimos gasped when he saw a focused blast of immense power tear through the sky and collide with Wrath, who never saw Blue Spekter coming for him.

"No!" Deimos shouted as something jerked him back. He desperately fought against the unseen snare that pulled him through the cold sky. His body suddenly spun around, and an orange-yellow-glowing hand closed around his throat. His velocity abruptly shifted forward and down.

"You need to let us help you, Carlos. There's a microchip inside your head controlling you," Helion said.

"What would you know about it?" Deimos snapped.

"Everything. Victor put one of those things inside my head, and it malfunctioned. I hurt many people. But we've had this conversation, haven't we?"

"You failed to see the unique gift Victor gave you, and you betrayed The Order. All enemies of The Order—"

"I know, I know, Jesus Christ, I know. I can't tell you how many times I said that to the people I love."

Deimos nervously glanced down and saw the fast-approaching ground. "Let me go!"

"Sorry, can't do that."

Distraught, Deimos blindly swatted at Helion, causing the hero to wince and duck to avoid the slap strikes.

"Stop being annoying," Helion shouted, shaking Deimos.

Deimos brought his full body into the fight, kicking, punching, and slapping at Helion, desperate to distract him or make him let go.

"Oh my God, would you knock it off?"

"Let me go!"

"Fine," Helion replied, shoving Deimos downward.

Drawing a deep breath and preparing to fight back, Deimos slammed into the ground, the wind momentarily knocked out of him.

Helion landed next to him, scowling.

Deimos grunted and pulled himself together, then flipped to his feet and raised his hands.

Helion didn't hesitate to throw the first punch, forcing Deimos to block and dodge.

"Argh," Deimos uttered, barely seeing the roundhouse kick coming his way. Helion's foot smacked the side of his head, and Deimos blindly thrust his fists at Helion, who easily blocked his strikes.

"Need a hand?" the familiar voice of Blue Spekter asked.

Deimos gasped and backed away, his shaking fists covering his face. "Get away from me."

"Nah, I just remembered something." Helion made a funny smile. Then he took one step toward Deimos and said, "Freeze asset one."

Desist.

An intense urge to stop what he was doing and embrace relaxation overwhelmed him, and he froze, keenly aware of his autonomously lowering arms and relaxing hands as his posture straightened up.

Compliance.

"Holy shit, it worked," Helion blurted out, stepping back with shock.

"You'd think they would have changed that pass phrase by now," Blue Spekter said with a shrug.

"Right?"

Compliance.

Helion shrugged. "Better do this quickly. There's no telling how long 'sleep mode' will last."

Blue Spekter chuckled.

Deimos passively watched Helion step behind him, unable and unwilling to interfere.

Compliance. The whispered word repeated calmly in Deimos's head like a mantra, keeping him at peace.

"Deimos, we're gonna check to see if you're hurt. Don't do anything, okay?"

"I understand."

Blue Spekter chuckled at his response, but Deimos didn't know why.

"I found it," Helion said behind him. "Oh, weird. It feels more like a caterpillar than the bug she used on us—or the one I already pulled out."

"Can you get it out?" Blue Spekter asked.

"I think so." Helion tapped Deimos's shoulder. "Hey, kneel down."

Deimos silently complied.

"Here goes nothing."

Deimos felt a wave of energy move through the back of his head until it focused inside his head. A flash of white light and unfathomable pain seared through his body, electrifying every nerve with an unbearable and overstimulating experience of everything—hot, cold, pleasure, and pain.

His mind screamed in agony while his brain short-circuited. Unsure of how to process the sensation, his brain simultaneously released every neurotransmitter, paralyzing him.

Fight back!

The words came from some place deep in his mind, but he could not obey their insistent message. Overwhelming pain and a confusion of sensations flashed and surged through him. He wanted to run, walk, sleep, jump, jog, giggle, cry, eat, drink, open presents, box someone, yell at someone, laugh with friends.... The unyielding flood didn't stop until something tore through the back of his head and his body collapsed to the ground—an elusive sensation he didn't realize had actually happened when mixed with everything else he felt.

Crackles and pops echoed in his head, and the painful experience subsided as he lay breathing quietly, staring at a clump of ferns.

He blinked several times and heard the distinct sound of footfalls around him. Two figures squatted in front of him, but he couldn't tell if they were real or part of the fading torture.

"Carlos?" one of them asked.

He jerked with surprise, lifting his head off the ground. "Yeah?"

Chapter 28
Three Times Is Enough

"H ey, how are ya?" Blue Spekter asked.

Carlos cleared his throat and felt nothing wrong with his body. The back of his head was sore. He pushed himself into a side-sitting position and looked at Blue Spekter. "Fine, I think. Did I crash? Wait, I flew?"

"Uh…," Blue Spekter uttered.

Carlos looked up, then jumped to his feet with surprise. "I flew!"

"Yeah. We know. Do you remember why?"

Carlos shook his head, then reached up with his left hand and scratched his head, moving his hand to the back of his head and suddenly remembering the sharp pain. "I, uh—"

"Looking for this?" Helion asked, holding up his right index finger.

Carlos's enhanced vision saw an almost imperceptible microchip. Memories flooded Carlos's mind, and he remembered. "Oh, shit, Deimos!" Carlos shouted, shaking his body and limbs as if exorcising demons.

"I'm confused. Do you have an evil split personality or something?" Helion asked, standing.

Blue Spekter stood as well.

Carlos laughed. "No, Deimos was the name Victor picked for me. I must have liked the name or something when we discussed it. Sorry."

Blue Spekter spoke up. "Cute. But that doesn't explain how you suddenly learned how to fly. They dosed you with orgone, and you escaped after they declared you dead. You barely used powers then, let alone learned how to fly."

Carlos tapped the side of his head. "The chip downloaded things into my brain."

"Seriously?" Helion asked, wincing.

"It was more like… impressions, not instructions. But it was clear enough for me to understand how to will myself to fly, for example."

"Huh."

Carlos glared at Helion. "Pulling that thing out hurt. A lot."

Helion shrugged. "Sorry."

"Thanks," Carlos said. "I don't want to go through it again. Three times is enough."

Suddenly, Blue Spekter whipped around, followed by Helion.

"What is it?" Carlos asked.

"Wrath," Helion replied.

Then Carlos winced, touched his head, and nearly doubled over. The proximity sense seemed unusually strong in his mind, probably because his brain was still settling down. When he became accustomed to the sensation, he straightened and saw Wrath cautiously walking toward them.

"What do you want?" Blue Spekter angrily asked.

Wrath stopped and stared at the three boys, his gaze lingering on Carlos.

"What do you want, creep?" Carlos asked, summoning small snaps of electricity between his fingers.

"Deimos?" Wrath asked.

"No, I'm Arcbright."

Wrath's shoulders slumped, and his head dipped. "Shit."

"Do you believe you can take all three of us?" Arcbright taunted, drawing a look from his companions.

"No," Wrath admitted, then vanished from their sight—and their minds.

"Where'd he go?" Arcbright asked, surprised.

"Clever," Helion added.

"Just as well," Blue Spekter said. "We would have taken him, but we have no way of holding him."

"Oh my gosh, Jesse and Janie! The farm!" Arcbright blurted out. He leaped into the air, his body glowing and snapping with powerful yellow energy, and the two other heroes followed him. He stopped about one hundred feet up and looked around. "Wait, where is it? Where are we?"

Blue Spekter chuckled and pointed east. "This way."

The trio flew east until they saw the burning woods near the farm. Emergency services had arrived and responded, but they could not save the barn. The large field was wrecked, pockmarked with several large craters from battle.

"I'm gonna help contain the fire over there," Blue Spekter said, veering off toward the burning woods.

"Okay," Arcbright responded absentmindedly. He spotted Jesse sitting in the back of an ambulance with a blanket wrapped around him. Medics attended to him, and Janie stood nearby and watched.

Arcbright came in hot and nearly crashed when his proximity sense detected Catamount. He caught himself and jogged over to Janie.

"You can fly?" Janie asked, wonder filling her eyes.

"Yeah." He smiled proudly. "Pretty cool, huh?"

"Some of your friends aren't very nice," Jesse said, frowning as a medic pumped a blood pressure cuff and listened.

"They're not my friends. At least, the redhead and the other guy aren't. Their super villain names are Tempest and Wrath."

"I knew she was trouble the first time I saw her," Jesse said, shaking his head. His gaze fixed on something behind Arcbright.

Arcbright turned and saw Catamount standing guard over a defeated Tempest, who sat on the ground with a modesty blanket draped over her shoulders.

"I'll be right back," Arcbright said. Then he stormed toward Tempest, fingers clenched into fists.

Helion followed him.

Tempest saw him coming and smirked. "Hi, handsome, fancy meeting you—"

"I have a message for you to deliver to Nightmare."

"Send him an email," she replied sarcastically. Then the color drained from her face, likely as she realized the Guardians had removed the new control chip.

Arcbright pointed at the house. "Tell him to leave them alone. If he wants me, I'm in Portsmouth, not Spec. Got it?"

Tempest pursed her lips, the fight draining out of her. "Fine. So... you're letting me go?"

"It's not like we have a prison for super villains. Yet," Helion said.

Tempest narrowed her eyes. "I see." She looked around. "Where's Wrath?"

"He flew off with this tail tucked between his legs," Helion answered, crossing his arms over his chest. "Nice blanket."

His answered appeared to upset her, and she stuck her tongue out at him in disgust.

"It's clear you can't take us on. Remember that the next time you decide to play baddie. We show up, you lose, every time." Helion punctuated his last words with hand claps. "Now take the blanket and go."

"You're just letting her go?" Arcbright asked, astounded.

Tempest scrambled to her feet, hesitating. Her gaze darted nervously between Helion and Arcbright, showing she mistrusted them.

"It's not a trick. Get out of here," Helion said.

She wrapped the blanket tightly around herself and took off, choosing to fly northwest

Arcbright shook his head. "I don't believe this. Should we follow her or something?"

"Unnecessary. I put a tracker on the blanket," Catamount said, smiling as Janie and Jesse approached.

"You did?" Helion asked, stunned.

"You have your orders, and I have mine," Catamount replied.

"But what if she finds it?" Arcbright asked.

Catamount shrugged. "Then she finds it. The chance that she doesn't offers a greater opportunity to find Nightmare's base of operations in Spec or wherever she goes next."

"Is that the last time we'll see her?" Jesse asked, sidestepping to Arcbright. Then he pointed at Blue Spekter, who was manifesting water out of thin air and dousing the flaming forest at the far edge of the field. "By the way, your friend's trick is really neat."

"I think she understands the stupidity of coming after you again. She's going to leave you alone now," Arcbright said.

"Good," Janie said, her tone short and angry.

Arcbright sighed. "I'm sorry about the barn, Jesse. Maybe we could—"

Jesse waved a dismissive hand. "The barn was old. Everything in the barn was old. I'm old. It's one less thing for me to worry about." He turned and looked at the field. "I think it's time I rent out the field to some of the local farmers who can actually do something with it. Maybe I'll come out and water their crops with my garden hose." He chuckled at his own joke. His demeanor and expression suddenly changed to panic and concern, then sadness. "Aw, Mabel."

"Oh," Arcbright said, saddened at the loss of the sheep who had kept him warm when he first arrived at the farm.

"I hope she went peacefully," Jesse said. "Poor old girl hadn't been feeling herself these past few weeks. Still, I am gonna miss her."

Janie put an arm around Jesse's shoulder, and the old couple shared a silent moment together.

Blue Spekter flew over from the smoking woods and quietly landed near the group.

"So, what will you do now?" Jesse asked, glancing at the heroes but focusing his gaze on Arcbright.

Arcbright smiled. "Fight alongside the Guardians and make sure Nightmare and his thugs don't hurt innocent people."

"That's a great way to use your gifts," Janie said with a proud smile.

"Don't forget about us," Jesse said. "With no barn to keep me busy, I'm gonna get bored quick."

"I'll come visit, I promise." Arcbright hugged them each in turn, then watched Janie and Jesse walk hand in hand to their home.

"So, you're joining us, huh?" Blue Spekter said with a smile.

Arcbright nodded. "Yeah. Not being in control of myself was the scariest thing I have ever experienced. If that's what Nightmare wants, well, screw him. But, uh, there's one thing we gotta do first."

"What's that?" Blue Spekter asked.

"We gotta take care of Uncle Hector. His entire organization needs to be put out of business for good. I can't have Abuela living in fear for the rest of her life. Can you find out if Tara is still tracking him?"

"Stand by," a female voice said in their earcomms.

Surprised, Arcbright made a funny face, then mouthed, "Who's that?"

Blue Spekter laughed and said, "If Potter has to do something, he has people monitor our conversation for important requests like that."

"What's more important than this?" Arcbright asked. He gestured to the destroyed landscape around them.

"Probably had to poop," Helion said mischievously.

The voice spoke again. "Confirmed, Arcbright. Hector's phone has moved around town but recently returned to the Court Street residence. And yes, Director Potter is, uh, indisposed."

"Pooping," Blue Spekter replied with juvenile amusement.

Helion giggled, and Catamount rolled her eyes, unable to hide a smirk.

"Thanks, voice in my head," Arcbright said, trying not to laugh.

"I'm Lieutenant Amanda Flagg, sir."

"Nice to meet you," Arcbright replied.

"Likewise."

Blue Spekter took over the conversation. "Lieutenant Flagg, can we mobilize a police response in fifteen minutes?"

"Fifteen minutes?" the young lieutenant echoed. "I, uh… Director Potter is on his way back. Please stand by."

"Nice try," Arcbright said.

Blue Spekter shrugged. "I tried."

The sound of a distant conversation reached their ears, followed by the sound of someone hurriedly pulling on a headset.

"You want to do what?" Potter asked.

"Take down Hector's ring right now," Blue Spekter replied.

"That's a hard no," Potter replied. "It's the end of the day, and they do not assemble the SWAT team this late. There's no way in hell we could provide backup or protect the innocent if all hell breaks loose in the neighborhood. You all know Chief Applegate would have my head for approving that action without her direct approval."

"Fine," Arcbright replied.

"But doesn't mean we can't set up something for tomorrow," Potter said.

"Really?" Arcbright asked. "That's great. The less time they have to plan, the better."

"What do you mean?" Potter asked.

"Hector used to bribe cops," Arcbright replied. "They'd tell him whenever the police planned to move against him or the business. I'm sure nothing has changed."

"I see. Then we only tell Chief Applegate and have her assemble the SWAT team for backup, but we give them no location or target details until they're rolling. They'll move in only after the Guardians have infiltrated the house and assessed the situation and the resistance."

"Chief Applegate sounds like a fun person," Arcbright quipped.

Helion rolled his eyes and groaned.

Potter chuckled. "Yeah, hilarious. Finish up in Spec and come home. I suspect you'll have a busy day tomorrow."

Chapter 29
Las Navajas

The next day, Arcbright walked to the Las Navajas house wearing black jeans and a white T-shirt, despite the frigid weather. He liked that his powers allowed him to heat or cool his body as he wished. Despite Abuela's vocal protestations, he refused to wear a coat. He didn't want to risk bullet holes in his favorite leather jacket.

He stopped in front of a historic blue-and-white house that, according to the GPS tracker Tara had given him, was his uncle's hideout. His enhanced vision noticed a figure peering at him from behind a sheer curtain. He closed his eyes and listened, hearing the panicked scuffling of the gang members inside.

"They know I'm here," he discreetly said.

Suddenly he heard more scuffling, guns cocking, and hastily shouted commands coming from all directions. He glanced around and realized Hector had bought out the entire neighborhood for the Las Navajas members.

He updated everyone listening through his earcomm, which included Director Potter, Chief Applegate, Blue Spekter, Catamount, and Helion.

"I don't think we have enough personnel or firepower," Chief Applegate replied nervously. "I will not send my people into a shitstorm only to have them carried out in body bags by you four bulletproof heroes."

"Technically, I'm not bulletproof yet," Arcbright said.

255

"Perhaps we should wait for the military?" Potter asked.

"Oh, hell no! What do you want, more stray bullets to rip through houses? I don't think so," Applegate said.

Arcbright asked, "Do they always argue like this?"

"Yep," Helion answered.

"It's not like you gave us a lot of time to prepare," Applegate tersely replied.

"The more time you take, the more time he has to escape," Arcbright said.

A window slid open on the second floor of the house. "What do you want, Nephew?"

Arcbright saw the familiar frame of his uncle behind the curtain over the open second-floor window. "I just want to talk."

"I have nothing to say to you."

"You tried to kill your own mother!"

"Walk away while you still can, Nephew."

"Or what? You'll have one of your goons shoot me?"

"Las Navajas are many. You are alone, and we've seen you bleed."

"Too scared to face me yourself?"

"Of course not." The business end of a rifle poked out the window.

A single shot rang out, and something sharp struck Arcbright's chest. Surprised, he stepped back, wincing in pain. "Ouch." Then he gasped and looked down at the bullet-sized hole in his T-shirt. He stared at it, refusing to believe Hector had shot him. Then he noticed there was no red blood staining his T-shirt.

"Are you okay?" Blue Spekter asked.

Arcbright laughed nervously, lifting his shirt to confirm his suspicions. A smashed bullet fell to the ground. "I'm fine. I'm finally bulletproof."

A second shot rang out. As if time slowed, Arcbright's enhanced vision saw the copper bullet traveling toward him seconds before it struck his bare abdominal area, crumpling upon impact. It stuck to his skin for a second, then fell to the ground, bouncing until it came to rest near the first bullet.

Arcbright squatted, picked up the bullet, and inspected it. "Holy shit, I'm finally bulletproof."

"Awesome," Blue Spekter said.

"Pretty ballsy way to find out, kid," Chief Applegate said.

Arcbright stood and shouted to his uncle, "You ruined my shirt!" He held out the damaged fabric.

Silence.

Uncle Hector still hid behind the curtain. Then the front doors of every house in the neighborhood opened, and the well-armed Las Navajas gang members cautiously stepped out, their weapons aimed at him.

"I have no quarrel with any of you, but I will speak to my uncle." He pointed at the window, smirking.

"You're gonna have to get through us, ese," one gang member shouted. He spat some chewing tobacco on the ground and grinned, revealing an incomplete set of yellow-brown teeth.

"Hope you're ready." Arcbright cringed at the disgusting sight. "See your dentist much?"

The man cursed, aimed, and fired several rounds, each of which harmlessly smashed into Arcbright's body and clattered to the ground. Infuriated, the man angrily pursed his lips, then shouted, "Shoot the mother—"

Gunfire rang out across the neighborhood, and bullets crisscrossed the space between Arcbright on the street and the historic houses. The first few rounds struck Arcbright, but within seconds they stopped short, hovering in the surrounding air.

Helion, standing unseen on a roof, captured the bullets in a telekinetic field that slowed and stopped the bullets in midair. They collected around Arcbright, frozen in Helion's powerful grasp.

"That's so cool," Arcbright said.

"I count at least thirty," Blue Spekter said, hovering invisibly thirty feet above Arcbright "I think it's safe to assume there are more gangsters inside."

"Gangsters?" Applegate echoed.

"He's young," Catamount replied.

"You know what I mean," Blue Spekter said.

When the gunfire stopped, Hector's men hesitated and stared at the sphere of bullets encircling Arcbright, momentarily forgetting about reloading their weapons.

"What are you idiots doing?" Hector shouted from inside his hideout, his voice betraying fear and uncertainty. "Reload!"

Helion released his hold on the bullets, and they fell to the ground, bouncing and pinging until the last one came to rest.

Arcbright grinned and looked at the men. "My turn."

"Reload!" Hector shouted again.

Arcbright reached up, eyes blazing with powerful yellow energy, and pulled electricity from the overhead wires.

The gang members panicked and fumbled with their clips as Arcbright snapped several low-voltage arcs of electricity at the goons guarding his uncle's hideout. The gang members fell to the ground, their bodies quivering as if tased.

"We got this, Arcbright. Go get Hector," Blue Spekter said.

"Thanks."

Helion leaped from his nearby rooftop, and Blue Spekter descended, ready to deal with the rest of Hector's militia.

Arcbright noticed his uncle no longer stood in the window. The front door slammed shut, and he heard multiple locks clicking into place. Smirking, he glanced up at the overhead power lines and tapped into the grid, sensing his destination. The hair on his arms stood on end as he willed himself to move. A bright flash surrounded him as his body transmuted, traveled, and solidified in a second bright flash inside the house. Someone swore, another shrieked, and then gunfire immediately pelted him. He raised his arm to protect his eyes. "Where are you, Hector?"

The gunfire stopped, and someone moved swiftly toward him from the right, attempting to tackle him. Arcbright simply looked at the man, whose determined expression shifted to horror a split second before he crashed into Arcbright, his bones breaking when he hit the immovable and stronger superhuman.

"Ouch, that musta hurt," Arcbright taunted as the man fell and looked up at him, clutching his shattered collarbones. Sensing Catamount moving toward him, he looked toward the back of the house and realized Hector had tried to run, but Catamount had expected this and was covering the rear exit.

The gang members he could see took aim again, but Arcbright impatiently reached out and zapped them with a bolt of neutralizing electricity. They collapsed to the floor, their weapons clattering on the hardwood.

"Get away from me," Hector shouted, running back through the house. When Hector came around the corner, Arcbright glared at him. Hector hurriedly raised a large Desert Eagle handgun and pointed it at Arcbright's face. "You've ruined everything!"

Then Hector fired three rounds, and the bullets smashed into Arcbright's face and neck. These bullet strikes hurt more than Arcbright expected, forcing him to take a step back and raise a hand to shield himself.

Hector seized the moment and tackled his distracted nephew, shoving the muzzle into Arcbright's left temple. Leaning close, he shouted at his nephew, "You can burn in hell, Carlos!"

Hector pulled the trigger, and Arcbright screamed when he felt the bullet strike his temple, fearing the worst. But the bullet exploded and fragmented, creating an unexpected recoil that tore the gun from Hector's hand and broke his trigger finger. Hector yelled in surprise and agony as several pieces of shrapnel pierced his hand, arm, and face. Crying out, he stared at the unnatural bend of his finger. The Desert Eagle fell and clattered on the floor.

"Ouch, looks like that hurts," Arcbright said dryly. He climbed to his feet and hauled Hector up by his collar.

Catamount quietly stepped into the room and nodded at him.

Hector trembled and whimpered, paralyzed with fear. Uncle and nephew quietly stared into one another's eyes for several long seconds.

Arcbright spoke softly. "You killed your sister. You killed your brother-in-law. You tried to kill me. You tried to kill your mother. What kind of man are you?"

Hector suddenly found his strength and scowled. "The kind you'll never be." Then he spat in Arcbright's face.

"I could kill you right now," Arcbright snarled, passing a low but noticeable current through Hector's body. Hector's eyes widened with alarm as the current made his muscles tense and twitch.

"Carlos, breathe," Catamount counseled quietly.

Arcbright snapped his head in her direction and felt heat and warmth rising within him. Electricity momentarily danced across his body as anger swelled like waves within him.

His own words to Quinn and Blake echoed in his mind. *This is my moment—I'm choosing to be a superhero. I just hope my actions back my words when push comes to shove.*

Arcbright's face immediately softened with realization and mercy, and he looked upon his angry, terrified uncle. "But you're right, I'll never be the man you are. I'll be better." Then he threw Hector at the front door, his body trembling with rage. He nodded at Catamount, then exhaled, letting go of his anger.

"Good man," Catamount added.

"I've got Hector," Arcbright said, knowing the rest of the team would hear him. He picked Hector up, ripped open the door, and shoved him outside. Metal from the locks clattered to the floor.

"And we've got the situation under control out here," Helion said.

"How'd you do it?" Arcbright asked, shocked at the number of men sitting quietly on the ground. He grabbed his uncle's arm and marched him toward Helion.

"Eh, word gets around that we're bulletproof," Helion replied. "These guys surrendered the minute you disappeared in an electrical… whatever that was. That, and I might have ripped all their weapons from their hands."

Arcbright laughed. "Cool trick. Where's Blue Spekter?"

"Checking the houses to make sure they're clear of Las Navajas before the police come pick everyone up for a joyride to prison," Blue Spekter answered.

"I'll check the remaining houses on this side," Catamount said.

Arcbright stopped near Helion and threw Hector into the center of the surrendered men.

"You're all cowards!" Hector snarled, glaring at his men. Some of them scowled at him. Others ignored him, resigned to their fate.

"Okay, night night." Arcbright snapped his fingers, and a sizzling arc of electricity jumped from his hand to Hector's shoulder.

Hector immediately dropped to the ground.

The nearest men gasped, while others squinted against the bright light and pulled back when they felt intense heat.

Helion stared dubiously at Hector's motionless body. "Dude, did you kill him?"

Arcbright rolled his eyes. "Felt like it, but nah. He's taking a nap."

"Oh."

"Um, you guys can come now," Arcbright said.

"Who are you talking to?" Helion asked.

"Chief Applegate."

"We haven't cleared all the houses, but I've only got one to go," Blue Spekter replied in his earcomm.

"Me too," Catamount replied.

"Oh, sorry," Arcbright said.

"Trying to get us killed, kid?" Applegate asked.

"Uh, no. Sorry."

"She's joking," Helion replied.

"You think so?" Applegate asked.

Helion winked at Arcbright, who smirked.

A drone flew overhead, briefly hovering over the unhappy gathering of Las Navajas members.

"Who do you think that drone belongs to?" Arcbright asked, raising a hand. Electricity snapped between his fingers.

"It's mine," Potter replied. "Please don't destroy it."

Blue Spekter dashed out of the last house and surveyed the situation. A moment later, Catamount walked out of the house she was checking and raised her thumb.

"All clear, Chief Applegate," Blue Spekter said. "Send in the SWAT team. You'll need about sixty sets of handcuffs and a big bus. We'll stick around to ensure your officers' safety."

"Understood, Blue Spekter," Applegate replied. "Thank you, everyone, for keeping my officers safe."

A moment later, flashing lights on cruisers and unmarked SUVs spilled onto the street, stopping on either side of the surrendered men. Officers in body armor cautiously climbed out, stunned at the sight of gang members quietly waiting to be arrested.

Blue Spekter turned to Arcbright, smiled, and extended his hand. "Job well done, buddy."

Chapter 30
Sign Me Up

"I n total, sixty-nine cartel members and their ringleader, Hector Rodriguez, were arrested thanks to the heroic and careful actions of our city's Guardian superheroes, Blue Spekter, Helion, Catamount, and a new hero, Arcbright." Camilla Brenhurst reported on the unusual scene in the Haymarket Square neighborhood of Portsmouth that morning. Her camera crews had arrived as the police cuffed and loaded the last of the gang members onto buses Applegate had brought in for the mass arrest.

"That's what I'm talking about," Carlos shouted, jumping up and swiping his fist through the air. He accidentally hit the large and very full bowl of popcorn on the coffee table.

"Mijo?" Abuela asked from the kitchen of the rental home the STF had provided for Carlos and his grandmother until workers could repair their damaged home in Atlantic Heights.

Quinn and his boyfriend Keegan and Blake and his sweetheart Ravone cuddled on the plush couches nearby. Blake reached out with two fingers and settled the bowl of popcorn before it flipped over the edge of the coffee table.

"They mentioned me on the news!" Carlos exclaimed. "I'm a freaking Guardian!"

"Mijo!" Abuela echoed, this time as a reprimand.

"Sorry!"

On the television, the image of antisuperhero Senator Wilmott appeared next to Camilla for a split-screen interview.

"Ugh, not him again," Ravone whined.

"Joining me now is Senator Orville Wilmott. Thank you for your time today, Senator."

"Of course, Camilla. Any chance to set the record straight about how dangerous these so-called heroes are is my absolute pleasure."

Camilla's left eyebrow twitched.

"Of course, Senator. We're well aware of your vehement opposition of the existence of superheroes in our world today. But in the cartel takedown earlier today, no one died—neither gang member nor police officer—because of the heroes' presence. How can they be dangerous if they protect our officers?"

"Well, you see, Camilla, you're only reporting on half the story. You're ignoring the massively destructive battle that took place in multiple locations in beautiful Virginia that—"

"Senator, I'm sorry, but that news story highlights a significant battle between superheroes and extremely dangerous super villains. It seems you'd like to lump them all together. Why is that?"

"Let's remember the danger these unstoppable individuals present to all of us. They're teenagers—"

"Catamount is not a teenager."

"Irrelevant, and don't even get me started on that deceptive vixen." Camilla barely maintained her composure at the word "vixen." "And just where exactly did this newcomer Arcbright come from? How many more 'heroes' should we expect, and why are they hiding?"

"Senator, we have confirmed reports that the super villain Nightmare had taken Arcbright and irradiated him, hoping to create a superhuman to serve his—"

"And that opens the door to an even bigger problem. Who is vetting these individuals, and what are their political motivations?" Wilmott asked, ignoring her argument and cutting her off.

"The government, Senator, through the Superhuman Task Force. The Guardians have the full support of our government."

"Do they? They never asked me. How many senators were involved in the decision-making process? When did Congress become involved? How do we know the STF isn't working for the Guardians?" His tone became more excited, exasperated, and angry with each question. "How do you know they're not holding the government hostage?"

"With all due respect, Senator, this kind of rhetoric is akin to fearmongering," Camilla replied, reining in her frustration.

The veins at the senator's temples nearly burst with anger, and his nostrils flared. "Young lady, this conversation is over. Don't think of speaking with me again until you've learned some manners, missy!" The senator ripped off the lapel microphone.

Camilla's image filled the screen. "Well, folks, it seems the dialog over superhumans, specifically the Guardians, will prove challenging for some. Reporting live for News Nine, I'm Camilla Brenhurst."

"He's such a jerk," Blake said, exasperated.

"And a misogynist," Ravone added, frowning.

"No matter what, we keep doing the right thing," Quinn said.

"That's a nice thought, but you may never win over haters like him," Keegan said.

Quinn sighed. "We'll try."

"Nightmare won't make it easy, will he?" Carlos asked.

"What do you mean?" Quinn asked.

"He stalked me and decided I'd be easy to convince, then zapped me with orgone and left me for dead."

"Creepy," Ravone said.

"That's not the creepy part," Carlos said.

All eyes studied him. "What is, then?" Ravone asked, as if afraid of the answer.

"How did he stalk me? How did he know I'd be a perfect candidate?"

Silence.

"Quinn, you figured out Hector had someone on the inside keeping tabs on me. Someone close—Everleigh. What if Nightmare has someone on the inside... say, at school... close to us... acting like his eyes and ears?"

"You think there's another superhuman at school?" Blake blurted out.

Carlos shrugged. "Don't know about the superhuman part, but someone's watching us—all of us—and feeding information back to Nightmare."

Quinn shook his head. "No. That's impossible."

"Whatever remains, however improbable, must be true," Blake said, pursing his lips.

"Exactly," Carlos said, clapping his hands once and pointing at Blake, nodding vigorously in agreement.

Quinn threw himself back on the couch, hands on his forehead. "This is not what I signed up for."

"Not that we signed up for it," Blake added.

"Me either," Carlos chimed in. "Well, sorta?"

"If there's another superhuman at school, that means Victor probably made them around the same time he made that mini super-army we fought over Rangeley," Quinn said.

"Can't you sense them?" Keegan asked.

Keeping his hands on his head, Quinn shook his head. "Not if you learn how to hide yourself from others, which Nightmare learned to do fairly quickly."

"Or he made them just after, given we know he survived," Ravone said.

Quinn dropped his hands to his sides. "Yeah, maybe. We couldn't find him, and we don't know where the other reactors are, so who knows? It's a complete guessing game at this point."

"What about the tracker you said Catamount put on Tempest's blanket?" Keegan asked.

Quinn shook his head. "She dumped the blanket. They found it in the woods several miles away."

"Damn," Keegan muttered.

Carlos cleared his throat. "Nightmare also made those new chips pretty quickly and figured out how to download superpower information into people's brains. When Tempest stuck one in me and I became Deimos, I learned a lot about what I could do. I can't wait to play with the rest of my powers while training with you guys."

"Why Deimos?" Blake asked, furrowing his brow. "I mean, the name. I don't get it."

Keegan spoke up. "Deimos and Phobos are the two Martian moons. Also, Deimos is the god of dread and terror in Greek mythology."

"Well, that makes sense," Carlos said, nodding to himself. Everyone waited for him to continue. When he noticed the silence, he chuckled. "Oh, uh, well, I vaguely remember him saying the name would help me embody the perfect weapon to use against the Guardians."

"Do I want to know what Phobos is in Greek mythology?" Quinn asked, playfully wrinkling his nose.

Keegan chuckled awkwardly. "He's the god of fear and panic."

"How do you know all this?" Ravone asked.

Keegan shrugged. "I like ancient cultures."

"You so smart," Quinn quipped, rubbing his boyfriend's chin.

"So, if there's a Deimos, does that mean there's a Phobos villain lurking out there?" Blake asked.

"I hope not. Assuming there is someone else at school, four super villains is enough. At least right now, we're evenly matched," Quinn replied.

Abuela entered the living room, carrying a large tray full of delicious-smelling snacks she had prepared for them. The teenagers sat up, their mouths watering in anticipation and delight.

"Thank you so much, Mrs. Domínguez," Ravone said, jumping up to offer a hand.

"Sí, sí, I want to keep my superhero grandson and his friends healthy and strong!"

"Thanks, Abuela," Carlos said, helping Ravone transfer the snacks to the coffee table.

"I made you some Takis Fuego, spicy tamarind balls, chorizo, tortitas de papa con queso, papadzules, and some Mexican fruit salad."

"What's that?" Blake asked, eyeing an orange fruit.

"This is just cantaloupe, dear, to cut the spiciness if you need it," Abuela said with a wink.

"Oh."

Carlos ruffled Blake's hair, and they shared a laugh.

"Your grandma's amazing," Keegan said.

"Yeah," Carlos said, nodding in agreement.

They dove into the snacks, and Abuela watched, her face glowing with pride. "I will bring you more?"

"More?" Blake asked, astonished.

"Best not to argue with the chef, guys," Carlos said.

"No argument here," Blake added quickly. "You'll soon discover the need for more grub, especially after using powers a lot."

"My food is not grub," Abuela said, sounding hurt.

Blake sat upright, appearing concerned he had insulted Abuela. "Oh, huh… I meant—"

"She's kidding," Carlos said, stuffing his mouth.

"Oh." Blake relaxed and sheepishly grinned.

Abuela smiled and did a little dance. "I'm cool, I'm funny."

They all shared a laugh.

"Gracias, Abuela," Carlos said.

"De nada, mijo." Then Abuela went back into the kitchen.

"So, what do we do next?" Carlos asked.

"We train. We prepare. We get ready to finish the fight and stop Nightmare forever," Quinn said.

"Do you think that's possible?"

"I have no idea, but I hope so. I don't want to do this for the rest of my life."

"Well, you can count on me. I'll fight alongside you."

"Me too," Blake added.

"Us too," Ravone said. "Probably more like cheerleaders from afar, but we'll be there too. Right, Keegan?"

"Cute cheerleaders," Keegan said with a grin.

"The cutest," Quinn added, winking. Then he turned to Carlos, his expression serious. "You really want to be a Guardian, huh?"

Carlos nodded. "Ten hundred percent. Becoming Deimos showed what I don't want to be."

"Okay. Then it's time we get you fitted for a supersuit."

Carlos nearly choked on his chorizo. "Seriously?"

Quinn nodded. "Yup."

"Hot pink spandex with neon green swirls?" Ravone asked, a mischievous smile dancing on her face.

Quinn burst into laughter.

Carlos's face scrunched with surprise. "Dear God, no."

"Well, it needs to stand out from this lot." She jerked a thumb at Quinn and Blake. "How about pastel blue and clementine orange?"

Carlos shook his head, unsure if she was joking.

"Well, I'm sure we can find you something pretty."

Blake snickered, and Keegan rolled his eyes with amusement.

Ravone chuckled. "Don't worry, you'll get an awesome supersuit that, uh, suits your tastes."

"Thanks," Carlos said. Then he pointed at the large flat-screen television. "So, do you think we can just be normal teens for the rest of the day and watch a movie or something?"

"Please," Blake said.

"Definitely," Quinn added.

They settled themselves on the couches: Quinn and Keegan snuggling together, then Carlos, followed by Blake, who put his arm around Ravone. They had already agreed to watch the latest Disney movie because it had nothing to do with superheroes.

As Cinderella's castle filled the screen and the music swelled, Carlos smiled, glancing at his new friends. Whoever he was before—the angry

Carlos, the confused Ethan, or the vengeful Deimos—he had finally found a family who accepted him for who he was and who he could become.

The End

This adventure has ended, but the **Superhero Age** series continues with
LEGEND OF THE CRIMSON BLAZE

Post-Credit Scenes

(JUST LIKE MARVEL)

Scene 1

Hector Rodriguez studied the cracks in the worn concrete floor of his prison cell. His right foot bounced nervously as he angrily counted seconds in his head, eagerly waiting for his cell door to open for the morning.

The bell in the white cinderblock hallway rang for three long seconds. A moment later, the cell doors—except his—buzzed and slid open. Hector raised an eyebrow but didn't bother to care. He had become used to the constant and supposedly random inspections the prison guards liberally conducted. When the last of the other prisoners had filed out, Hector drew a deep breath and waited.

At last, one set of footsteps with the sound of leather-soled dress shoes echoed in the hallway.

Hector sat up, curious, then jumped when his cell door buzzed and slid open with a scraping, grating sound of metal on metal, desperately in need of lubrication.

A man wearing a black suit stood in the open cell doorway. His medium-length black hair was parted from the left and styled with shiny hair gel. Hector saw the stubble of a mustache, soul patch, and chin-strap beard on his statuesque face. He had tucked his fingers into his pants pockets, thumbs hooked on the fabric.

Hector silently glared at the overdressed stranger. After a moment, the man smirked. "Hello, Hector. My name is Victor Kraze, and I'm here to make you an offer."

Scene 2

Director Potter stared at nothing, his fingers steepled. The mystery of who Wrath could be eluded and frustrated him. In addition, someone had infiltrated the STF, but he couldn't figure out who because they knew how to cover their tracks.

A knock at the open door drew and focused his gaze. "Yes, Lieutenant?"

Lieutenant Amanda Flagg entered, beaming with pride. "We found it, sir."

Potter's eyes widened, and he sat up. "What? But you suggested this was a lost cause."

Flagg placed an official file folder on the director's desk. "They buried this dossier in an inconspicuous box that was listed in the catalog as being related to the Ranalli mafia. I think it's what you're looking for, sir."

"Thank you, Lieutenant. Well done."

Flagg saluted and closed the door behind her.

Potter drew a deep breath and hesitantly reached out to open the dusty dossier. When he flipped open the cover, his mouth dropped open when he saw the words **LEGEND OF THE CRIMSON BLAZE,** in bold capital letters on the first page, next to a hand-drawn portrait of a very familiar—and surprisingly unchanged—woman.

"Found you," he smirked, pulling the dossier close to read it.

Before You Go

Please Leave a Review

The world needs to know how you feel about this book. Don't let them down. Leave an online review wherever you bought this book or on Goodreads today.

Subscribe to My Newsletter

Want to learn about my newest releases before anyone else? Then subscribe to my newsletter by scanning the QR code below with your smartphone's camera. I promise not to spam you! Your readership is too important to me.

Damien Benoit-Ledoux Books

Buy Direct

Did you know most of my books are available for less than you'll find on popular retail distributors? When you buy directly from me, you save money because I don't have to pay a distributor for their services. It's a win/win for both of us!

Buy my books directly from my online store by scanning the QR code below with your smartphone's camera or visiting this link: https://damienbenoitledoux.myshopify.com/

Live Long and Prosper.

Online Bonus Content

Explore the Spekter Superhero Universe Online!

The Spekter Superhero Universe is a fantastic superhero universe that contains several published or in-process novels bout amazing superheroes and deadly super villains. I carefully designed the website to support the series universe by providing all kinds of background information about the characters and the places of their world that I couldn't include in the novels. I hope you enjoy what you discover here, and happy reading!
worldanvil.com/w/the-spekter-superhero-universe-damientronus

I can also be found online at the following social media sites:

- Facebook: facebook.com/damientronus/

- Goodreads: goodreads.com/damientronus

- Instagram: instagram.com/spektersuperheroes

- Patreon: patreon.com/damientronus

- Twitter: twitter.com/damientronus

Acknowledgements

Huge thanks to those who made this novel a success:

- My husband and handsome hero Tim, for his constant encouragement and willingness to share in this part of my life. I truly appreciate your support as I jockey between our lives, our sons, work, and several novels. I love you, through all of time and space…

- Eric Juarez – for explaining how bullets work in the real world.

- Walter E, Eric L., Eric P., and Eoghan K. – my crew of fellow geeks who put up with my unprovoked brainstorming.

And to my professional production team:

- Cover Designer: Miblart

- Editor: Dawn Vogel – https://historythatneverwas.com/

- Proofreader: Alexandra Ellis – https://rabbitrune.wordpress.com/

About the Author

Damien's mind is a magical and nerdy place where fantastic heroes defend amazing worlds from dangerous villains who run amuck in an epic struggle to take over the universe. Recently, the brightest and best from this colorful cast of characters have made their way into notes, plots, stories, and novels for you to read and enjoy.

Damien strongly believes the real world we live in should be a place where LGBTQA equality and acceptance are second nature and never questioned. When he's not working or spending time with his husband and their dog, Damien weaves this philosophy into the exciting lives of his characters and the fantastic space battles and romances they endure so they'll stop taking over his dreams at night.

And finally, he wants you to remember a very important thing:

No matter how bad your day is at work, it's always important to be grateful that you don't work for a Sith Lord.

Milton Keynes UK
Ingram Content Group UK Ltd.
UKHW040954040823
426331UK00001B/119